11-16

The Spirit
the Season

The Spirit of the Season

DANA CORBIT

Guideposts
New York, New York

The Spirit of the Season

ISBN-13: 978-0-8249-4744-6

Published by Guideposts
16 East 34th Street
New York, New York 10016
www.guideposts.org

Distributed by Ideals Publications, a Guideposts company
2630 Elm Hill Pike, Suite 100
Nashville, Tennessee 37214

Library of Congress Cataloging-in-Publication Data

Corbit, Dana.
  The spirit of the season / Dana Corbit.
    p. cm. — (Tales from Grace Chapel Inn)
  ISBN 978-0-8249-4744-6
  1. Sisters—Fiction. 2. Family—Fiction. 3. Bed and breakfast
accommodations—Fiction. 4. Pennsylvania—Fiction. 5. Christmas stories.
I. Title.
  PS3603.O733S65 2008
  813'.6—dc22

                                    2008005861

Design by Marisa Jackson
Cover art by Deborah Chabrian
Typeset by Nancy Tardi

Printed and bound in the United States of America

10 9 8 7 6 5 4 3 2

Thank you to Karen Solem for your vision and guidance, and to Priscilla Drobes and Leo Grant for demanding my very best.

GRACE CHAPEL INN

A place where one can be
refreshed and encouraged,
a place of hope and healing,
a place where God is at home.

Chapter One

Christmas spirit filled the chilly air of Acorn Hill, Pennsylvania, the town positively humming with anticipation. Shoppers rushed along Hill Street and up Acorn Avenue, gaily wrapped packages clutched under their arms. Storefronts from Fred's Hardware on Hill to Time for Tea on Berry Lane were decked out in their festive best with bright red bows, Christmas trees and multicolored lights combining to create a holiday atmosphere. Streetlamps draped with garland and holly and an authentic layer of winter white made the town appear as if it had been wrapped in the season and tied with a bow.

Alice Howard couldn't help smiling as she hurried alongside other shoppers Saturday morning, her boots crunching over the packed snow and shopping bags filling her arms. Neither the cold that required her to wear a bulky parka and mittens nor the wind that ruffled her bobbed, reddish brown hair beneath her knit hat could bother her today. She had only to breathe in the frosty air, tinged with the aroma of cinnamon and spices wafting from Good Apple Bakery, and she was at peace.

She loved this town and this time of year when the community celebrated God's most precious gift to their world through the spirit of giving. Her own spirit lightened with every smile from neighbors and downtown business owners, each wave and each "Merry Christmas." Some shoppers probably preferred to take the short drive to Potterston or even to make a day trip into Philadelphia, but Alice tried to make as many purchases as possible in town. Here she could shop among friends and receive hugs along with her change.

Just as she passed Acorn Hill Antiques, Rev. Kenneth Thompson pushed open the door of the Coffee Shop and buttoned his long wool coat over his navy pullover and gray pants. The minister of Grace Chapel waved when he saw Alice and stepped forward to greet her.

"Good morning, Alice." He reached over to pat her shoulder. "What's the hurry?"

"Good morning, Pastor Kenneth," she answered as she pondered his question. "You know, I'm not sure. With only nine days until my favorite holiday, I guess it's just hard to resist the Christmas rush."

As if to emphasize Alice's point, waitress Hope Collins hurried out of the Coffee Shop, her short-cropped hair in its new strawberry blonde hue sticking out every which way from beneath her pink knit stocking cap.

"Hi, Alice. Hi, Reverend. I'd love to chat, but I'm doing some shopping on my break." With a quick wave, she was on her way.

A smile softened Rev. Thompson's patrician features, and mirth danced in his hazel eyes as he watched Hope's exit. "Yes, we all do seem to be in a hurry during this holy season."

Except for the minister, perhaps. He appeared relaxed, taking the time to watch a flurry of activity down the street outside Wild Things and then waving to his landlords, Joseph and Rachel Holzmann, owners of the antique shop, who were hanging a large wreath beside the front door. He was still smiling when he turned back to Alice. "We have to take time to enjoy this special season." Then he added, "I have to pick up something at the pharmacy. May I join you?"

"Of course. I'm heading for Fred's Hardware." Alice walked beside him, purposely slowing her gait to match his and pausing with him from time to time to enjoy the companionship and the surroundings. *What is your hurry?* she asked herself.

She didn't have to be home early, because no new guests were expected at Grace Chapel Inn until after the holidays. Even the remaining guests—soon to depart—kept mostly to themselves, requiring little of the devoted service Alice and her sisters, Louise and Jane, offered.

"Your sisters aren't shopping with you today?"

"Not today. They insisted they could handle the chores this morning so I would have time to finish my Christmas shopping."

The pastor glanced down at her bags. "It looks as if you've finished quite a bit of it."

Her cheeks warmed. Restraining her spending when selecting gifts for her family had always been a particular challenge for Alice. She always discovered a more special gift just after she'd finished wrapping her first selections. Her navy parka made a swishing sound as she shrugged. "Some of these are for my Secret Santa match."

Rev. Thompson, who had been reaching out to relieve her of her packages, paused at her comment, but then his hand closed over the bag handles anyway. "I promise not to peek just in case I'm that lucky recipient."

"Well, if you're sure you won't snoop," Alice said as she gratefully accepted help with her burden. "Thank you."

"You're most welcome." The minister carried her packages effortlessly as he continued walking. "I'd better get started on my own shopping, because if I give my recipient hymnals every day, I might become a Secret Santa suspect."

"You have plenty of choices at Grace Chapel—Sunday school books, vintage study Bibles, even personalized packets of offering envelopes."

They chuckled together over her joke.

"Vera Humbert must be delighted that her Secret Santa program is going so well," he said.

"There certainly are a lot of secrets floating around town." As they crossed Chapel Road, Alice glanced back at the white clapboard structure that was Grace Chapel. A few of the lovely stained-glass windows were visible from where they stood, as was a pretty manger scene displayed prominently on the lawn.

"Father loved that old crèche." She recalled how her late father, Daniel Howard, pastor of Grace Chapel for more than sixty years, adjusted the hay in the manger until it was just right for the baby Jesus doll. "He liked the fancy one that we used to decorate inside the sanctuary, the one that Ronald and Florence Simpson donated, but he especially loved the message that this one announced to passersby: 'Jesus is at the center of our celebration.'"

Rev. Thompson glanced at the church once more and then looked back at her. "I'm pretty partial to the manger scene outside as well. Is it going to be a busy Christmas at the inn?"

"Busy? Oh no." She shook her head to emphasize the point. "We're expecting a relaxing Christmas this year. Louise's daughter Cynthia is coming in from Boston, and since there are no other reservations for the week of

Christmas, we'll be closing the inn through the holidays. Is everything ready for the Christmas services?"

"Nearly. Christmas and Easter are my busiest work weeks, but I love every minute." His face took on a contented but faraway look. "I always feel a little like the angel announcing to the shepherds in Luke 2:10: 'Do not be afraid. I bring you good news of great joy...'"

"That thought must make you very happy."

"It does. Just like your work with the ANGELs brings you as much joy as it does the young ladies who participate in the group."

She smiled. God had blessed her in so many ways while she worked with those wonderful middle school girls.

At the entrance to Fred's Hardware, she turned to face her minister. "Well, I have a little more shopping to do, and you just might *not* want to know about these top-secret purchases." She raised an eyebrow to appear even more mysterious, though she was only kidding. All of her Secret Santa gifts would be going to Zack Colwin, owner of Zachary's, a supper club.

Rev. Thompson nodded, returned her shopping bags and took two steps back. "Then I'd better be on my way." With a wave, he turned, crossed Hill Street and headed toward the pharmacy.

Though Alice could now return to her mission, she no

longer felt so caught up in the frenzied holiday pace. She wanted to stroll instead of speed walk, to stop and admire glittery light displays instead of letting them race by in a blur, to take the time to enjoy the Christmas season as Rev. Thompson had suggested. She looked forward to a joyful and serene celebration of Jesus' birth with Louise, Jane, Cynthia and her Aunt Ethel.

Louise and Jane were in the kitchen sharing a late lunch of homemade cream-of-cauliflower soup and fresh chicken-salad sandwiches when Alice shoved the kitchen door open and worked her way inside. Though Alice had been out all morning and into the afternoon, Jane was surprised to see that her sister appeared energized rather than exhausted. With her hair tousled as she removed her hat and with her cheeks pink from the wind, Alice looked far younger than her sixty-two years.

"Well, there's our bag lady after all." Jane gestured to the shopping bags Alice had settled onto the black-and-white checkerboard tile floor. "We were just discussing whether to send out a search party."

Alice stopped and studied them. "Why? Is something wrong?" Louise shook her head, making her short silver hair flutter as she stood up from the table.

"No, no, dear," she said as she crossed the room to rest her hand on Alice's shoulder. "Everything's fine. We were just worried you might be frozen like a Popsicle by now."

Unfolding the wire-rimmed glasses that she wore on a chain, Louise slipped on the spectacles to take a better look at her sister, who was removing her mittens. She took hold of Alice's hands. "My goodness, you are nearly frozen."

"So you didn't need me for anything?"

"Of course not," Jane said. "If we had, we easily could have tracked you down."

Alice smiled. "I suppose that's true."

Louise opened the cabinet and pulled out another place setting. "Now sit down and have some soup, and we'll have you warmed in no time."

Jane stood to fill a bowl from the saucepan on the stove. "And when you're nice and toasty, you can tell us about your adventures downtown."

"As long as you two tell me about everything I missed this morning at home."

Jane chuckled at that. "What an exciting story that will be."

All three sisters laughed, and Louise steered Alice into the place they had set for her at the table. Then, for nearly an hour, they shared stories of the interesting and the mundane, of breakfast dishes and fresh linens, of holiday window displays and Christmas secrets.

They were clearing the table and putting away leftovers when the telephone rang.

Alice glanced over at the kitchen extension. "Do you want to answer it, Louise? Maybe it's Cynthia."

Louise glanced down at the pile of soup bowls and plates in her arms and shook her head.

Alice lifted the receiver. "Grace Chapel Inn, may I help you?"

At the sink, Jane watched her sister's smiling expression turn to one of concern. Instead of meeting her gaze to answer some of the questions forming in Jane's mind, Alice turned away, winding the cord around her fingers.

"I'm afraid that won't be possible. The inn will be closed that week."

With her back still to her sisters, Alice stood quietly for several seconds, listening and occasionally nodding. Jane glanced over at Louise, who lifted an eyebrow, her blue eyes reflecting the same concern that Jane felt.

"Oh, that's too bad ... that would be just awful."

Jane couldn't help fidgeting and tucked a few strands of long, dark hair behind her ears to give her hands something to do. The look Louise sent her way told her she wasn't alone in worrying.

With the three of them present, why had Alice been the one to answer the call? The middle Howard sister was the caregiver in their family, the worrier who couldn't turn away a stray cat or dog, let alone a guest who might need the respite they provided at Grace Chapel Inn. That benevolent nature made Alice perfect for her job as a nurse at Potterston Hospital, but it didn't provide her with strong skills for saying no.

Come on, say good-bye, Jane said silently to the back of her sister's head. She thought her message had gotten through when Alice pulled the phone away from her ear, but Alice only asked Louise to hang up the extension after she took the call at the front desk.

"Alice, wait," Jane called after her, but Alice only held up her index finger as a signal for her to wait a minute.

After Alice left, Jane turned to Louise, who was still holding the extension. Clearly, her oldest sister was tempted to listen in on the conversation. They both were. Good manners prevailed, though, and Louise returned the phone to its cradle.

"Why do I have a bad feeling about this?" Louise asked.

"For the same reason I do—because Alice is too tender-hearted for her own good."

While they waited for their sister, Louise and Jane returned to their work cleaning up the kitchen. Louise flipped on the inn's one television to check the world news, but the anchor was talking about the impending baggage handlers' strike that could cause headaches for holiday travelers. Grateful that Cynthia was driving instead of flying from Boston, they agreed to shut off the set.

As Louise placed the last cup in the dishwasher, Alice returned, a sheepish expression on her face.

Louise crossed her arms. "All right. Tell us what's going on."

Alice tilted her chin down and looked up at them from beneath her lashes, her kind brown eyes cajoling them before she spoke.

"Well, you see, there's this family from San Diego, the Ericksons. They flew all the way into Philadelphia International Airport for their two-week ski vacation at a resort in the Poconos."

"How nice for them," Jane interjected, knowing full well her sister wasn't finished.

"Yes, it would have been, but it didn't turn out as they'd planned," Alice continued. "The resort was double-booked. Now they can't find a hotel room, and with worries over a possible strike at the airlines, they're having trouble changing their return flights. Paul and Sandy had promised their children a chance to see a white Christmas, and now they're worried they'll have to break their word."

"That is too bad," Louise agreed.

As much as she wished she could keep a cool distance, Jane felt as bad for the weary travelers as Alice did. But she didn't have a plan to solve their problems, as her sister's expression suggested she might.

"Fortunately, the Ericksons were able to locate our inn on the bed-and-breakfast Web site, and we have two guest rooms available."

"And *unfortunately*, we are closing for the holidays," Jane said.

Stepping forward, Louise rested her hand on Alice's forearm. "Now, sweetie, you did direct them to other accommodations in Potterston, right?"

"Of course I did. They don't have any vacancies either." She placed her hand on top of Louise's.

Jane sighed, her wonderful Christmas holiday melting away like old snow. "So what you're saying is this family really has nowhere to stay except here?"

"Oh, they could stay in a rental car as they drive the twenty-seven hundred miles back to San Diego. Maybe young Dylan and Claire could even open their Christmas gifts in the backseat, and their dad could watch through the rearview mirror."

"Sounds like a holiday to remember," Jane quipped. "Next you're going to tell us it would be downright un-Christian for us not to let this poor family spend Christmas here."

"I wouldn't have phrased it just that way, but . . ." Her smile was victorious, but Alice never gloated.

"Then it's settled," Louise said. Though the role of mediator in the family most often belonged to Alice, Louise could step into it easily. "We'll offer the family an opportunity to stay here for the duration of their vacation."

Alice watched Jane until she nodded her acceptance.

"Good," Alice said. "Let's prepare the Symphony Room and the Sunrise Room since they share a bath. The Gilberts will check out of the Garden Room tomorrow. Since you changed the linens this morning, we have only to prepare the flowers and—"

"Shouldn't you contact the Erickson family to let them know they can have the rooms?" Louise asked. "Or did they tell you they would call back?"

Alice gripped her hands together and chewed her bottom lip as she stared at the floor like a child caught with the forbidden cookie still in her hand.

Jane studied her before folding her arms across her chest. "Alice Christine Howard, are the Ericksons in a taxi on their way here this very minute?"

"They could be, or they still might be caught up at the resort."

Louise blinked. "You told them they could stay here and that we would open the inn over the holidays without even asking us what we thought?"

"That's exactly what she did," Jane said.

Her hopeful expression wavering, Alice looked back and forth between her sisters. "No, it wasn't like that."

As frustrated as she was with her sister for changing their plans, Jane couldn't help softening as she saw Alice's hurt expression. This was Alice, after all, someone who'd never done a hurtful thing on purpose in her whole life. Stepping forward, Jane touched her arm. "So tell us what it was like."

That contagious smile returned to Alice's face. "I wasn't discounting either of your opinions. I just believed in the two of you. Once my wonderful sisters knew the whole story, I just knew they wouldn't leave the Ericksons out in the cold, or without a place to stay."

Jane couldn't help asking, "What if you didn't know us as well as you thought you did?"

Louise tilted her head and studied Alice. "Yes, what if we refused to give up our vacation to open the inn for your guests?"

"I planned to cross that bridge when I came to it. I would have pleaded, begged and bargained."

"If none of that had worked, you would have sent your *wonderful* sisters out to the front porch and made us send the guests away ourselves," Jane said with a chuckle.

"There is that too," Alice agreed. "It would have been hard to turn away two children at the door."

Jane glanced back at Louise. "That sister of ours, she's pretty smart."

"That makes three of us," Alice said with a laugh.

Louise suddenly straightened as if she was coming to attention. She glanced about the kitchen. "The three of us have also just become very busy. We have four unexpected guests coming in an hour, so we need to get to work."

Alice and Louise started off to do their chores, while Jane remained in the kitchen. She shook off the last of her frustration over losing her holiday. She had to concentrate on her work. Extra groceries would be necessary to make breakfasts for her guests, and she needed to check her tea supply.

The situation probably wasn't as bad as she thought anyway. If they had planned a ski vacation, the Ericksons probably would be the type of guests who spent all their time on adventures away from the inn. That would leave her, her sisters, her aunt and her niece alone to savor the afternoons, sipping tea and sharing stories.

A smile brightened her face as she completed her grocery list. Perhaps it would still be a merry Christmas at the inn after all.

Chapter Two

By the time the taxi pulled into the drive at Grace Chapel Inn, Louise was putting the final touches on the guest rooms while Alice fluffed pillows for the over-stuffed burgundy sofa in the living room. In the Sunrise Room, Louise smoothed her hand over the blue, yellow and white patchwork quilt displayed in an oak frame, and took one last glance around the room to make sure everything was in place. After she locked the room, she descended the stairs, adjusting her pearls and smoothing her aquamarine-colored sweater set as she went.

Alice stood in the front hall waiting for her when she reached the landing. "I was just coming to get you."

"I heard a car." Louise glanced at the door. "I thought Jane would make it back from Potterston before our guests arrived."

"She'll have plenty of time to meet the Ericksons dur-ing the next two weeks," Alice said.

Louise set her lips in a line as she walked toward the door. She and Jane had let Alice talk them into changing their plans for closing the inn, then prepared the rooms.

Now Louise needed only to ready herself to entertain their displaced guests.

Alice opened the door though the visitors had yet to knock. Neither sister was prepared for the travel-weary family they found on the porch.

"I told you this was a bad idea," the man was saying while he glanced around the inn's grounds, clearly disgruntled. "There's probably not even a Starbucks here."

The woman, wearing a long, hooded coat, stared down at a gadget in her hand and navigated it with what looked like a small, silver pen. "At least one of us—" She stopped herself when she noticed the Howard sisters standing at the front door. "Hello."

"The Erickson family, I presume," Alice said too brightly.

"You guessed right," the woman answered, her voice sounding as forced as Alice's. "I'm Sandy Erickson. This is my husband Paul, and these are our wonderful children, Dylan and Claire. Dylan is eleven, and Claire is ten."

For the first time, Louise paid close attention to the two younger Ericksons, a pair of sullen preadolescents whose faces peeked out of the hoods of blue and magenta parkas. Both said requisite hellos, but they didn't give a *wonderful* first impression.

An uncomfortable sensation settled deep inside Louise. *This is going to be a very long visit*, she couldn't help thinking.

"What kind of hostesses are we, keeping you out here

on the porch?" Alice opened the door wider and ushered their guests into the front hall. "I'm Alice Howard. I spoke to you on the phone. This is my sister, Louise Howard Smith. You'll meet our other sister Jane later."

"Thank you so much for opening your inn to us," Sandy said as she pushed back her hood and unzipped her coat. A petite brunette with brown eyes appeared from beneath layers of padding. "We don't know what we would have done if you hadn't."

"We're glad to help," Louise answered.

Sandy took a deep breath and let it out in a long sigh. "It's going to be so nice being here where we can kick back and enjoy the slower pace of a small town. With Claire's soccer and dance practice, Dylan's hockey and art lessons, plus piano and voice, we're always on the go."

"My, that does sound busy," Louise agreed. She'd raised her own daughter a long while ago and wasn't really up on children's overcrowded schedules these days, but it seemed like a lot.

"Yes, we're busy, but the children are so well-rounded." Sandy reached out to give each of them a warm squeeze.

"Well, if you want relaxed, you've come to the right place."

For the next few minutes, the woman's husband and children stood in the entry, removing layer after layer of winter outerwear. Louise wondered what would be revealed when they had removed it all. Paul turned out to be tall and trim with a thinning cap of golden blond hair cropped close to his scalp. The two children both had their mother's curly brunette hair, but only Claire's eyes were dark replicas of Sandy's. Dylan's were an interesting hazel combination of his mother's brown and his father's blue.

Alice gathered their coats in her arms. "Pennsylvania weather is a bit of a change from what you're used to in Southern California, isn't it?"

"Let's just say I'm glad I left my short-sleeved shirts and swimsuit in San Diego," Paul said with a chuckle.

"Maybe fewer movie stars swim in it, but I think I'll stick with the Atlantic if I have a yearning to swim in salt water," Alice told him. "I might not have great geography skills, but I think it's closer."

The Howard sisters joined the family in a laugh that released some of the tension in the room. Louise felt herself relaxing by degrees. She couldn't blame the family for being stressed after a full day of frustrating travel. "You must be tired. Let's get you registered so we can show you to your rooms. We'll give you a tour later, when you've had time to get settled."

"That sounds wonderful," Sandy said. She admired the wide staircase and then pointed to the nineteenth-century beech coatrack that Daniel Howard had acquired years before. "If the rest of the house is as lovely as this, I can't wait to see it. I was reading on the Web site that it is a late nineteenth-century Victorian and listed on the historic register."

"This was our mother's childhood home and the place where we were raised," Alice explained. "When we renovated it to make it into a bed-and-breakfast, we followed the guidelines from the county's historic preservation committee."

Sandy stepped over to her children and put her arms around both of them. "Isn't that great, kids? You might even have the chance to learn about nineteenth-century architecture while you're here."

"Great," the children chimed with far less enthusiasm.

Louise glanced from mother to children and wondered if she should mention that they might find more enjoyment without the architectural studies. Something more than travel exhaustion was affecting this family, and she was tempted to indulge her curiosity, but a knock at the door interrupted her.

After a second knock, Ethel Buckley pushed open the door and took off her knit hat to reveal short, bottle red hair that she patted into place. She glanced with curiosity at the young family. "Oh, I'm sorry. I saw the cab leaving, and I thought Cynthia must have arrived. I wanted to be among the first to welcome my favorite grandniece."

Alice smiled at Ethel's *apparent* mistake about Cynthia, then guided her aunt inside and closed the door. Ethel slipped off her coat, revealing a rose-pattern sweater and gray wool skirt as well as her intention to stay. Taking the coat, Alice rested her free hand on her aunt's arm. "Paul and Sandy Erickson, I'd like to introduce our dear aunt, Ethel Buckley. She lives in the carriage house next door." She turned back to her aunt. "Aunt Ethel, this is the Erickson family. Now, Louise must have told you that Cynthia won't arrive for a few more days. She's driving, not flying, so she won't need a cab."

"Of course. Now I remember. I'm so forgetful sometimes."

Louise smiled as she faced her father's only surviving sibling. Though Ethel kept her exact age under tighter security than most governments kept their classified documents, she was maybe only a decade older than Louise's sixty-five years. As for her forgetfulness, she probably had a better memory than any of her three nieces, especially when referring to Acorn Hill history and tidbits of gossip. "The Ericksons are from San Diego and will be staying with us through Christmas."

Ethel clapped her hands together. "This is a new development. Didn't you say you would be closing the inn for the holidays?"

"Plans have changed," Louise said simply, trying to hold back a smile. Her aunt's forgetfulness about their Christmas plans also appeared selective. "Now, Alice, why don't you show our guests to their rooms? Aunt Ethel, if you'll wait in the living room, I'll make some tea. I'm sure Jane has something tasty in the kitchen to go with it."

Alice hung up Ethel's coat, then led the Ericksons up the stairway. Ethel appeared annoyed at missing an opportunity to learn directly about their California guests, but she allowed herself to be led into the living room. She settled on the burgundy sofa with a pillow propped behind her back.

Just as Louise started toward the kitchen to make the tea, she heard another knock. "This is a popular place today," she said as much to humor her aunt as to release the tightness in her own chest.

Before she reached the door, whoever was outside knocked again, this time more insistently. "I'm coming," Louise called out, but the door swung open before she reached it. Florence Simpson rushed in, her face ruddy and tear stained, her penciled eyebrows and carefully applied makeup looking now like a surrealist painting. Even her dark brown hair, usually perfect from being set weekly and tinted monthly, appeared matted.

"Florence, are you all right?" Automatically, Louise reached out her arms, but Florence skirted past her.

"Where is Ethel? Is she here?" She didn't bother wiping her wet face. "I went to the carriage house, and she wasn't—"

"I'm right here, Florence. What is it?" Ethel stood in the living room doorway, her eyes wide and her posture stiff.

"It's over." Florence closed her eyes and shook her head. "My marriage is over."

Louise glanced up the staircase. What would their new guests think of relaxing at Grace Chapel Inn now? She didn't even bother trying to convince herself that they had not overheard. To make the rest of the conversation more private, Louise took Florence's long fur coat and closed the door to the living room.

"Here, you sit and take a few breaths," Louise said. "I'll make the tea, and then perhaps we'll make sense of whatever has happened." Her voice sounded surprisingly calm and her words reasonable, though she felt unsettled by Florence's frantic outburst. She forced herself to remain steady as she passed through the dining room, with its old Queen Anne-style furniture and green walls, and continued through the swinging door into the kitchen. Having descended the back stairway, Alice was already at the stove, putting on the teapot.

"What's going on in there?" Alice whispered.

"It's Florence."

"I heard that much all the way upstairs."

Louise stepped closer and kept her voice low. "Her marriage is in crisis."

For a few seconds, Alice's hands, which had been setting the tray with a pretty tea service, stilled. "Oh, that's just awful," she said finally.

Louise admired her sister. Alice was simply being herself and empathizing with others in pain. Louise stopped Alice's hand just before she placed the fourth cup and saucer on the tray. "No, I want it to be just the three of you in there. You're closer to Florence than I am, so maybe you'll be of more help."

"But I don't—"

"Alice, the three of you serve together on the church board. You certainly know Florence better than I do. You want to help, don't you?" Louise waited for her nod before she continued. "Well, then you go ahead, and I'll bring in the tray when I have everything ready."

Just as the swinging door to the dining room closed behind Alice, Jane entered through the back door, carrying two stuffed bags from Gierson's grocery store in Potterston. Her tidy ponytail was windblown now, and stray strands clung to her jaw.

"Did our new guests arrive?" she asked as she set down her bags.

"They're here as well as Aunt Ethel and Florence." Louise held a finger to her lips for a few seconds and then whispered the details as she knew them. "I thought that Alice might be a voice of reason, so I sent her to help."

Jane's blue eyes sparkled. "You didn't want to get caught in the crossfire, did you, Louise?"

"I suppose that's true as well. But Alice does know Florence better than either of us, so I'm hoping she'll be of assistance."

"Aren't you going to carry the tea service into the parlor?"

Louise frowned at the tray still sitting on the counter. "Perhaps I'll wait a few minutes longer." She pushed the swinging door open a crack. The din of voices made her uncomfortable and suggested that the last thing the women in the parlor were interested in was tea. "Yes, waiting a few minutes would be a good idea."

They remained just inside the kitchen door, close enough to rush in if they were called, yet out of earshot.

Just how have we gone from planning a quiet family Christmas to dealing with two troubled families? Louise wondered. She couldn't answer that question, but she knew one thing for certain—the situation at the inn was becoming more complicated by the minute.

Alice perched on the edge of her chair, watching her aunt trying to coax something intelligible out of her friend, who didn't look like the Florence Simpson Alice knew at all.

Instead of the tastefully expensive clothes she usually wore, Florence had donned a gray knit top and matching pants that she reserved for lounging at home.

Alice felt like an eavesdropper on what should have been a private conversation between her aunt and Florence. She wasn't even sure why Louise believed she would be of any help. A marital crisis was new territory for someone like her who had never married. Jane had confided only little of her own difficult divorce, so Alice couldn't have felt more ill-equipped to say or do the right thing. Instead she listened and prayed.

"Now, Florence, dear, you're going to have to calm down if you're going to tell us what happened," Ethel said as she sat next to Florence on the sofa and patted her hand.

"He should have defended me. But no. He betrayed me. He thought it was so funny. Not funny—"

Ethel waved her hand to interrupt her friend. "You're going to have to go more slowly and try to start from the beginning."

Another tear trailed down her cheek as Florence took a deep breath and tried again. "I was downtown shopping. I walked up behind Ronald, but he couldn't see me. Hope Collins and Nancy Colwin were saying awful things about me—things Ronald overheard—but instead of defending me, he *agreed* with them."

"Now Florence, this doesn't sound a bit like Ronald, or Nancy and Hope for that matter," Alice couldn't resist saying, despite her plan to listen rather than participate. "Maybe you misunderstood—"

"Misunderstood? No, I think I know my husband's laughter when I hear it," Florence retorted.

Ethel frowned at her niece. "Alice," she said in a tight voice, "why don't you go check on what's keeping Louise with the tea."

Relieved to escape, Alice took quiet steps through the dining room only to have the swinging door open outward as soon as she reached it.

Both Louise and Jane were standing there, holding one tray between them. "Oh, I was just about to bring this out," Louise said.

Alice lifted an eyebrow, wondering just how closely her sisters were listening to the conversation. She wiped her nervous hands on her jeans and straightened her sage-colored flannel blouse.

Jane tilted her head in the direction of the living room. "Shouldn't you be getting back? Aunt Ethel might need you."

Resigned, Alice carried the tray into the living room and rested it on the coffee table. Clearly the conversation hadn't progressed; her aunt was still asking Florence to tell her what exactly the women had said. "Some nonsense about the constructive criticism I've given concerning their restaurants. As if it is *my* fault, the customer's fault, that neither the Coffee Shop nor Zachary's tried hard enough to provide a pleasant dining experience."

"Of course not," Alice and Ethel chimed.

Florence nodded as if at least that part of their discussion was settled. The conversation paused long enough for Alice to pour the tea. Florence held the fragile cup in her trembling hand. "Then that waitress, Miss Collins, said, and I quote, 'Acorn Hill would be better off without Florence's form of help.' They didn't stop there, either. They actually said that I gave your nieces trouble when they decided to turn this lovely home into an inn."

Alice stiffened, her cup halfway to her lips. Ethel glanced at Alice surreptitiously, but neither said anything. Florence had given the Howard sisters trouble at every turn. She called an emergency church board meeting to question whether they had the authority to turn the house into an inn. Later, she questioned the colors they'd chosen to paint the house. She even suggested they might be using questionable funding for their project.

Too upset to notice the exchange, Florence set her tea aside. "After Ronald heard all of those awful things, my *dear* husband, instead of defending me, started laughing and agreed with them."

Ethel set her own cup and saucer aside with a *clink* of fragile china. "He *agreed*? Are you quite sure? What else did he say? Is there any chance at all that you misunderstood his actions?"

Florence shook her head vigorously, and tears welled in her eyes again. "The first words out of his mouth—after he laughed—were, 'You're right.' I didn't bother to hang around to hear the man berate me any further."

Ethel scooted closer to Florence and put an arm around her shoulder. "Dear, shouldn't you be with Ronald now, telling him you're angry and giving him the chance to explain?"

"There's nothing to explain," she said. "A man who says such things about his wife in public doesn't love her and wants everyone to know he doesn't. Ronald was signaling to everyone in town that our marriage is beyond repair."

"Oh, Florence, you can't judge Ronald that quickly," Alice blurted before she could stop herself. She might not have ever made vows herself, but she believed in the sanctity of marriage and hated the tragedy of any marriage failing.

Giving Alice a censuring glance, Ethel turned her attention back to her friend. "Fiddlesticks, Florence. You love Ronald. You always have. Yes, your marriage has had its moments—they all do—but you can't give in this easily."

Instead of arguing the way she normally would have, Florence simply lowered her head and appeared defeated. "Nothing about our marriage has been easy for years. We usually tolerate each other, but since Ronald retired, we haven't been able to do even that. Almost every private conversation becomes an argument. Lately, Ronald purposely disagrees with me in public." She lifted her tea, sipped it thoughtfully. "Today was just the last straw."

"But you've been in counseling with Rev. Thompson, right?" This time Alice didn't even care if she earned another frown from her aunt. She wanted to help in any way she could, and just sitting there wasn't helping.

"I did announce that, didn't I? Well, I was really the one in counseling. Ronald only went a few times."

Ethel came to her feet. "None of that matters. You'll go and talk to your husband, and you'll find a way to save your marriage."

"I've already told him I'm leaving him." She glanced down at her watch and then came to her feet to look out the window. "My taxi's waiting outside."

"Where are you going?" Ethel asked her, shaking her head.

"I have a first-class ticket to Orlando, and the flight takes off at seven thirty PM. My aunt Darlene, who lives in Grand Island, said I could stay with her."

"Are you coming back?" Ethel's voice sounded desperate now. "Are you filing for divorce?"

Though Florence had been edging toward the door, she hesitated at the last question, as if it hurt her to hear the word spoken aloud. "I might," she said in answer to both questions. "It's all up to Ronald now."

With tearful hugs to both Alice and Ethel, Florence slipped into her coat and hurried out the door. Alice watched her go, noting that if Florence was wearing her fur for a trip to Florida, then she clearly wasn't thinking straight.

The taxi was pulling out of the driveway when Jane and Louise hurried through the living room. Ethel stared out the front window, watching the disappearing taillights.

"This is simply terrible," Louise said as she approached their aunt from behind and touched her shoulder.

With the backs of her hands, Ethel swiped at her own tears. "I always knew they had problems, but I never expected it to come to this."

Louise pulled a lace handkerchief from her sweater pocket and handed it to her aunt.

Alice turned to Louise. "How much did you hear?"

"Enough."

Ethel turned away from the window, a fierce look in her pale-blue eyes. "There has to be something we can do."

"Sometimes, no matter how hard we try, it isn't enough," Jane said sadly.

Louise frowned. "Jane's right, I'm afraid."

Their aunt straightened to her full five feet five and

planted her hands on her plump hips. "This isn't one of those times. Florence Simpson is the most stubborn woman I've ever laid eyes on, and I know in my bones that she is on the wrong track. I don't know what idiotic nonsense she overheard Ronald spouting. He'll just have to apologize."

Alice gathered her aunt into her arms. "You heard the things Florence said. Florence and Ronald have been having problems for a long time. Maybe their marriage truly is in crisis."

"I'm ashamed of you three." Ethel stepped back from Alice. "A little challenge comes your way, and you're ready to give in."

Louise held her hands wide. "We're just trying to be realistic."

"There is nothing more real than this," she said. "My friend is losing her marriage. I refuse to let it happen without helping her to fight for it."

Alice stared at her aunt, wishing she could help but not sure what she could do. "How are you going to convince her when she's a thousand miles away?"

"She won't be. I'm going to Florida too, and Ronald Simpson is going with me, whether he wants to or not."

Chapter Three

This is a bad idea. This is a bad idea. Because she'd repeated those words in her thoughts dozens of times since she and Ethel piled into her small, blue Toyota and headed across town to the Simpsons' home, Alice wasn't surprised that the message continued to play as they stood on the front porch and rang the bell. Twice.

"He's probably just not accepting visitors this late." Alice balled her gloved hands in her pockets and jangled the keys with her right hand. She didn't know why she was bothering to try that tack again. The possibility of breaching good manners hadn't convinced her aunt not to come in the first place, nor had any of Alice's other arguments on why they shouldn't rush over to the Simpsons' house and try to intervene.

Alice refused at first when her aunt, who wasn't a licensed driver, asked if she would take her to Ronald's house, but Ethel only threatened to walk alone in the dark. Because Alice worried as much about Ronald's well-being as about her aunt's safety, Alice reluctantly collected her car keys.

"It's been a long night for him—for all of us. Maybe Ronald needs some time alone."

Her aunt turned her head to face Alice. Under the glow of the twin porch lanterns, Ethel's features tightened. "The last thing that Ronald Simpson needs right now is to be alone. He needs to face the fact that as we waste time around here talking, his wife is jetting off to Florida without him."

Alice wanted to remind her that people dealt with crises in different ways, but she kept the thought to herself. No use wasting words that would go unheard. Still, as they stood outside the massive red-brick structure and she felt her fingers freezing joint by joint, Alice guessed that a try was better than no effort at all. "I don't think he's going to answer. Why don't we try again tomorrow?"

"Tomorrow may be too late."

Even as her teeth began to chatter, Alice pondered her aunt's words. In years past, her father had often used those same words to encourage people to look to God. "Now is the day of salvation," he would preach from the pulpit, letting the words from II Corinthians trail away. There was no guarantee anyone would see tomorrow, just as there was no guarantee Ronald Simpson would open that door before she and her aunt were transformed into ice-sculpture porch ornaments.

Finally, the heavy front door opened a crack. "I don't

want to buy anything, so go away," boomed a voice behind the wood.

Ethel didn't bother with greetings as she pushed the door open. "Well, that's just fine, Ronald, because we're not selling anything."

The man inside posed a startling contrast to the trim and fastidiously dressed fellow Alice saw on Sunday mornings. His blue oxford shirt was unbuttoned over a white T-shirt, and his shirttail hung over his hips. Wrinkles lined his tan trousers, and a dried brown stain on one knee suggested he'd spilled a cup of coffee and hadn't bothered to change. What was left of his thinning red hair stood up, and his brown eyes were red-rimmed, as though he'd been grinding his fists against them for hours.

If not for the freckles dotting his nose and the empty pipe dangling from his lips, Alice would have been tempted to back up and check the house number chiseled into the brick. She'd always thought his freckles gave him a kind face, and she remembered that he always smelled of sweet-scented pipe tobacco. He enjoyed his smoking habit in part because it was known to annoy his wife.

"Florence isn't here, Ethel, so you might as well go home," he growled.

"Why, Ronald, is that any way to treat your guests?" Ethel pushed past Ronald into the grand foyer that

Florence had decorated with heavy textured wallpaper with daylily designs. "Let's all sit on that lovely divan in the living room and have ourselves a nice chat."

Never known for his fortitude in the face of aggressive women—his wife a case in point—Ronald stood with his jaw slack, watching Ethel make herself at home. She shrugged out of her heavy coat and pulled off her stocking cap, shaking her hair and sending snowflakes flying.

"And to think that the weatherman says it's still a few days until winter officially starts," she said as she took several steps across the plush, caramel-colored carpeting in the formal living room. "I think Pennsylvania knows better." From the way she talked, an outsider might have concluded that they were, indeed, having a friendly conversation. However, only one of them was talking.

Shrugging apologetically at Ronald, Alice stepped inside after her aunt, but she remained on the runner near the door in case their host ushered them out into the snow.

Ronald followed Ethel into the living room, where she was settling herself onto the sofa. For her part, Alice hovered in the entryway, an unwilling observer who would not become a participant if she could help it.

Ronald looked bewildered, clearly uncertain how he was supposed to handle his forceful guest. "I'm sorry, ladies, but I'm really not in the mood for guests. If you haven't heard, my wife has just left me and—"

"Why do you think we're here?"

Ronald grunted and threw his head back. When he straightened again, he looked even more exhausted. "Oh, great! I've already been raked over the coals enough for one day. Now she's sending in reinforcements. Believe me, ladies, I've heard it all."

Ethel merely leaned back into the sofa. "Believe me, Ronald Simpson, you haven't heard even part of it, but you're about to . . . right now."

He appeared to crumble as he lowered himself to the sofa. "Go ahead, then. Tell me what I did was rotten, as if I don't already know that and haven't apologized for it a dozen times today."

The room fell quiet as they all waited for Ethel to begin. She had her chance, and she didn't often waste an opportunity to give her opinion on the actions, good or bad, of those who lived in Acorn Hill. Alice wiped her shoes on the entry runner and slipped into the living room, settling into the plump chair across the coffee table from them.

Her nervous gaze flitted over the heavy brocade draperies with their gold rope tiebacks, then toward several oil paintings with gilded frames. She supposed the accent lights directed at the still-life paintings were meant to hint at their value, but Alice recognized that Jane could do equal justice to a bowl of fruit with her oils. On the far wall, more lights illuminated the two dark china cabinets that displayed some of Florence's prized heirlooms. The irony struck Alice that all of these pretty possessions hadn't seemed to bring the Simpsons happiness. Finally Alice's gaze returned to her aunt, who still appeared to be considering her words.

"I don't care what you did or said. What's done is done." Ethel tossed away the past with a wave of her hand. "You're just going to have to make it right."

"I told you Florence has left. You said yourself you already knew that, which means she either stopped by or called you from the airport."

"And you're just going to accept that?" Her voice was eerily calm, her posture rigid.

Staring at his hands in his lap, Ronald appeared unaware of the tension brewing. "I guess I have to, don't I? My wife didn't give me much choice."

"Wrong!" Ethel propelled herself off the couch with the same intensity that she expelled the word from her lips. Ronald's head snapped up as she stepped right in front of him and wagged her index finger at him. "You don't have to accept that. You got yourself into this mess, and you're going to help get yourself out."

Ronald blinked. "How am I supposed to—"

Ethel waved a hand to cut him off. "Pack your bag, Ronald. You are coming with me to Florida to get your wife back."

For a few seconds, he only worked his mouth before setting his jaw. As he came to his feet, looming over Aunt Ethel, Ronald suddenly appeared taller to Alice than she remembered.

"What would you say if I told you that I don't want to chase after my wife to Florida, and that nobody can make me?"

As Ronald stared down at Ethel, his jaw clenched, and she peered up at him, looking as if she was trying to stretch herself taller, Alice felt an overwhelming urge to giggle but managed to control it. She still half expected them to circle around each other like boxers in a ring. Only this time they would be trading barbs instead of punches.

This was certainly a side of Ronald that he didn't usually present to the people of Acorn Hill. He didn't even make a habit of standing up to his wife, so why he picked this moment to lock horns and why he picked Ethel as his opponent, she couldn't imagine. Alice wanted to tell him he would be outmatched in a war of words, but she figured he was about to find that out anyway.

"Then I'd say you're a fool," Ethel snapped.

Ronald's eyes went wide. "You have no right—"

"Don't I? If you felt that one of your nieces or nephews was making a huge mistake, wouldn't you feel you had a right to step in and say something?"

"That's different. They're my family."

"Well, you two are my friends. I refuse to let you give up on a marriage you've been building for nearly fifty years because of one mistake."

He turned away then and shoved his hands back through what was left of his hair, leaving some strands standing on end. "It's more than that, and you know it." Pausing, he paced, leaving tracks in the plush carpeting. "Our marriage has been rocky for years. Maybe this 'one mistake' was just the breaking point."

"Maybe, but only if you let it." Ethel's hands were fists at her sides, and her voice had climbed an octave. "You don't even realize what you're throwing away. If I had a chance for even one more day with my Bob . . ." Ethel stopped herself, appearing upset that she'd revealed more than she intended, and she turned and retreated into the front hall.

Alice's heart constricted. Clearly, for Ethel the situation was personal. She'd lost her husband more than a decade ago and then moved into the carriage house to be near her brother. But in that moment of her aunt's emotional out-burst, it occurred to Alice that maybe they both should have taken their friends' problem personally. She'd been against

Ethel's plan from the moment she suggested it. She encouraged her aunt to stay safely out of the volatile situation, but Ethel insisted on barreling in without an invitation. Now Alice had to wonder which one of them was right.

Rising, Alice made her way over to Ronald, who was still facing the wall and pretending to study one of those bowls of fruit. She placed a hand on his shoulder and cleared her throat. "Ronald, do you want to save your marriage?"

He dropped his head but didn't face her. "I don't know." His words were barely more than a whisper.

"You don't know if you want to or if you can?"

"Neither."

Her heart ached for Ronald, for Florence, for all of the circumstances that had led them so far from the great expectations of newlyweds. "Is it worth a try?"

His only answer was a noncommittal grunt, but it must have been enough for Ethel, because she started clapping. Alice turned back to find her aunt standing in the doorway, her heavy emotions replaced by a grin.

"Then it's settled. We're off to Florida. First, I'll call the airlines, then—"

Ronald reached out a hand to signal for her to stop. "Wait, I never agreed to…" He let his words drift away because Ethel had already hurried down the hall to where she knew the Simpsons had a telephone. Turning back to

Alice, he lifted his hands, palms up in a helpless gesture. "I never agreed to go anywhere with her."

Alice could sympathize as someone who'd been bowled over by her aunt a few times before. "No, you didn't agree, but you didn't exactly disagree either."

"A loser by default then." He looked heavenward with an exaggerated expression of defeat.

Alice returned to her chair and watched Ronald plop down on the sofa in a way he probably never would have had Florence been in the room. At least Ronald was trying to find his sense of humor in her aunt's wild plan. He would probably need it when he faced Florence in the Sunshine State. "How can you say loser when you're going to get to enjoy sunny skies and warm temperatures just days before Christmas?"

He answered with another grunt as he stared at his hands, but at least he wasn't refusing to go. Alice shook off the image of Ethel marching through the airline terminal and pulling a hog-tied Ronald behind her. The current plan sounded much more dignified.

Ronald was tapping a nervous hand on his leg. Alice glanced at her watch. *What is taking her so long?* she wondered. She could hear her aunt's muffled voice as she spoke into the hall phone, likely haggling with a ticket agent. Alice smiled, realizing that she knew her aunt so well. Ethel was searching for a bargain just as surely as she would ask Alice to drive her and Ronald to the airport. No point in wasting money for long-term parking, she would say. Alice planned to agree without balking too, because she was still feeling guilty for trying to talk her aunt out of helping. At least this time, Alice would know she was doing the right thing.

Finally, Ethel reappeared in the doorway, a strange smile pulling at her lips.

"I suppose you got the tickets," Ronald said.

That Ethel only patted her hair and continued to smile as if she knew something that they didn't made Alice ill at ease. Had Ethel come up with an even crazier plan? Alice tried not to imagine Ethel and Ronald aboard a small plane and skywriting I'M SORRY across the central Florida sky. "Are you planning to go right after church tomorrow?" Alice posed it as a question, though she knew how much her aunt hated missing services.

"Of course," Ethel said and then cleared her throat.

Alice turned back to Ronald, who was now perched on the edge of his seat. "Leaving after church will work for you too?"

"As good a time as any."

None of them mentioned that he wasn't keen on leaving at all. Before he could, Alice turned back to her aunt. "Then you'll have the chance to talk to Lloyd at church and let him know about the trip. What time is your flight?"

Ethel's eyes widened as if she'd only then remembered Lloyd Tynan, Acorn Hill's mayor and the man with whom she'd been "special friends" for some time now. Her pale cheeks took on a girlish pink outside their twin circles of rouge. "Lloyd does worry. He'll definitely want to know what we three are up to."

The pointed way that Ethel studied her niece, and the reference to "we three" heightened Alice's discomfort. She'd picked an odd way to segue into a plea for a ride, but Alice decided to save her the trouble. "If you need me to drive—"

Her aunt beamed. "I thought you'd never offer."

Alice frowned. "You never said when the flight is scheduled."

"No, I didn't."

"Well, we need to build in plenty of time in case there's traffic," Alice continued, perplexed.

"I don't think that will be necessary."

Annoyed by her aunt's reticence, Alice walked over to her. "Just what are you saying?"

"With the pending baggage handlers' strike, flying appears to be out of the question." She paused, not seeming upset by that obstacle. Finally, she pinned Alice with her stare. "I thought it would be nice if the three of us drove to Florida together."

"I still don't see how Aunt Ethel talked you into doing this."
Jane shook her head at Alice and then frowned across the
church parking lot at the relative in question. Ethel's stiff
posture and Lloyd's tight expression suggested the two of
them were having a disagreement, but Jane had no doubt
her aunt would counter each of his arguments against the
trip. Still, she was relieved to see that she wasn't the only
one who thought this trip was a bad idea.

Alice followed Jane's gaze to their aunt and her gentleman friend. Like Alice, Ethel had dressed casually for
church so they would be comfortable when they started
their trip right after services.

"I didn't even realize I'd been had until... I'd been
had," Alice admitted.

Jane had experienced her aunt's legendary powers of
persuasion often enough to commiserate with her sister.
Poor Alice couldn't have stood a chance against Ethel's
arguments.

Their aunt must have sensed them talking about her,
because she waved and then held up her gloved index finger in a signal to Alice that she would be along shortly.

Behind Ethel, congregation members continued to spill
out of church, chatting and laughing. Unfortunately, the
Howard family had little to laugh about as the new week
dawned. First, the sisters had lost their private holiday, and

now they weren't even sure the three of them would be together for Christmas.

Alice stepped closer to Jane and wrapped her in a hug. "Everything's going to be fine, dear sister." Alice's expression, some strange combination of a grimace and a grin, suggested that even she wasn't convinced of her optimism. "You know I couldn't just let the two of them take off without—"

"A chaperone," Louise finished for her, as she joined her sisters. "No, a chauffeur."

"Or a referee." Jane glanced at the far side of the parking lot where a yellow taxicab sat waiting for them. In the back, she saw Ronald slumped, brooding. "I thought you were renting a car for the drive to Florida."

"The only place we could pick up a rental car on a Sunday is at Philadelphia International." Alice stared at the ground while she zipped her coat higher to cover her throat.

Jane was frustrated on her behalf. "You couldn't get a flight, but you still have to go to the airport?"

"Unfortunately. It will add more than an hour to the trip in driving time alone." Appearing impatient to get going, Alice glanced first at her aunt and then at Ronald.

"Didn't you tell Ronald he was outmatched when he took on Aunt Ethel?" Jane said.

The three turned to watch their aunt again. If body language held true—Ethel's posture was ramrod straight while Lloyd was beginning to slouch—she was getting the better end of that "discussion" as well.

Louise turned back to Alice. "How were you able to cover your shifts at the hospital?"

"A few of the other nurses were begging for some overtime to pay for Christmas presents, so I started by calling them this morning before church. Those ladies recommended others to call, and before long, the shifts were filled."

She didn't explain further, but Jane suspected Alice had called in some favors and created more favor deficits that she would be repaying long after her coworkers paid off their credit-card bills. She only hoped that Ethel recognized the sacrifices Alice had made.

Alice plunged her hands into her pockets. "I never would have forgiven myself if something awful happened to them along Interstate 95."

"How would you have protected them?" Louise asked kindly.

Even Jane resisted the urge to point out that a sixty-two-year-old woman wouldn't be much of a guardian for her two slightly more senior traveling companions. Besides, Jane figured their aunt could take care of herself and that any carjacker targeting her should beware.

Alice swung her purse around like a weapon, and all three of them dissolved into girlish laughter.

"Besides, someone had to drive after Aunt Ethel discovered she couldn't get airline tickets," Alice added.

Jane glanced at Ronald again. "I take it Ronald didn't offer."

"He did agree to take over when I need a break."

"How good of him," Jane grumbled. Did this man have any idea of the sacrifice her family was making for him?

Louise touched Alice's shoulder. "Aunt Ethel and the Simpsons really are lucky to have you, dear. And you're right. Aunt Ethel is trying to do God's will. It's only right that we should help her any way we can."

As much as she would miss her sisters in the last days before Christmas, Jane couldn't argue with their logic. She fleetingly wondered if her own marriage might have survived if friends like these had intervened, but she pushed the thought away. "If nothing else, you can bandage their cuts from flying dishes," she said to lighten the conversation as much as her own thoughts.

"What can I say?" Alice answered with a shrug. "I'm a regular Florence Nightingale."

They were still bantering when Ethel shuffled over to them. "Alice, are you going to spend the day laughing with your sisters, or are we going to get on the road?"

"I'm ready whenever you are. Ronald's in the car, waiting for us."

Ethel looked toward Ronald. "At least he hasn't made a break for it."

Surprised that their aunt had made a joke, they all laughed again. Louise glanced at the two people who would be traveling with her sister. "Yes, Alice, it's a very good thing that you could go along on this trip."

The Howard family exchanged hugs and admonitions to be careful. Alice even promised to send e-mail messages from the laptop that Ronald had insisted on packing in the backseat.

Jane watched as the taxi pulled out onto Chapel Road. She grew lonely even before it disappeared. She'd been separated from her sisters before, over plenty of holidays and even for years at a time, but she'd grown accustomed to their being around now. Louise and Alice were an important part of her life, just as they had been when all three were girls and her two older sisters mentored her in the absence of their late mother. Alice planned to be home in time for holiday services, and if it was God's will, she would make it. Still, the melancholy sound of Elvis Presley singing "Blue Christmas" seeped into her thoughts as she returned with Louise to the inn.

Chapter Four

A tomblike stillness settled over Grace Chapel Inn Sunday afternoon while Jane and Louise finished their light lunch in the kitchen. Their guests were gone when the Howard sisters returned from morning services, and the family hadn't come back to contribute the sounds of their voices and movements.

Sunday afternoons were supposed to be quiet times of rest. Usually Louise looked forward to these relaxing hours, but today she felt restless. She took a bite of her chicken Caesar salad, barely tasting it, her thoughts and worries focused on her absent sister and aunt and the couple they had gone to help.

The family housecat, Wendell, was the first to break the silence, mewing under the kitchen table as he wound his way around Louise's legs. When Louise peeked below the table, the gray tabby with coal black stripes sat and looked at her expectantly. "Wendell, you know it's not polite to beg at the table. Looking cute is not going to get you any of my chicken."

"Obviously, he's going to the wrong source," Jane said with a smile. "I've already left him some scraps in his bowl. He prefers his chicken spiced a certain way."

"Only Father's cat would have such a sophisticated palate."

Jane crumbled a few more pieces of chicken into the tabby's bowl before turning back to her sister. "Is the candle in the front window still lit?"

"As far as I know. I lit it as soon as we got home from church. I can still smell the peppermint." Since they opened the inn, the Howard sisters had followed the German tradition that directed Christian innkeepers to burn a candle through Christmas Eve to light the way for the Holy Family and to provide a safe haven for stranded guests.

"We can't let it burn out," Jane said.

Louise nodded. Neither had to mention that the tradition took on a special significance this year now that Ethel and Alice were away. Perhaps the flickering flame would help their loved ones find their way home sooner.

Jane slapped her hands on the top of the table, causing Louise to flinch. "This place needs some music, don't you think? I've been humming 'Blue Christmas' all afternoon."

"I doubt we need anything to make us bluer." Louise twirled her fork in her uneaten baby spinach leaves. "But you're right. Maybe we should have some music. What would you like me to play?"

"'I'll Be Home for Christmas'?" At Louise's frown, she shrugged. "Okay, maybe not that. How about some traditional Christmas carols? That will get us back into the spirit. Maybe 'O Holy Night' or 'What Child Is This?'"

The smile playing across Jane's lips disappeared when she glanced at Louise's nearly untouched plate. Neither of them was very hungry, it seemed.

"I was also looking around the house, and I'm rethinking our decision not to put up all of our holiday decorations this year," Jane said. "Maybe it made sense to go with the less-is-more concept when we weren't going to have any guests for Christmas, but now I feel the need to make a bigger statement."

Louise studied her for a few seconds. "Do you need a little decorating therapy?" She suspected Jane's gesture was for her benefit, to help draw her from her melancholy mood, but she let Jane keep her secret. Besides, Louise had a little secret of her own that she hoped would raise everyone's spirits.

"Some people use scented candles to relax," Jane said. "I'll do just fine with some ribbon, garland and tinsel."

"That sounds like a great idea. I don't suppose you'd be up for, *ahem*, a little entertaining therapy as well."

Jane's eyes widened, making it clear she'd picked up on her sister's sudden surplus of enthusiasm. "Louie, is there something you're not telling me? Just what are you roping me into?"

Louise couldn't help grinning. Her sweet youngest sister was the only person she permitted to call her by that nickname. "Okay, I'm caught. Vera cornered me at church and begged me to let her host the reveal party for the Secret Santa program at the inn."

"Reveal party?"

"It's where each recipient finds out who has been giving him gifts and has a chance to give a present in return." She paused to take a bite of her salad, suddenly a little hungry. "If it wouldn't be too much trouble, she'd like to have it here before services on Christmas Eve."

"Not too much trouble," Jane repeated with a chuckle. "And I take it you, like our dear Alice, have already agreed?"

"What should I have done?" Louise raised her hands in mock defensiveness. "The Christmas craft exchange Florence usually hosts had to be canceled because of Florence's sudden departure. Aunt Ethel hosted it the last time Florence had to be out of town, but well . . . you know."

"Vera pulled out the heavy ammunition, didn't she? Now I know how she keeps all her fifth-graders in line."

"She said if she couldn't find a place to host the reveal,

then another Acorn Hill Christmas event would have to be canceled."

"She could have planned it at her house."

Louise studied Jane for several seconds to see if she was kidding, but Jane's blank expression gave away nothing. The woman could hold a straight face in a comedy routine. "Now I know why she didn't ask you first. You would have been a much tougher egg to crack."

"I would have given in just as easily as you did," Jane admitted. "Besides, planning for an event will give us something to do instead of worrying about Aunt Ethel and Alice."

Relieved Jane wasn't upset with her, Louise pressed forward with her plan. "I thought we could make it something casual—just cookies, coffee, tea and hot chocolate."

"Sounds fine to me."

From the front part of the house, they heard a rustling that suggested the Ericksons had returned. Though Louise had been bothered by the quiet, now she wished for silence again. Strange. Perhaps the Ericksons were only stopping in briefly before they headed out on another adventure. It was unkind for her to hope so, but something about Sandy Erickson's intensity left Louise exhausted.

"Put on your work hat," Jane whispered. "Our guests have returned."

Louise nodded and listened for sounds of movement. Voices lingered in the foyer for a few minutes, but no one seemed to be moving to the stairs.

"Hello, Howard sisters, are you home?" Sandy called from the front hall. A few footsteps more and she reached the main entry to the kitchen. "Oh, there you are."

Jane popped to her feet with the agility of a runner, which she'd been for years. "Mrs. Erickson, how nice to see you."

Louise had introduced their guests to her youngest sister the night before, as they crept down the stairs just after Ethel and Alice rushed out the front door. Though the children showed their first signs of interest since arriving at the inn, their parents appeared a bit flustered by Florence's noisy visit.

Now Sandy looked back and forth between them, an amused expression on her face brushed pink by the chilly wind. Maybe she could relax after all. Maybe Grace Chapel Inn was going to be a good place for her to do it. Sandy's gaze moved to the half-filled plates still on the kitchen table. "Oh, please forgive me. I didn't mean to interrupt your lunch."

Louise looked back at the plates and waved a hand. "We just finished. Is there something we can do for you, Mrs. Erickson? Do you need something for your rooms?"

Or do you want to vacate them today because of the ruckus last night? she thought.

"It's not that. Please, both of you, call me Sandy."

"Please return the favor by calling us Jane and Louise," Jane said.

The two younger women traded smiles, leading Louise to observe that, at fifty, Jane was probably no more than a decade older than Sandy Erickson.

"We were hoping you would have time to give that tour you offered. The children are very excited to begin their study of nineteenth-century architecture. They're particularly interested in the antiques and furnishings of the period."

Louise could hardly imagine the Erickson children begging to learn more about Grace Chapel Inn, but Sandy appeared as if she was tempted to rub her hands together like an excited child with a pile of presents on Christmas morn. Sandy Erickson was a puzzle, all right, but Louise wondered if with all of her worry over Florence, Ronald, Alice and Aunt Ethel, she had the energy to put the pieces of the puzzle together.

"I suppose I could give a tour now." Louise paused to glance at her sister. "That is, if you'll clear away the lunch dishes, Jane."

"I'd be happy to," Jane answered too quickly.

Louise brushed imaginary dust off her shirt cuffs. "Well

then, we'll get started." But to Jane she added, "Then you can catch up with us as soon as you're finished."

"Oh no, I wouldn't want to intrude," Jane said, a smile just beneath the surface of her straight face. "Besides, as the oldest sister, you know the family home best of all."

Following Sandy from the room, Louise frowned at Jane over her shoulder. Her sister winked and giggled. Some things never changed no matter how many years passed.

Their tour nearing completion, Louise and the Ericksons relaxed in the library. "Claire, what do you think of these lovely fountain pens?" Sandy sifted through the box of pens that rested on Daniel Howard's desk. "Wouldn't it have been wonderful learning to write with a fountain pen?"

Claire shrugged, unimpressed. She and Dylan hadn't appeared interested in anything else Louise had told them about the childhood home of her mother, Madeleine Berry Howard, either. Their own mother only wanted them to be interested. Their father, on the other hand, appeared just as unimpressed as his children. He sat in the leather desk chair, but he was far from relaxed as his gaze flitted about the room. Sandy motioned with her hand to encourage the children to speak up, but when they didn't, she asked a question of her own. "What proportion of the furnishings has to be appropriate to the period for the home to be included on the historic register?"

Louise watched the children's eyes glaze over as they had when she'd spoken of the Greek Revival, Gothic Revival and Federalist houses designed during the early to mid-nineteenth century, but she decided to answer anyway. She'd started this tour, and she was determined to finish it before retreating to restore herself with a cup of tea. "The county historic preservation committee focuses solely on the house's exterior. Though the house was painted peach for years, in the renovation, we restored it to its historically accurate, though unusual, colors. It caused a bit of a stir in town."

Dylan turned his head up to her and drew his eyebrows together. "People in the olden days painted their houses purple and brown?"

It wasn't the most positive observation, but it was better than none, Louise decided. "They did like color, and they had such interesting names for the ones they chose. For instance, the color on the roofline trim is called *eggplant*. The body of the house is painted in a color called *cocoa*. On the shutters, though, they just called that color *green*. Pretty unoriginal, don't you think?"

Dylan agreed to that but gazed out the window, demonstrating that Louise had lost his attention again.

"Did you notice the sign on the door to this room?"

she asked to pull him back. She pointed to the sign that read THE DANIEL HOWARD LIBRARY. "This was the office where my father wrote the sermons he preached at Grace Chapel for more than sixty years. And those pens your mother pointed out were my father's collection. He even had some very special ones, including two Parker 51s and a coin-filler Waterman. My aunt Ethel, my father's sister, bought him that mahogany box so he could keep his pens in it."

The children cast curious glances at the pens. Sandy had already moved on to study the collection of framed photos of Daniel Howard as a boy and as a seminary student, and of Louise's parents before they married. Louise took the opportunity to open the box of pens again. She lifted a fawn-colored Parker 51 and rolled it between her fingers before offering it to Claire. The girl studied it for several seconds and then passed it on to her brother.

"Did your father collect these other things too?" Claire pointed to the old black-leather Bible and the dated globe that also rested on Daniel Howard's big mahogany desk.

"Those weren't part of a collection, but they did belong to him. He used that old Bible to research his sermons." She wondered if the Ericksons found time for Sunday school and church in their busy schedules. Just because she hadn't seen them at Grace Chapel this morning didn't mean they hadn't attended services at another church.

Because Dylan had started glancing around the room as if he was losing interest, Louise tried to engage him again. "Do you two collect anything like dolls or race cars?" She tried to remember some of the most recent cartoon-character trading cards, but the names escaped her.

"Posters," the two of them said in unison.

"You mean like of kitties in baskets, or inspirational sayings?"

Excitement filled Claire's little, round face for the first time since her family arrived. Her lips curved and her dark eyes crinkled. "No, of Mia and Beckham."

"Of Gordie and Federov." Dylan's hazel eyes gleamed with amusement.

Paul took pity on Louise when he noticed her perplexed expression. "Mia Hamm and David Beckham are soccer legends. Gordie Howe and Sergei Federov are heroes from hockey."

As understanding settled over her, Louise nodded. "Oh, of course, from your special interests." At least they appeared to be interested in something. "You probably don't know the names from my special interest—Bach, Beethoven, Rachmaninoff and Puccini."

Claire grimaced and glanced in her mother's direction to see if she'd been caught. "We know those names too. I can play a few of them."

"Me too," Dylan added.

"I love the works of the classical composers," Louise continued. "Just like you like to play your sports or watch your favorite players compete. Whenever I'm feeling low, I can go play one of my favorites, and my mood is instantly better."

"You're the one who plays the lovely baby grand piano in the parlor," Sandy said, brightening.

"I'm the one. I love music. I've played all my life and am involved in the music ministry at Grace Chapel."

"Oh really?" Sandy came closer. "Are you self-taught, or did you have a piano teacher?"

Louise was surprised to feel herself bristle at the woman's innocent inquiry. She studied Sandy, wondering why she was so interested, before answering. "I have a music education degree from the conservatory in Philadelphia. I've played professionally and have even tried my hand at composing."

"Do you also give private lessons?"

Before the words were fully out of her guest's mouth, Louise had an answer. "Yes, I do, but—"

"How wonderful! Don't you think that's wonderful, Paul?"

"Great." He barely looked up from the desk where he was fidgeting with Daniel Howard's pen collection. After several seconds, he stood up and stalked over to the window.

His disquiet unsettled Louise.

"I told you that both of the children played, didn't I? They're very well-rounded. Dylan has been playing for six years, and Claire was so excited to start that she began at age four."

The glum expressions on the children's faces suggested that they dreaded the latest turn in the conversation. Didn't they enjoy playing? Music had always given her peace and comfort, even after her mother's death, when she'd suddenly become responsible for an infant sister, and especially during the lonely times after the death of her husband, Eliot. Did Claire or Dylan find joy or peace when they played?

Sandy continued, clearly oblivious to Louise's discomfort. "It would be just great if you could work the children into your teaching schedule while we're here. We'd pay you your regular rate, of course. You know how much they lose if they don't have their daily practice."

So much for a relaxing vacation, Louise thought. First, they had an introduction to nineteenth-century architecture, and now Sandy wanted piano lessons for them. What next? Would Claire be expected to do soccer dribbling drills through the parlor while Dylan took shots on an imaginary goal on the frozen Fairy Pond? Somehow she suspected they'd prefer doing those things rather than taking piano lessons from her.

Louise demurred. "Oh my, this week is awfully busy as we get ready for Christmas. We're planning a small party for the community's Secret Santa program on Christmas Eve. Your family is welcome to attend, of course."

"Thank you. We'd like that," Sandy said politely, but she looked disappointed. "Oh well. If you find you do have the time after all, just let us know. The children would love working with someone of your caliber."

"I'll be sure to let you know. They're more than welcome to practice on my piano . . . if they're in the mood to play." She watched for reactions from the children, but both of their expressions were carefully blank. Still, in her heart, she believed they were grateful she hadn't offered to instruct them.

Well-rounded. Sandy had used that term a second time to describe their children. Well-rounded was a good thing, Louise reminded herself, but the Erickson children seemed to be involved in too many things to find joy in most of them. They were simply too busy. Overscheduled. Maybe that was just how a great many children were today, so busy expanding their minds and becoming the best at everything that they didn't have time to play.

This isn't your business, she reminded herself. Paul and Sandy had the right to raise their children as they saw fit, just as she and Eliot had enjoyed that freedom with

Cynthia. She just wished someone could make them realize that they might be missing out on the true joy of being together while they raced off to the many activities that separated them. Not her, of course, but someone. For now she rested in the knowledge that she wouldn't be finding time this week to teach extra piano lessons.

The dull gray of the snowy Pennsylvania countryside whirred past her as Alice drove the emerald green sedan they'd rented for the trip. Now, on the way to I-95, Alice was relieved to have escaped the Philadelphia airport traffic, as congested as ever, even on a Sunday. If only the sun would peek out from behind the steel helmet of sky that covered them, but Alice realized sunlight would only contrast with the dark mood of one of her passengers. Bringing in the cavalry to save the Simpsons' marriage lost some of its impact when the one who had the most to gain or lose joined them against his will.

Alice wasn't exactly an enthusiastic participant either and was still surprised by the series of events that landed her in this position as chauffeur to two argumentative passengers.

Ronald sat in the backseat looking sullen, like a teenager forced to visit relatives over summer vacation. At least he was less disheveled than he'd appeared the night before. His slacks and shirt were clean, and his hair had been combed, but he still wore the haunted look of a man who hadn't slept and probably couldn't now if he tried.

"If we had to do this, couldn't we at least have flown?"

"I told you that with the strike looming, we couldn't get tickets," Ethel said for the third time since she climbed in the rental car. "Besides, it's Christmas."

"My runaway wife got tickets."

In the front seat, Ethel turned her head to answer that one. "Florence was also willing to pay top dollar for first class. There is simply no excuse to waste that kind of money when we could easily make the drive in two days. Even with the rental car and stopping for the night in North Carolina, we'll still save money."

Alice glanced at her aunt sharply. *You mean we could have flown?* Somehow she managed not to ask the question aloud. Someone needed to watch out for Ethel during her multistate journey to ensure she didn't attempt amateur marital counseling. On the other hand, Alice would gladly have traded this road trip for a flight, even if she was a white-knuckle flyer.

"Are you saying we're driving sixteen hours, not counting stops, when we could have flown there in less than three?" Ronald boomed.

"This way is more romantic, don't you think?" Ethel smiled.

"You and I obviously have a very different definition of romantic," he grumbled.

Ethel's smile morphed to a frown as she looked over her shoulder again. "So you're an expert on romance now? I can tell you what you did to your wife was definitely *not* romantic. If you weren't going to defend your wife against those disparaging comments, the least you could have done was keep quiet and not make things worse."

The top of Ronald's balding head reddened, and he crunched his round face into a scowl. "I did defend her... eventually. I talked about all the things she's done on the Grace Chapel board, the donations she makes every year to local charities and the way she announces to anyone who will listen the joys of living in Acorn Hill."

Ethel waved away his comments with a flip of her hand. "It was too little too late as far as I'm concerned. Nothing could take away the fact that you laughed at your wife's expense. Laughed and then agreed."

"And I apologized for that."

"So you say."

"I kept apologizing while she was packing. She wouldn't even listen to me."

Ethel snorted. "After what you said, I wouldn't listen to you either."

"Nobody asked you."

Having already endured enough battles for one day, Alice jumped into the conversation. "Ronald, you never told us about the conversation you overheard."

Ronald made a dismissive sound from the backseat. "The two women were comparing stories about scenes my wife has made in each of their eating establishments. At the Coffee Shop, it was over a slice of overly tart blackberry pie. Then at Zachary's, my Florence took offense at a filet mignon that she found too rare at first and then overcooked after she had sent it back."

"Not a kind conversation, but…" Alice let her words trail away, deciding it would be best not to finish. As her father always said, if she couldn't say something nice, then she should keep quiet.

"But true," Ronald finished for her anyway. "She's always flying off the handle about something. Just look at the rampage she's gone on after what she *thought* she overheard. I can't believe she would even think I could be so disloyal as not to defend her."

As much as Alice wanted to help, she was uncomfortable giving relationship advice when her long-distance relationship of sorts with Mark Graves was the closest she'd ever come to a serious attachment. "Her feelings were hurt, Ronald. That's why she jumped to conclusions."

Ethel piped up again. "If you hadn't given her a reason, then she wouldn't have jumped."

Ronald gripped the back of the driver's seat and straightened behind it. "Alice, let's turn this car around and forget the whole thing. Florence and I have had troubles for a long time, and she's made her decision. Maybe we should just live the rest of our lives apart."

Alice tightened her hands on the steering wheel. No, they couldn't give up this easily. Ronald and Florence had loved each other too many years for their friends to let them give up without a fight. "We're already on our way. Let's just see the trip through. Then you and Florence can decide together what you want to do."

"Okay," he said finally.

Thank You, God. If not for You, we wouldn't have made it this far. She didn't know what He had in store for this trip or for the Simpsons. Still, she found comfort in knowing the situation was in God's hands.

Chapter Five

"Did she write anything yet?" Louise crowded in behind Jane as her sister sat in her office chair and booted up her computer.

"Give me a minute, okay?" Jane didn't look up from the screen, but she sounded annoyed. Either that or she was as eager as Louise was to receive word from Alice and her traveling companions. "The Internet is supposed to make information travel fast, but the computer has to be turned on and connected for it to work."

"Can't you make it go any faster?"

Jane sighed as she always did when they discussed any of those technological innovations that fascinated Jane but remained a mystery to Louise. Louise wasn't particularly interested in how it worked as long as it produced an update on Alice's status as soon as possible.

"I wish she just would have called," Louise lamented as her sister clicked a few things with her computer's mouse.

"I hope she's had a chance to write." Louise busied herself while she waited, adjusting the guest book on the reception desk.

"I'm checking my e-mail account since Alice will be writing from hers," Jane explained, though she hadn't been asked. She stared at the screen for several seconds and then started chuckling.

Louise moved in order to look at the screen. "What is it? Did something come from Alice?"

"Yes, it did. She wrote last night." Jane stood up from the desk and indicated with her hand for Louise to take her seat.

Lifting her glasses to the bridge of her nose, Louise studied the screen.

Dear Sisters,

I hope all is well at the inn. I am writing from Ronald's fancy wireless computer right in the lobby of our motel. We just arrived in Fayetteville, and it is late. The trip is going fairly well. The atmosphere in the car has been a bit tense. Ronald drove through most of Virginia and part of North Carolina, so I am not overtired. He is already resting in his room, and I will soon join Aunt Ethel in ours. We look forward to arriving tomorrow evening. How I miss relaxing at home with the two of you. Say a prayer for us.

Yours,
Alice

Louise frowned. "She uses the words *a bit tense*. If I know our aunt at all, that would be like calling the Mississippi River *a little stream*."

"You're right about that."

Turning her head, Louise looked up at Jane over her shoulder. "I wonder why she's being so diplomatic."

"She probably doesn't want us to worry."

Louise stood up and let her sister take her place. Jane's fingers flew over the keys as she wrote a return message, noting that the Ericksons were now their only guests and that everything was fine at the inn. After she shut off the computer, Jane stood and faced her.

"So everything's really fine?" Louise asked.

Jane smiled. "Just being diplomatic, and all good diplomacy goes two ways."

Jane carried a shopping basket through the narrow aisles of the General Store Monday afternoon. She didn't mind the cramped displays that placed dried fruits and nuts just across from bath towels, choosing to think of her search as a treasure hunt.

Her outing had two benefits: It gave her the chance to shop for Secret Santa gifts, and it allowed her a brief escape from the guests back at the inn.

As if it wasn't bad enough having Florence and Ronald's marriage in crisis and Ethel and Alice on a frenzied mission to save it, now Jane and Louise were stuck at the inn with guests who had developed cabin fever the minute they'd checked in. Jane was relieved to have time away from the Ericksons, who claimed to want relaxation but were prowling around like caged animals instead.

For a short time, she wanted to forget about all of the concerns and focus on something fun like selecting trinkets for her Secret Santa recipient, local librarian Nia Komonos. Because Alice and Ethel entrusted their recipients into Jane's care when they left for Florida, she looked forward to choosing additional small gifts for Zack Colwin and Rev. Thompson as well.

She put several tiny boxes of chocolates in her cart and then started down the next aisle toward the display of Asian spices and other exotic products that the General Store had begun stocking at her request. Spices were probably redundant gifts for a chef, but as a chef herself, Jane suspected that Zack would appreciate the gesture. She added containers of marjoram and turmeric to the other items in her cart.

A jingle of bells announced the arrival of another customer, but glancing over the top of the shelving, Jane didn't see anyone. She moved to a small section of personal-care items and started picking through a basket of perfumed lotions. Maybe Nia would appreciate some of those.

"Hi, Ms. Howard."

Meghan Quinlan stood at the end of the aisle, a heavy-looking purse clutched under her arm.

"Hello, Meghan." Jane approached the sweet nine-year-old daughter of Logan and Jessica Quinlan. But when she reached her, Jane blinked. The child looked the same, with curly auburn hair and sparkling green eyes—looks she shared in common with her two younger sisters—but the coat she wore didn't quite button. Also, there was a small gap where her sleeves came short of reaching her mittens. Her jeans, though clean, were frayed and revealed far too much of her boots to have fit properly for a long time.

Meghan shifted under the examination and shuffled her boots. "Are you buying Christmas presents?"

Jane forced herself to glance back to the basket of lotions, sorry for her lack of manners. "Yes, just a few last-minute things. How about you?"

The little girl grinned as she pointed to her purse. "I'm shopping too."

"Aren't your mom and dad with you today?"

Meghan stiffened. She glanced around as if she was worried about being caught.

"Not this time?" Jane encouraged.

"No, not this time."

"Christmas secrets, huh?"

A tentative smile settled on the child's pale pink lips, and she hugged her purse to her.

"I'll let you get started then," Jane said.

Meghan waved and moved past her to the rear of the store, where a small toy section was located.

Jane tried to return to her own shopping, even sniffing a few of the lotions and breathing in wild berries and vanilla, but she couldn't shake thoughts of the child in the back of the store. She'd been acquainted with the Quinlans for quite a while now. They were an upstanding, hard-working family; Logan and Jessica always seemed to take such pride in caring for their daughters. So why was Meghan shopping alone while wearing clothes she should have handed down months ago to her sisters?

Finally, Jane just dropped the wild berry lotion into the basket, hoping Nia preferred the fruity-smelling type, and moved on to the back of the store. She fully expected to encounter Meghan playing with a few of the display toys. Older sister or not, Meghan was only a child after all.

Jane was surprised when the child hurried around the corner and ran right into her. Meghan's purchases scattered and her purse landed with a thud, part of the plastic bag filled with coins spilling on the floor.

"Oh, Meghan, I'm sorry."

"That's okay. At least all of it didn't spill."

The two of them crouched, tucking the coins back into the bag and gathering the purchases into a pile. Even after they were finished, Jane couldn't help glancing back at the items Meghan had chosen—two three-pair packages of tiny anklet socks, two packages of underwear with princess characters on them and two sets of balls and jacks.

She wondered if they were gifts for Meghan's sisters. If they were, why was a child buying underwear for Christmas? This didn't make sense. Logan Quinlan had a good job at Potterston Feed and Grain. She seemed to remember, though, that the grain warehouse had announced some lay-offs last spring. Could Logan's job have been affected?

When she glanced up again, Meghan was chewing her lip and studying her.

Jane lifted a few of the packages. "You had an awful lot of things in your arms. How about I share my basket with you?"

At first the girl shook her head, but then she shrugged. "Are you sure we won't mix up our stuff?"

Jane held back a smile. "No, probably not. I'll try to remember which things are yours. We'll separate our purchases at the cash register."

Meghan appeared to think for a few seconds. "Okay."

Jane paused at a display near the cash register to select

a pen-and-pencil set for the minister and a mirrored compact for the librarian. As she did, she caught her fellow shopper checking out her items.

"Who'd you buy all that stuff for?" Meghan asked.

"I'm playing Secret Santa to a few of my friends. I get to leave surprises for them without their knowing who they're from. Doesn't that sound like fun?"

"I like playing Santa." Meghan started stacking her items on the counter.

"You're doing a great job of it. Did you already buy wrapping paper?"

The look on Meghan's face said she hadn't, so Jane lifted a roll of it and a package of tape from bins next to the register. "These will be my Christmas gifts to you."

"Thank you." The child appeared much too grateful for such simple gifts.

Together they dumped the bag of coins onto the still conveyor and started counting them out.

"Boy, you have a lot of money here," Jane told her. "I bet you've been saving for a long time."

Meghan beamed. "It's the money from my piggy bank."

"That's nice of you to shop with your very own money." Jane put four more quarters together.

Meghan smiled again, but this time less brightly. Another

pang of worry filled Jane as she wondered just how limited funds were for the Quinlans.

With all of the money counted, Meghan came up seventy-four cents short. Jane reached into her own purse and made up the difference. While the cashier rang up Jane's purchases, Meghan waited so they could walk out together.

On the sidewalk outside the General Store, Meghan turned back to her. She had pulled her coat as close to buttoning as possible. "Thanks for my Christmas present."

Jane was moved by Meghan's obvious gratitude for such a simple act of kindness. "You're welcome," she choked out. For now she needed to tuck away her worries about the Quinlan family, but she vowed to find some answers.

"Would you like me to drive you home?"

Meghan looked away. "No. That's okay." She paused for several seconds before she added, "My dad's picking me up in a little while."

Though Jane suspected she wasn't being truthful, she smiled and prepared to part company. "Well, you have a Merry Christmas, Miss Meghan." Jane hugged her and started walking toward the inn.

"Ms. Howard," Meghan called after her.

Jane stopped and turned around.

"Can you tell me who your secret presents are for? I won't tell anybody. I promise."

Jane gave her an exaggerated wink. "Secret Santas never tell."

Alice rubbed her right eye beneath her sunglasses while focusing the left one on the seemingly never-ending asphalt ribbon of I-95. If only she could close them both, just for a little while, she wouldn't mind missing some of the scenery that had changed from snow-clad pines to sunny palm trees. To Alice, who'd never before visited the Sunshine State, the first palm tree she spotted, somewhere north of Jacksonville, had been quite a novelty. That newness had worn off completely now that she was nearing an exit for St. Augustine.

Before leaving North Carolina at just past eight o'clock that morning, they'd stuffed their coats, hats and gloves in the trunk with their luggage, realizing that much of their clothing was "out of season" in their new climate. Alice's neck ached. Her arms ached. Even her heart ached after the hours of painful discussions. At first she monitored them as an impartial observer, then she eventually participated as a concerned friend. Now even the bright sunshine and cobalt sky striped by scattered cirrus clouds couldn't give her any relieving calm. Her emotions were stretched tighter than a high wire, and they hadn't even faced Florence yet. Alice was invested in this situation, however, and she would take the loss personally if Ronald and Florence gave up the fight.

"You're still awake, aren't you, Alice?"

Ronald's voice from the backseat startled Alice from her thoughts. The hand that had been rubbing her eye moved to her lips to hush him as she glanced at her aunt in the passenger seat. Ethel was sleeping with her head at an odd angle that probably would have her waking feeling worse than when she'd nodded off an hour before. As sore as Alice felt after the two-day drive, she could just imagine how uncomfortable Ethel and Ronald, both at least a decade her senior, must have felt.

"Barely," she whispered finally.

Looking no more rested after his own brief siesta, Ronald leaned as far forward as his seat belt would allow.

"There's a rest stop coming up," he said in a soft voice. "Why don't you take the next exit and let me drive?"

"Are you sure? I haven't seen any signs for a rest stop. We should be there in a few hours anyway."

"Just over two hours, depending on the traffic on Interstate 4."

She peeked at him in her rearview mirror. "You've been there?"

His smile was a sad one. "A few dozen times. Darlene is my wife's favorite aunt, you know, even if they don't have a lot in common."

Alice wondered what he meant by that, but he didn't elaborate. Ronald had talked about a lot of things he would have preferred not to share in the last two days, and she didn't want to press him on something less critical. Florence's aunt, however, did give them a safe topic for discussion, one that didn't involve power struggles, miscommunication or blame. "When was the last time you visited her?"

He hesitated as if trying to remember. "Oh, nearly ten years, I suspect. You know how it is. You have good intentions of visiting with family more often, but schedules get in the way. Before you know it, you're a decade older, and your relatives seem like strangers."

Alice grimaced. So much for the safe topic. She'd dug this hole, though, so she had no choice but to continue. "Do you have good memories of those visits?"

"The best. Early in our marriage, when Darlene and Boyd's twin girls were still toddlers, we visited as often as we could. My wife fancied herself the girls' doting aunt, though in reality those girls were Florence's first cousins."

Alice tried to make sense of all that Ronald was saying, but the incongruity of his comments had her puzzled. Had

Florence's aunt and uncle become parents late in life for them to have young children when the Simpsons were newlyweds? Also, the picture of Florence as a "doting aunt" seemed out of character. While she was still trying to find an appropriate way to pose either of those questions, Ronald continued as if he hadn't noticed her hesitation.

"Florence loved those girls. Karen and Sharon are their names. Boyd's gone now, and his daughters are in their fifties and nearly finished raising their own families." He paused for so long that it seemed as if he'd said all he cared to on the subject, but then he continued. "That was when there were still possibilities. Before Florence gave up hope."

"Hope? What do you mean?"

"That we would be able to have children."

His words were so succinct, so simple, and yet there was nothing simple about the message they delivered. The Simpsons had wanted children? She assumed they'd chosen a childless life. Florence didn't even seem to *like* children and certainly didn't make a lot of effort to be near them. "Oh, I didn't know."

"You weren't supposed to. It was easier for us to live as if this were the life we chose—the adventure of travel, the opportunity to collect rare possessions—rather than deal with people feeling sorry for us."

"They wouldn't have—" Alice stopped herself, realizing even she felt sorry for them over something they'd come to terms with decades before.

"Don't get me wrong. We accepted God's will for us . . . *eventually*."

The way that Ronald stressed the last word made Alice wonder just how hard they'd worked to find that acceptance and what it had cost their marriage. "Did you ever consider adoption?" she couldn't help asking.

"At first, Florence wouldn't hear of it, but by the time she softened to the idea, I was more reluctant. We had our life. We were comfortable in it. I couldn't see changing everything. It was the only . . . oh, it doesn't matter."

For several long minutes, he said nothing. Either there was no more to say or he couldn't find the words. Ahead on the right, the exit for a rest stop came into view, but instead of tapping her brakes to disengage the cruise control, she drove past it. She sensed that Ronald hadn't said all he needed to, but she felt certain that whatever else was on his mind would be lost if she turned off the highway and parked the car.

"You missed the exit," Ronald pointed out needlessly.

"I know."

"Why didn't you stop?"

Alice felt nervous, the way she always did when in a

confrontation. Maybe she shouldn't push Ronald. Ethel had certainly pushed him enough, and Florence would do her share as soon as they reached Grand Island. Still, she'd come to help, and she sensed that it would help him to finish whatever he'd started saying. "I didn't think you were finished talking."

"I was."

Alice didn't want to seem antagonistic. Even so, she couldn't just drop the issue. "Were you? You began to say something else. It was the only *what*, Ronald?"

At first he didn't answer. Then he sighed. "It was the only time I ever put my foot down with my wife. She never forgave me for it."

Alice considered the information. She would have asked more, but Ethel startled in her sleep and then came fully awake.

"Ow!" She clamped her hand on her neck. "How could you let me sleep like that?"

"Sorry." Alice glanced at her aunt with a pitying look. "I didn't know how to move you."

"You could have figured out a way. Now my neck's going to ache all day," Ethel griped.

"Well, Sleeping Beauty has joined the land of the conscious," Ronald said, causing Ethel's scowl to deepen.

Pulling down the visor mirror, Ethel set to patting her

red locks into place. Finally, with an exasperated sigh, she flipped it up again. "How much farther do we have to go?"

It must have been Alice's exhaustion that made her aunt's comment seem so funny; she couldn't help chuckling. "You sound like Jane when Father took the three of us to Normandy Beach in New Jersey. She kept saying 'Are we there yet? Are we there yet?'"

Ethel glanced sidelong at her. "Well, are we?"

"It's not much farther," Ronald answered for Alice.

Turning around in her seat, Ethel focused on Ronald. "Are you ready for this?"

"I'm ready. Your niece is going to take the next exit and park so I can drive the rest of the way."

Who could argue with an order like that? The man in Alice's rearview mirror suddenly appeared stronger, more determined. No, this trip was not Ronald's idea, but he suddenly seemed eager to get on with it. His enthusiasm—or at the very least, lack of reluctance—gave Alice hope. Maybe this meeting with Florence would go easier than they'd expected, and they would be back on their way to Acorn Hill before they knew it. Maybe.

Chapter Six

*B*ack at the inn, Louise was sitting alone in the kitchen, clipping coupons, when Jane opened the back door and stepped inside. Louise lowered the scissors to the table and glanced at her sister expectantly. "Did you have a nice time?"

Jane slipped out of her coat. "Well, I bought some Secret Santa gifts, if that's what you mean."

She studied Jane for several seconds. For someone who had left to escape tension, Jane appeared to have kept her share and brought it back home with her. "What happened while you were out?"

"Nothing—" Jane appeared to stop herself before the denial was out of her mouth.

Louise recognized that something was bothering her sister. Jane would tell her when she was ready. While she waited, Louise lifted her scissors and clipped a sizable laundry-detergent coupon. If they used it on Tuesday, double-coupon day, it would be a really good bargain.

"Can I tell you in a few minutes?" Jane asked. "I'm still processing it myself."

"Sure," Louise answered. "Perhaps I should wait to update you on what happened around here while you were gone."

"Something happened? You have to be kidding. Haven't we had enough drama here for one week?"

Louise studied another offer. "Oh, this isn't anything so dramatic," she assured Jane. "Patsy Ley just called to reserve a room for Pastor Henry's cousin and his wife for five days beginning Wednesday."

"More guests?"

She could definitely relate to Jane's tired frown. "Patsy heard from Vera that we're hosting the reveal party and that we have guests through the holidays, so she thought two more wouldn't matter."

Jane's only answer was a somewhat weary shrug. Louise had to commiserate with her. The accumulation of small changes made them far busier than they'd planned to be for Christmas. "Anyway, Patsy assures me that Kevin and Jill won't be around the inn much. Apparently, Patsy and Pastor Henry invited several relatives for the holidays, but none could accept. Then several changed their plans, so suddenly the Leys are expecting the rectory to be overflowing."

Resting her hands on the edge of the counter, Jane let her shoulders droop as if Louise's words weighed them down. "Soon there will be no room at the inn, either."

"You're right. I told Patsy she could have only one room, since Cynthia will be staying here as well."

Jane removed price tags from the small boxes of chocolates and a container of hard candies before looking back at her again. "Have you heard from Cynthia yet?"

"Not yet." Louise continued to clip, this time a combination offer for several cans of tomato soup. "I'll call her tonight. I still don't know when she's coming in." Louise didn't want to admit that she was beginning to worry. Her daughter was thirty-four now, and Cynthia could take care of herself. Still, it was a mother's prerogative to worry, and Louise always availed herself of that right.

Lowering her voice, Jane pointed toward the door. "Did anything new happen with our interesting guests while I was gone?"

"They're still lurking, pretending to relax. Sandy's even mentioned piano lessons again, but I managed to put her off for now." Louise held her hands wide, scissors gaping in one and coupons in the other. "I hate to disappoint her, but I don't think the children are interested in lessons."

"Or anything that involves spending time with their parents," Jane added.

Louise nodded. "I really think that Dylan and Claire are so overscheduled they don't know what to do without the frenzy of activity. Their parents appear equally lost. The children seem to sense that they should want to relax and play and are rebelling a bit, but they don't really know how to have simple fun." She gazed out the window, the troubled family filling her thoughts. When she glanced back at Jane again, her younger sister was smiling.

"You're looking for a way to help, aren't you, Louie?"

"I'd like to do something if I can."

"I know just what you mean—I have a cause of my own."

Jane folded her arms, rubbing her hands along her upper arms as if she was chilled. "I saw little Meghan Quinlan at the General Store by herself, and I'm worried there's something very wrong at the Quinlan home." She described the child's appearance and strange purchases, and then shared her suspicions with her sister.

Louise set her scissors aside, stepped over to Jane and rested a hand on her arm. Jane covered that hand with hers.

"It sounds as if a few families might benefit from our help," Louise said. "I guess Alice and Aunt Ethel aren't the only ones God is calling this Christmas season to reach out to the 'least of these.' He has laid on our hearts the need to help three different families." She mulled over the thought, feeling honored and humbled by it. "'For I was hungry and you gave me something to eat, I was thirsty and you gave me something to drink, I was a stranger and you invited me in'" (Matthew 25:35).

Jane smiled as though she too, remembered how many times their father had quoted that passage to the three of them. "I don't know all of it, but I had to memorize Jesus' words in Matthew 25:40 for Sunday school. '. . . I tell you the truth, whatever you did for one of the least of these brothers of mine, you did for me.'"

Louise thought for a few seconds and then turned back to her sister. "Do you think Jesus' words include troubled families and overscheduled children?"

"I think He meant us to help many people in many ways."

Not sure how she was going to provide such help, Louise lowered her gaze to the array of gifts on the counter. In one hand, she lifted the pen-and-pencil set while she collected the mirrored compact in the other. "Now these will be welcome gifts. It must be hard selecting things for your own recipient as well as Aunt Ethel's and Alice's. If you need any more ideas, just give me the names and I'll be more than happy to help."

"Not so fast, lady. I'm not going to tell you who any of the recipients are."

"Don't blood connections count for anything?" Louise asked.

"Not this time."

Louise grinned. "I moved back here for nothing then."

"I only know the identity of Aunt Ethel's and Alice's recipients because they trusted me to fill in for them." Jane crossed her arms in a friendly standoff. "You'll find out the answers on Christmas Eve, just like everyone else."

"Then I won't be confiding in you who my recipient is either," Louise said, mimicking her sister's pose.

"Well, then don't."

If Jane had stuck out her tongue right then, she might have repeated a scene from her childhood, when she was occasionally a bit mischievous. She had the same twinkle in her eyes at least.

"Have you purchased all your Secret Santa gifts yet?" Jane asked.

"Not yet." Louise didn't mention she hadn't even started.

"When will you finish?" Instead of waiting for an answer, Jane began to separate her bounty of trinkets and sweets into three sets of color-coded gift bags—one red, another green and the third a plaid mixture of both. "I've received nothing from my own Secret Santa so far—not even a card. I don't want to be greedy, but I expected at least a little surprise by now."

"I agree. That is odd," Louise acknowledged. She'd received a lovely snowflake Christmas ornament and a basket with coffees and teas from her Secret Santa. Both Ethel and Alice had received gifts from their benefactors before they left for Florida.

Louise shrugged, unable to hide her mild concern. "I wouldn't worry too much about it. Maybe your Secret Santa just got a late start like . . ." She let her words trail away, but Jane glanced over at her.

"You mean like you?" Her eyes narrowed. "Are you my stingy Secret Santa?"

"No. Wrong Mrs. Claus here. I've been so busy planning for Christmas with Cynthia—and then with our surprise guests—that I haven't gotten down to work on it."

Jane rubbed her chin. "Do you think there's a possibility my name was accidentally excluded from the exchange?"

"I wouldn't think so." They had, after all, watched Vera toss their names into the hat one by one. But her own recipient, Viola Reed, would soon be thinking the same thing as Jane if Louise didn't get started.

Louise couldn't have been more delighted to draw Viola's name. They were dear friends, after all. The irony of it was the very fact that they were such close friends. It was more difficult to select trivial gifts for Viola. Nothing was special enough or personal enough. Certainly books, which Louise could select for her friend blindfolded because of their shared passion for nineteenth-century literature, wouldn't work. It just wouldn't do to buy books for a woman who owned Nine Lives Bookstore.

Maybe something for one of her cats? she thought. If Viola loved anything as much as her precious books, it was her collection of felines, all named for literary characters. Louise couldn't help smiling at the thought. She could just picture Anna, the ivory Siamese with light-blue eyes, and Gatsby, the seventeen-pound, black-and-white male, and even Tess, the beautiful calico, battling over a tinkling caged ball or a feathered chase toy. She would have to buy toys galore for all of them.

"Well, something seems to be making you happy."

Louise glanced over to see Jane studying her. "It's nothing. I just had a moment of inspiration. Now I have to find some time to shop."

"If you're inspired, I certainly hope you're shopping for my Christmas present. Even if I'm not your recipient, I'm still on your Christmas list, right?"

"Maybe." Louise didn't want to spoil the fun by revealing she'd purchased and wrapped all her gifts for family members before the leaves even started to turn. She liked having all her shopping finished before the Christmas rush started. It didn't sit well with her at all that she'd fallen so far behind on her other purchases.

She was helping Jane to add color-coordinated tissue paper to her gift bags when the phone rang. Their gazes met, and Jane frowned, suggesting that Louise wasn't the only one becoming wary of phone calls.

Louise answered on the second ring. "Grace Chapel Inn."

"Hi, Mom."

Relief rushed through her, as she smiled into the receiver. "Hello, sweetheart. I'd planned to call you tonight."

"I saved you a call then. You were getting worried, weren't you?"

Louise could almost see her daughter's scolding finger and could certainly hear the laughter in her voice, even if it sounded a little unnatural. "When should we expect you?" she asked her daughter.

Cynthia made a muffled sound into the receiver. "Late tomorrow."

Louise couldn't help asking, "Are you feeling all right? Are you sure you're okay to drive alone?"

"Mom, you always worry." Cynthia paused, probably smiling at the phone. "Besides, I won't be alone."

"What do you mean?"

Again, there was a muffled sound. "I didn't think you would mind, so I've invited Greg to come home for Christmas with me."

"Greg?"

"Greg Hollister."

Her throat suddenly dry, Louise cleared it before she spoke again. "I don't remember your mentioning that name before."

"I guess I didn't," Cynthia admitted. "That's why I'm having you meet him now."

"Are you serious about this young man? How long have you known him? Is he even—"

"So many questions, Mom." Her nervous titter did not escape detection. "I have to go right now, but I can answer them all tomorrow." She paused, seeming to confer with someone on her end before speaking again. "Don't worry. You'll love him."

"Wait," Louise began, but her daughter must not have heard, because she spoke at the same time.

"Can't wait to see you. I love you, Mom. Bye now."

"Good-bye." Louise slowly lowered the phone into its cradle. Jane was watching her.

"Who am I to try to help another family," Louise said, pausing before she added, "when I apparently have no idea what's going on in my own?"

The moment of truth arrived Monday evening along with three weary travelers. The last vestiges of sunlight cast shadows on the Florida subdivision of stone-block ranch homes painted in beige, creamy white and hues of gray. Surrounding them, the neighborhood fairly burst with color from flowering trees and bushes and even green lawns that didn't seem to realize it was winter. As twilight began to take hold, Christmas lights danced in some of those trees, their flickering lights out of place next to still-blooming flowers.

When Ronald pulled into the drive of a cream-colored house with a peach front door and shut off the engine, the silence within the sedan was oppressive. Though Alice felt the need to stretch her muscles, she was simultaneously filled with the irrational temptation to stay in the car with the doors locked.

The impulse was silly, and she knew it, yet she couldn't

help herself. The next few moments posed a wide spectrum of possible outcomes, from a love story as tender as that of Ruth and Boaz to the bloodletting in the Battle of Jericho. She wondered just how many of them would be left standing if the walls crumbled.

"Are we just going to sit here, Alice, or are we going to get out and ring the bell?" Ethel frowned at her as she pulled the door handle. She climbed out of the car not appearing sore at all. Maybe the nap had refreshed her after all.

At least her aunt hadn't singled out Ronald for her comment, though he was taking his time getting out of the driver's seat. His shoulders were braced, and his mouth was pressed into a grim line. He was going in for battle, all right, and he didn't appear convinced he'd be victorious. Though Ethel probably didn't even know about the Simpsons' marital disappointments that had built a foundation for resentment, she still was ready to offer Ronald her compassion.

The first thing that struck Alice as she pushed open the car's rear door was the scent outside, earthy and alive, so unlike the icy tang of frozen earth and hibernating nature she remembered from home. If only the heady perfume of hibiscus and azaleas could keep her from missing the snow-covered housetops of Acorn Hill.

Ethel rang the doorbell while Ronald and Alice were still going up the walk. The front door came open just as she lifted her hand to push the doorbell a second time.

Alice stopped at the bottom step, staring at the woman inside the screen door, someone who was too young to be any aunt of Florence Simpson. Alice rubbed at her road-weary eyes, which seemed to be playing tricks on her. The image, though, stayed the same when she lowered her hands. The woman standing inside looked more like Ethel's long-lost twin than any relative of Florence's. Well, a mousy-brown-haired version of Ethel, wearing jeans and sneakers; but the two women's round faces were mirror images of one another just the same.

Ronald must have noticed the resemblance too, because he kept looking at Ethel and then at the other woman with a quizzical expression.

Ethel leaned close to Alice's ear. "Just what are you looking at?"

Alice glanced back at her aunt, surprised she couldn't see it. Anxiety filled the woman's pale blue eyes, also similar to Ethel's, until her gaze landed on Florence's husband. "Ronald—" She stopped herself, glancing nervously behind her as she stepped outside and closed the door softly behind her. "Is that you?"

"Of course it is." Ronald's voice sounded strained. "Grayer and more battle scarred but the same Social Security number as far as I can tell."

The woman smiled at Ronald's attempt at a joke, but her expression was equally tight. "What are you doing here?"

"I'm here to bring Florence home."

"Maybe you shouldn't have—" Again she stopped herself as if hurtful words didn't sit well with her. She swung her head toward Ethel and Alice. In a soft voice, she asked, "And your companions?"

"Same reason," he said.

The woman blinked a few times and then turned back to Ethel and Alice. "Ladies, please excuse my poor manners. I'm Darlene Irwin, Florence's aunt."

"Aunt?" Ethel lifted an eyebrow.

Darlene's smile was almost bashful, as she looked up at them from beneath her lashes. "Her mother was my oldest sister. Florence and I are really more like sisters, since we're only a year apart. I've always insisted that she not call me Aunt Darlene." She shivered visibly at the thought. "It makes me feel too old."

Oldest sister? Suddenly some of what Ronald had said earlier made sense to Alice. Darlene and Florence were planning their families at the same time because they were contemporaries. Things just didn't work out the way the Simpsons had planned.

Ronald cocked his head. "Where's my wife?"

Darlene glanced nervously into the house. "She's resting. She's had a really tough couple of days." As she said the last part, she avoided meeting Ronald's gaze.

As someone who avoided confrontation whenever

possible, Alice shared Darlene's discomfort. In her own case, Alice couldn't help feeling relieved that Ronald and Florence's meeting would be delayed, even if only for a little while.

Ethel wouldn't hear of it. "If our Florence is sleeping, then it's high time you awaken her, Darlene. We've been traveling two days to see her, and we don't intend to wait around here for her to take a nap."

Darlene blinked and picked at imaginary lint on her lightweight peach sweater. She might have been Ethel's twin in facial appearance, but, it seemed, the two personalities couldn't have been more different. Whereas Aunt Ethel was forceful and opinionated, Darlene was mild-mannered and agreeable. The irony of it was lost on Alice's aunt.

"Well?" Ethel pressed.

Instead of meeting the other woman's gaze, Darlene glanced at her niece's estranged husband. "Ronald?"

Alice expected Ronald to hesitate. He'd been coerced into being here in the first place, no matter what he might want Darlene to believe. He surprised Alice, though, by straightening his shoulders.

"Please, Darlene, I need to talk to her now."

"Very well. Please wait here." She pressed her lips together in a clear sign that she thought waking Florence was a mistake.

Alice had to agree. Florence Simpson was enough of a . . . challenge, even when she hadn't been awakened from a sound sleep.

When Darlene pulled open the door and started inside, the squeak of an interior door reached Alice's ear.

"Darlene, who's out there?" Florence called from the hall.

"Florence, dear, I was just coming to find you."

"Find me? You knew where—" Florence's words and her footsteps halted at the end of the hall the moment the guests at the front entrance came into view.

For several seconds, time seemed to be held captive, with no one speaking or moving. Florence was the first to escape it. She started shaking her head, slowly at first, then faster, then forcefully.

"No, no, no, no!" She yelled the words, shaking her head all the while. "Ronald Simpson, you are not going to come here, pretend everything is all right and take me back home, even if you did bring . . . witnesses." She took a step backward. "No. It's not going to happen, so get out—all of you. Now!" She whirled and started down the hall.

"Florence Simpson, you stop right there!" Ethel's stern voice didn't allow for any argument.

Alice, Ronald and Darlene waited for the fireworks to begin. Amazingly, Florence did as she was told, but she didn't turn around.

Without apology, Ethel brushed past Darlene into the house. "We haven't just driven nearly a thousand miles for you to toss us out on the street. Your husband is here to apologize to you, and whether you like it or not, you're going to let him do it."

Florence did turn around then, her expression livid. "You don't know anything about it. And you ... how can you claim to be my friend and then bring *him* here?"

Ethel took several steps forward, until only a few feet separated the two women—a standoff between two forceful characters in a dark hallway. "I'm not claiming to be your friend. I'm *being* your friend."

Florence's mouth opened and then closed.

"Good. Now that I have your attention, I have some things to say."

As she watched the exchange, Alice experienced a moment of shame. A few times in her life, especially since she and her sisters decided to open Grace Chapel Inn, Alice had wished Ethel would be a bit less forceful, certainly less involved in everyone else's business. Perhaps someone more like Darlene. In this critical moment, though, Alice realized it would take someone with Ethel's unique personality to bring Florence to her senses. God had created Ethel with a purpose. As always, the Lord had a plan.

"I don't need to hear this." Florence's words were little more than a whisper. She closed her eyes and covered her face with her hands.

"You do need to hear it. What Ronald did was wrong.

I completely agree with you on that one. But if you try to tell me what he did was unforgivable, you're going to get an argument there."

"He doesn't deserve any—"

"Deserve?" Ethel rubbed her index finger over her lips as if deep in thought. "What an interesting choice of words. Does any of us deserve forgiveness? I always thought that had to do with grace—mercy even. I thought forgiveness was a gift."

"That's not fair, and you know it."

Ethel's shoulders lifted and then dropped. "I never claimed it was, but that doesn't make it less true."

Alice fought back a smile. Only Ethel could turn a conversation like this one into a discussion of God's forgiveness, a gift that they all enjoyed, a truth with which even an angry Florence couldn't argue. Alice glanced at Ronald, who, like her, was still peering through the screen door. She turned toward the area where Darlene had been standing, but Florence's aunt had disappeared into what Alice guessed was the kitchen.

"You of all people must know that there's more to our problems than just one awful day." Florence started wringing her hands, her distress strangely out of character.

"That's why you should be talking to your husband instead of hiding inside this house like a coward."

Automatically, the Florence they all knew so well was back among them, with her eyes flashing. "Ethel Buckley, you know perfectly well that I am not a coward. How can you even say that? I've never been a coward, and I'm not about to start now."

"Then it's settled," Ethel said, pointing toward the screen door and to Ronald and Alice, looking in like a pair of children at a candy counter.

Florence's eyes widened as she realized that, in effect, she had agreed to speak to her husband. She started shaking her head, but finally she blew out an exasperated sigh. "Fine. I'll talk to him. The sooner he finishes talking, the sooner he'll be back on the road to Pennsylvania. Him and his fan club." She frowned first at Ethel, then at Alice.

The side of Ethel's mouth lifted. "Think what you will, dear, but my niece and I haven't come to plead Ronald's case to you. We're here for you too."

"Why couldn't you just have left me alone? I needed time alone, time to think. I needed—"

"Someone to convince you," Ethel said, "not to make the biggest mistake of your life."

Chapter Seven

*A*lice leaned back into one of the white wicker side chairs in Darlene's sunroom and wrapped her hands around the warm cup her hostess pressed into her hands. Twinkling Christmas lights encircling the tall row of windows cast soft glimmers across Ethel and Darlene as they sat on a wicker sofa opposite her.

The low lighting, the soft floral cushions on the chairs, and even the cranberry Christmas candle with its flickering flame on the coffee table were all intended to create serenity, but despite her body's aching exhaustion, Alice couldn't relax. "Thank you again," Alice said.

From the moment that Florence had marched out the front door, having begrudgingly accepted her husband's invitation to take a walk, Darlene played hostess to her other uninvited guests. After she disappeared into the kitchen, she returned with a tray of fruit and sandwiches. In addition to her other kindnesses, Darlene accepted no arguments when they tried to turn down her offer of lodging. Now she insisted that they sit and rest in the sunroom. They did sit, but finding rest was another matter.

Outside the walls of windows, the Florida sun had long since disappeared, leaving behind a dark sky set ablaze with twinkling stars and a crescent moon. Even those displays of God's creations didn't bring peace, and all three women fidgeted.

"When do you think they'll come back?" Darlene asked, her soft words breaking the silence.

"They have a lot to talk about," Ethel said. "This might take some time."

Her aunt appeared so anxious that Alice longed to hug her and assure her that everything would be okay, but she wasn't sure Ethel would appreciate the gesture just then. She had to give her aunt credit. She'd recognized the problem and had taken on the challenge of correcting it, not letting any obstacles get in her way. Alice worried, though, about how Ethel would handle it if the Simpsons didn't reconcile.

"You've done all you can, Aunt Ethel. You know that, right?"

"But is it enough? I just don't know. There has to be something else we can do."

"There is. We can pray now that Ronald will be ready to say healing words to Florence and that she'll be ready to hear them."

Ethel shook her head, her eyes misting for the first time since Florence had shown up at the inn with her sad news. "They can't give up. They just can't."

"We can support and pray for our friends, but we can't decide for them about saving their marriage." Alice hung her head, feeling some of her aunt's frustration. "They have to do that themselves."

Darlene's smile was a sad one. "They used to have so much to talk about, but apparently they've been missing that for the last few years. How do relationships slip away like that?"

"Because we allow them to," Ethel answered, though Darlene's question was likely rhetorical.

Darlene sipped her tea. "They can't realize what they're losing, or they would try harder."

"They just can't see it," Ethel agreed.

Alice found herself studying the two women. Both had raised families, and both had buried husbands they loved. They knew of what they spoke. Both honestly loved Florence and wanted to help her save her marriage. As the two of them sat side by side, Alice still found their facial resemblance remarkable. She'd always heard that everyone had a twin. Well, her aunt need look no further for hers.

"Goodness, Alice, whatever are you staring at?" Ethel asked finally.

"The resemblance, of course," Darlene said with a smile.

Ethel's forehead furrowed as she set aside her cup. "What do you mean?"

Alice couldn't help chuckling. Any laugh, even a small

one, felt nice after all the tension they'd experienced that day. "You two are practically twins. Ronald noticed it. Florence would have too, if she wasn't so preoccupied."

Darlene faced Ethel, one of her knees slipping up on the couch. "Really? You don't see it?"

"See what?"

"That we look so much alike." Darlene straightened and stretched her neck so that Ethel could study her.

Aunt Ethel narrowed her eyes. "I don't see it."

"You have to picture Darlene with her hair cut short and with a Titian Dreams rinse on it," Alice said.

Ethel squinted her eyes and tilted her head for further study. "Maybe," she concluded.

Automatically, Darlene's hands flew to her mousy locks, which she patted nervously into place. "Titian Dreams —I'm not sure I could make such a...strong cosmetic statement as that."

Instead of taking offense, Ethel laughed out loud. "I guess it does take a certain disposition." She paused for several seconds, studying Darlene. "Wait, I saw a long mirror in the bathroom." With that she tugged Darlene out of her seat and pulled her into the house.

Alice waited with her hot chocolate, which was already lukewarm, while laughter and voices floated down the hall. The sounds made her smile. At least they'd found a distraction while they waited for Ronald and Florence.

"I have a twin after all," Ethel said when they returned and took their places on the couch.

"I'm almost as gorgeous as Ethel, but not quite," Darlene declared with a grin.

"It's the hair." Ethel patted her red locks and preened for the two of them.

"Of course," Darlene decided.

Though their natures couldn't have been more different, Alice sensed that the look-alikes had become fast friends.

The next few minutes passed by quietly, with the three women sipping tepid drinks and hoping the conversation between Florence and her husband was as pleasant as the one back at the house. Voices from outside provided the first indication of the Simpsons' return, their loud volume even more telling.

Florence appeared as if propelled through the sliding door into the sunroom. "If you think I'm going home with this insufferable man, then you've all got another thing coming."

Ronald stomped in after her. "As if I'd even want to bring that much of a headache home with me."

Florence whirled to face him. "Headache? You've been my headache for the last forty-nine years."

The three other women rose from their seats and moved close to the Simpsons, but the feuding spouses were too intent on their argument to pay attention to their audience.

Ronald crossed his arms. "Since I can say the same about you, why don't we both just take a couple of aspirin and call it a day?"

"Fine!"

"Fine!"

What did they just agree to? A perplexed Alice wondered. *Did Ronald mean they should give up talking for this one day, or that they should give up on their marriage altogether?*

Florence glanced toward the window and then looked back at him again, her expression masked in the room's shadows. "Don't you think the three of you should be going then?"

"Absolutely," he retorted. "I don't think we can get out of here fast enough."

Ethel opened her mouth but struggled to find the right words. She had to be madly searching for the right thing to say to keep her plan from resulting in disaster. Mild-mannered Darlene found her words first. "I don't think that will be possible."

Four startled faces turned to Darlene, who wore a small smile rather than the nervous expression Alice expected.

When no one else spoke up, Florence asked, "What isn't possible, Darlene?"

"You cannot send my guests away tonight, dear. I have offered them lodging, and they've accepted my invitation. The matter is settled." When Florence opened her mouth to protest, Darlene raised a hand to stay her. "Now I know you're tired. You'll want to get some rest, so go ahead into my room. I've moved your things in there, so you and I can bunk together. Ethel and her niece will share a room, and Ronald has the third bedroom."

Florence blinked a few times but then turned and hurried from the room.

Ronald rested his hand on Darlene's shoulder. "This is awfully gracious of you, but I think it would be best if we just stayed in a motel. Then tomorrow we'll get an early start back..." He let his words fall away as Darlene kept shaking her head.

"I said the matter was settled." Darlene didn't raise her voice at all, but there was finality in her words. "We'll talk about tomorrow when tomorrow comes. Now, it's been a long day, so I'm going to turn in." She stepped through the slider into the house but turned back to them before she closed it. "I've placed guest towels in each of your rooms. If you discover you're missing any necessary items, you'll probably find what you need in the medicine cabinet." With that she pulled the slider closed and made her way down the hall.

Ronald, Ethel and Alice stared after her in silence. Alice discovered that she had a new respect for Darlene, who had more than a little spunk buried beneath her mild demeanor. From the smile pulling at Ethel's lips, she guessed that her aunt felt the same. People weren't always what they seemed. Father had been right when he warned Alice and her sisters not to prejudge the people they met.

Ronald appeared stern. "I hope you know how much of a mistake all of this has been, even if your intentions were good. I expect both of you to be ready early tomorrow, because I'm heading back to Acorn Hill if I have to take the rental car myself." He didn't bother to look back at them as he stepped inside and closed the door behind him.

"I guess we have our work cut out for us," Alice said as she watched his retreating back.

Her aunt glanced at her, a scowl forming on her face. "You didn't expect it to be easy, did you? Florence is one of the most stubborn women I know, and Ronald's just proven he's got a few stubborn bones too. They aren't so different after all."

"Darlene was surprisingly spunky herself. Don't you agree?"

"Didn't your father and mother teach you not to judge a book by its cover? I'm sure Darlene's full of surprises, and we've definitely got an ally in her. They may not realize it yet, but they're fortunate to have her on their side."

"She's loved them both for a long time," Alice agreed.

"So she remembers how much they loved each other."

Loved. Alice tilted her head and pondered the tense of the word. Was love no longer the case? Wasn't love more about promises than feelings? She realized she just didn't know as she stared out into the starry night. "Do you think they still do?"

"Love each other? Of course they do." Ethel's voice didn't hold any doubt. "They've just forgotten the reasons they came together in the first place. That's where we come in."

"*We're* going to remind them?"

"That and we're going to help them remind each other."

Again, Alice felt out of her league in speaking of marital relationships. "It doesn't seem as if they *want* to be reminded."

"Oh, they want to be reminded, all right. They wouldn't be fighting each other so hard if they didn't have something worth fighting for."

If only she shared her aunt's confidence. "How can we convince them of anything when Ronald's insisting that we leave first thing in the morning and Florence will be more than ready to show us the door?"

Ethel wrapped an arm around Alice's shoulder and squeezed. "To quote Scarlett O'Hara, 'Tomorrow is another day.'"

Alice couldn't help chuckling. Because Aunt Ethel loved reading romance novels, it was only right that she should quote from *Gone With the Wind*. "Scarlett's right. It is."

"And if Ronald insists on leaving or Florence insists that he go, Darlene and I are going to have something to say about that." Ethel nodded with enough confidence for all of them.

Suddenly, Alice felt more hopeful. "That makes three of us."

Tuesday dawned looking like a midsummer's morn, not one predicting the winter season that would arrive in just two days. But even the dazzling sunrise, its palette of orange, magenta and gold adorning a sparkling blue canvas, failed to penetrate the gray pall over Louise's spirits. She viewed the show from the rear kitchen window, automatically pulling her baby blue cardigan tighter around her shoulders.

She poured juice into glasses and set them on a tray for Jane, grateful that her sister had offered to serve breakfast this morning as long as Louise took over cleanup duty. Agreeing had been easy, because the last thing she wanted to do was face the Ericksons and the reality that her family situation might be every bit as troubled as theirs.

Someone named Greg Hollister would be arriving with her daughter tonight to share an intimate family Christmas with the extended Howard family, and until last night, she'd never heard his name. The rational, ordered part of her pointed out that this was not the first time her family had invited strangers to celebrate Christ's birth with them, but the worrying-mother side insisted that this was different.

Just who was this Greg Hollister, and how well did he know her only daughter?

Don't worry; you'll love him, Cynthia's words came flitting through her thoughts. Didn't she realize that her comment alone gave Louise cause to worry? It signaled that this Greg was someone important to her, someone she hoped her mother would like. Louise couldn't imagine when her daughter had become serious enough about a young man to want him to meet her family. The last she remembered, Cynthia had said she was focusing on her publishing career and didn't have time for relationships. She mentioned accepting a few dinner invitations from men in her church's singles' group, but she never referred to those dates by name. Was this Greg one of those men?

Jane pushed through the kitchen door, carrying a tray of dirty dishes. She set it on the table in the center of the room. "Are you finished brooding yet, or should I make myself scarce awhile longer?"

Louise didn't think she would be finished for some time, but she forced a grim smile.

"That's the best you can do? Well, I'm sure there's something I can do upstairs. Let's see. I'll arrange the flowers for the Sunset Room. Cynthia's room."

Louise cleared her throat and turned back to the sink. "You mean Greg's room now."

Her sister winced. "Oh, another sore spot. The interloper is filling the last available room at the inn."

For several seconds Louise watched the water in the old soapstone sink pour over the cereal bowls and her rubber glove-covered hands. She rinsed the dishes lightly and then placed them in the industrial-strength dishwasher. Finally, she turned to face Jane. "That's not what this is about."

Jane took a seat at the table and folded her hands. "So tell me what it is about."

"We don't even know this Greg."

"Thus the holiday meeting."

Louise tried not to roll her eyes. "She has to be serious about this young man, or she wouldn't be bringing him from Boston to meet us."

"You don't know that for certain."

"I know," she said in a firm tone, sure that Jane, who didn't share her maternal experiences, would concede the point. Still, Louise felt guilty for using the tactic when Jane did as she expected.

Without saying more, Jane started helping with the dishes that were supposed to be her sister's job. After several seconds of heavy silence, Louise couldn't take it anymore.

"We don't even know if this Greg Hollister is a Christian or if he's a scoundrel looking for a woman to support him. Is he an acceptable mate for Cynthia?" She shook her head, her worst suspicion coming to her lips. "Cynthia's thirty-four now. Do you think she's being overly sensitive to her biological clock and lowering her standards?"

"Louise!" Jane gripped her sister's arms. "I do not believe that, and neither do you. Cynthia is as smart as she is lovely and kind. We all know what a great job you and Eliot did raising her. If this man turns out to be a serious boyfriend, and I'm not convinced he will be, then I just know Cynthia would choose a man who shares her faith."

The words penetrated Louise's glum thoughts. "Maybe you're right. She has mentioned dating men from her church group a time or two."

"You see—"

"But she's never mentioned *him*."

When Louise glanced up again, Jane was studying her with narrowed eyes. "The boyfriend isn't what this is all about, is it? You're upset because Cynthia didn't *tell* you about the boyfriend. That she left you out of the loop."

Louise didn't bother trying to deny that Jane, as she so often did, had leaped right to the heart of the matter. "We were always so close before this. She always told me everything."

This time Jane smiled and brushed her knuckles over her sister's cheek. "You're still close, close enough that your daughter wants to bring her friend or boyfriend or whatever he is to your home to meet you. This has to be painful for you to realize, but your sweet little girl is a full-grown woman now, and she doesn't have to share every secret with you."

"It still hurts."

"I know it does."

Louise glanced at her, grateful for her empathy. Perhaps she understood that this really was the second time for Louise to go through such a rude awakening. The first was when Jane herself had climbed out of the nest and flown without assistance. Louise thought she would be good at this by now. Cynthia had been leaving a little more each year since she started college, and she'd been on her own in the world for more than a decade. Perhaps Eliot's death had made Louise cling a little tighter, secretly relieved that her daughter was too busy to get married and start a family before now.

You still can't be sure of anything, Louise reminded herself. She wasn't and wouldn't until tonight, no matter how much brooding she did in the meanwhile.

Jane went to the dining room to collect the Ericksons' dishes, and she came back with another full tray. "Do you want me to do these for you? If you'd like to go upstairs and lie down—"

Louise lifted the tray from her arms. "No, I'm fine. Besides, we have too much to do around here for me to spend my morning moping."

"Great," Jane answered. "I was hoping I wasn't going to have to get the room for your *guest* ready as well as the one for the Leys. The Ericksons' rooms will need cleaning as well."

Louise started loading the items into the dishwasher. "I'll finish cleaning up in here and be right up."

"By this afternoon, you'll be free to shop downtown for your Secret Santa gifts."

"Maybe I will." At least it would give her something more constructive to do than worry about Cynthia's arrival. "Have you checked the e-mail to see if there's another one from Alice?"

"I haven't checked, but I'll do that as soon as we finish some of the other chores." Jane started out the door into the dining room but turned back and said, "I'm glad you'll be leaving the kitchen soon."

"Why do you say that?" Louise asked, cocking her head.

"You've spent so much time in here lately that the Ericksons have to think we *live* in the kitchen." A grin formed on Jane's lips. "You've been hiding out."

Chapter Eight

$\mathcal{N}$erves were as plentiful as Florida sunshine Tuesday morning at Darlene Irwin's home. Given the bank of clouds approaching from the west and the forecast for midmorning showers, the scales quickly tipped in favor of disquiet. Just outside the sunroom, though, a bed of azaleas bloomed, oblivious to all but the sunlight, dozens of pink blossoms stretching and opening in its direction. Farther out in the yard, a fifteen-foot crape myrtle tree stood majestically, covered with clusters of purple blooms. The hibiscus that formed a hedge between Darlene's and her neighbor's yards was covered with white double blooms.

Alice wrapped her hands around her mug and stared out at the flora that she was certain Jane would have appreciated even more than she did. In the presence of so much beauty, she hoped Ronald would give up the angry disposition that accompanied him when he'd stormed out for his morning walk before Darlene finished brewing the first pot of coffee. The fresh cup of tea in Alice's hands was her second.

She moved to the picture window, where an elegant Christmas tree stood draped with white lights and gold lamé bows. She stared out at the neighborhood. More beauty greeted her in a neighbor's bougainvillea, twisting and climbing along a trellis, its clusters of bright red blooms providing a suitable Christmas decoration. Another neighbor's jacaranda tree had incredible lavender blooms. Jane would like the jacaranda best, Alice decided.

"I don't know why you're pacing so, Alice," Florence called to her from the dining room table before she took a bored sip from her own cup. "My husband will return when he gets around to it. He's only trying to upset all of you with his little tantrum."

Alice jumped at Florence's words, ashamed that her thoughts had drifted from the problem at hand. Having spent little time in her life away from Acorn Hill, she couldn't help feeling homesick for Jane and Louise and the inn. She couldn't break her promise to them that they would share Christmas Eve on Sunday together. She'd also promised her supervisor and her fellow nurses covering her shifts that she would be back soon. The clock was ticking against them, and the Simpsons were no closer to reconciliation. Alice hated wondering if they ever would be.

Releasing the light window sheers she had pushed aside for a better look outside, she glanced back at Florence. She had little doubt that the tantrum Florence spoke of was directed at one woman alone, the very person who was too busy with her own fuming to pay attention. Florence emerged from her room the moment Ronald took his leave and had been dour since, but she was also uncharacteristically quiet until now. Her clothes today were unusually neutral as well, their lack of color and their simple lines a contrast to the bright colors, lace and ruffles she usually preferred.

"I was just noticing how lovely it is outside," Alice said as she walked back to the dining room. "It doesn't look at all how I usually picture Christmas, though."

"Not the Christmas scene in a Norman Rockwell painting anyway," Darlene said with a chuckle as she laid a platter of scrambled eggs and bacon in the center of the table. A round pan of steaming homemade biscuits already rested on the other end. "But after you've been down here a few years, you get used to the prickle of Bahia grass under your feet, and you stop missing the snow at Christmas. You even begin to realize that sandstorms were far more likely than snow on Joseph and Mary's journey into Bethlehem."

"You're right about that, Darlene." Ethel grinned up at her. "Now please stop fussing and join us."

Darlene hesitated as if she would prefer to stay busy, but finally she took a seat.

Alice was the last to take her place at the antique mahogany table in a room so formal and lacy that the whole thing looked like an oversized doily. She found the room strangely incongruent with the rest of Darlene's rooms, which were decorated for function and comfort. As she bowed her head for grace, Alice thought about how much Louise, who adored both formal settings and doilies, would have loved the room.

They had barely said "amen" and started passing the platters when Florence started talking. "It just serves Ronald right for pouting. He's missing out while we're enjoying this nice breakfast. I hope he starves."

Darlene lowered her fork and glanced pleasantly at her niece. "Oh, I must have misunderstood you, dear. I thought you just said you hoped your husband would starve, and I know that you, as a good Christian woman, would never wish such a thing on anyone, let alone the man you've promised to love, honor and cherish all the days of your life."

Alice choked on her biscuit and had to turn away and cough into her napkin. How she'd ever thought of Darlene as meek at the beginning of this visit she couldn't imagine. Whether they realized it or not, Ronald and Florence were fortunate to have Darlene rooting for them and their marriage.

Florence looked at her aunt in surprise. "You know that's not what I meant, Darlene."

"Of course not. I was sure I'd misunderstood." With that, Darlene lifted her fork a second time and took a small bite of her eggs.

"It's just that he makes me crazy is all. He marched in here yesterday as if I should forgive him just like that." She snapped her fingers. "He even had the gall to say—"

Seated next to Florence, Ethel interrupted her with a wave of her hand. "What else would you have him do? Ronald has already traveled through seven states to apologize to you."

Florence narrowed her gaze at Ethel. "Ronald has admitted to me that you *encouraged* him to make the trip. He didn't confess that you shanghaied him in that rental car of yours, but I don't think that's far from the truth."

Ethel arranged her silverware across her plate, a signal that she was finished eating though she'd barely touched her food. "Does it matter how he got here as long as he's here and willing to talk this out with you?"

"That man?" Florence asked in a loud voice. "The one who stormed out of the house this morning because he couldn't get away from me fast enough? The one who said he didn't want to take 'this headache' home with him? That's the man you're telling me is willing to talk?"

"You both said a lot of things last night, things you probably regret." Until the other three women turned to look at her, Alice wasn't even aware that she'd spoken her thoughts aloud, but she wasn't sorry for it. She hoped that Florence and Ronald regretted the things they'd said.

For all of Alice's effort, Florence continued as if she hadn't even heard her. "If Ronald thinks coming here and giving that one little apology is going to be enough to make up for what he did, then—"

"When *is* it going to be enough?" Ethel interrupted her

again. She gripped the table as if trying hard to remain seated. When her friend finally turned to look at her, Ethel asked, "*When*, Florence?"

"When he can take back what he did in front of those awful women in Acorn Hill." She crossed her arms like a defiant child, but her eyes were shiny. Pain seeped through cracks in her heavy veneer of anger, but she turned her head away lest any of them see it.

"We both know that can never happen." Ethel didn't move, but her voice softened. "Just as neither of you will be able to take back the things you've said and done since then."

Florence stared down at her plate, and though she slathered jam on her biscuit, she set it aside without taking a bite. "He agreed with those two vengeful women. He didn't even defend me." Tears slipped out in twin trails down her cheeks.

Alice was relieved when Ethel finally rested a hand over her friend's. She couldn't bear watching Florence suffer, even if she was being unreasonable about forgiving her husband. But her aunt's jaw was firm as she spoke again. "Now, dear, I want you to tell me which part of what those women said about you was untrue."

Florence's head jerked, and she pulled her hand away from Ethel's. The shock stopped her tears.

"All of it was true, wasn't it?" Ethel nodded, the matter already settled in her mind. "Remember, we had a long drive here, Florence. Your husband explained a lot of things about that unfortunate conversation to us … and indicated that Hope's and Nancy's comments, though unkind, were accurate."

"Why, that disloyal—" Florence began, but she stopped herself, burying her face in her hands.

Ethel regarded her for several seconds. "Funny that you would say that. If you would give your husband time to explain, you would know that he did defend you to those other women, whether you deserved it or not." Her words were true rather than supportive or comforting, but she reached out a second time to her friend, squeezing Florence's shoulder and then leaving her hand there.

Darlene, who'd only watched the exchange until then, pushed her plate away. "This is about more than just one unfortunate conversation, isn't it? I remember a time when you never questioned Ronald's loyalty to you … or his love. Whatever happened to that belief you had in him?"

Florence looked up from her hands, her face wet with tears. Still, the smallest of smiles lit her lips as if she too, could remember a time that her aunt described. "Belief and love are often lost over many years and through trying circumstances."

"Then find them both. Please." Darlene's voice sounded anguished.

"I don't know if I can. We can't even have a conversation without arguing."

Alice couldn't bear Florence's forlorn expression that so clearly mirrored Ronald's when he'd talked in the car.

"Have you considered counseling with Rev. Thompson again? I thought you found that helpful."

"That was individual counseling, not marital counseling. Ronald didn't attend on a regular basis."

Darlene kept shaking her head slowly until the other three women let her have her say. "No counseling is going to help you if you don't have a reason to want to make your marriage work. Try to remember, for both of your sakes, what made you love Ronald in the first place."

Florence's lips turned up, but her smile was a sad one. "It seems so long ago now."

Ethel straightened in her seat as if she spotted a seed of hope. "Not so long that you can't remember." She paused long enough to chew a bite of biscuit and, perhaps, to give her friend time to reflect. "I remember you talking about how funny he was. You and I used to trade humorous stories about your Ronald and my Bob."

"You're right about Ronald, Ethel." Darlene said with a smile. She turned toward her niece. "He was always sneaking in one-liners. I remember when you first brought Ronald to meet us, Florence. You were so nervous that we wouldn't like him. How could we not when you were so clearly head over heels for him?"

"He did make me laugh." Florence said it wistfully as if

she wished he were still lightening her spirits with a comedy routine.

Darlene turned to Alice and Ethel. "Ronald took ribbing from some of the other husbands for being such a romantic," she explained. "He brought Florence flowers and candy, even when there wasn't any special occasion. Boyd once told him to tone it down because he set the bar too high for the rest of the husbands."

"He hasn't done things like that in years."

Knowing a little about the resentment between them, Alice wondered when these gestures of affection had ceased. Had Ronald stopped doing things to make his wife feel special, or had she stopped appreciating his efforts? Had the couple allowed small things to become larger by not addressing them? She wondered if other marriages were like this one, not so much poisoned by someone's wrongdoing as allowed to wilt because no one expended the effort to make them work.

"Didn't you tell me one time that Ronald used to write you love letters with poetry so awful that you found it endearing?"

Alice stared at Florence, waiting for the answer. She shouldn't have been surprised to see Ethel studying Florence just as closely. It was hard enough to imagine Ronald as a jokester entertaining a crowd of friends, and now they were trying to picture the same gentleman as a lovesick poet.

Florence wore a faraway expression, her eyes brightening over happier times. Clearly, she had no trouble seeing Ronald Simpson as a poet and romantic, but her smile disappeared the moment the front door closed with a loud click. Suddenly, her arms stiffened at her sides, and she appeared to prepare for battle.

Alice coughed to cover her frustrated sigh. They seemed to be making so much progress with Florence, helping her to remember what she loved about her husband and what she stood to lose if they couldn't repair their rift. Now Alice prepared herself to watch all the progress melt away. "Good morning, ladies," Ronald said, carefully avoiding looking at his wife. "A storm is coming in."

At least he hadn't demanded that Ethel and Alice get into the car that instant. Darlene came out of her chair and stood, ready to be of service. "Would you like breakfast, Ronald? I can make you something fresh."

"No, thanks. I'm not hungry."

Alice studied him more closely. He should have been ravenous after his long morning walk. She couldn't have imagined it, but Ronald looked even worse than he'd appeared the night Florence walked out on him.

Darlene looked for a moment as if she might insist, but then she shrugged. "Well, coffee then. I just made another pot."

"Fine." He allowed her to press a mug into his hand and thanked her for it.

"Why don't you take a seat at the table? Are you sure there isn't something I could make you? Oatmeal maybe?"

"I'd best not," he said. "I need to take a shower and get ready."

If the room was fairly quiet before, it fell into total silence now. Ronald didn't even need to say that he intended to leave, to give up and return home. Alice caught her aunt's attention and held her gaze. Ethel's expression bore none of the hope it had when they began this journey. Perhaps she finally realized that no matter how much she wanted Ronald and Florence to reconcile, she couldn't force them to do it.

Ronald's shoulders slumped as he set down his mug. "Darlene, I'm sorry about all of this. I'm sorry for the intrusion, for the outbursts. All of it." His gaze swept the room this time, lingering just a moment on the back of Florence's brown hair, as if he was talking to her rather than to her aunt. Ronald turned and took a few steps.

"I'm sorry too, Ronald," Florence said in a quiet voice. "For a lot of things."

Jane sank into her office chair with an exhausted sigh Tuesday afternoon and clicked the icon to sign onto the Internet. Hours had passed since Louise suggested she check for messages, but they were so busy that until now she couldn't find the time.

"Louise, there's another message from Alice."

She waited to open it until her sister hurried into the room and Jane was able to offer Louise her chair. It was as good an excuse as any to convince her sister to finally sit down. With all the fluttering Louise had been doing around the inn, they'd barely taken the time to munch on a sandwich during the noon meal. "Alice is really worrying me," Louise announced when she stopped reading.

Startled by the comment, Jane leaned in and read over her shoulder.

> Dear Louise and Jane,
>
> I'm happy to hear all is well at the inn. We arrived safely in Grand Island. Darlene Irwin has been a lovely hostess and has invited us to stay here. Ronald and Florence are spending time together now, and we have high hopes they'll resolve their differences soon so we can return home shortly. Say a prayer for the Simpsons.
>
> > Longing to see you,
> > Alice

Louise was shaking her head when Jane finished reading. "If I know Florence Simpson at all, and I do know her, none of this is as simple as Alice is making it sound. I suppose she'll tell us when she's ready," Louise concluded. "She probably just doesn't want to worry us. We're not going to worry her either. She has enough on her mind with Aunt Ethel and the Simpsons without our adding troubles around the inn to her list."

"You're right, but—"

"As soon as she's home, safe and sound, we'll share everything, right?" She turned and waited for Jane's nod before she continued. "Now how do I reply to one of these letters?"

"You mean e-mails?" Jane winked at her, kidding her again about her lack of technological expertise. At her sister's frown, Jane replied, "Click on the *reply* tab."

"Of course."

With Jane reading over her shoulder, Louise composed a brief note that was every bit as vague as the two Alice had sent. Jane bit back a comment as Louise wrote of the "great surprise" that Cynthia would be bringing Greg Hollister to spend the holidays with them. Alice would see through that statement as quickly as Louise and Jane had read into Alice's.

Louise mentioned that Pastor Henry's cousin and his wife would soon occupy the Garden Room, while Mr. Hollister stayed in the Sunset Room. Trying to preempt Alice's likely offer of her own room for Cynthia, Louise said how much she was looking forward to the one-on-one time with her daughter as they shared a room. She mentioned that they had agreed to host the Secret Santa reveal party because Alice would have expected news from Acorn Hill. Louise closed her note with, "We can't wait for your return so we can share the celebration of Christ's birth with you. Come home soon."

After a message like that, Alice will probably hop the next plane out of Orlando, Jane thought. What she said was, "Sign my name along with yours, and then click on *send*."

Indicating that she and Louise should trade places, Jane closed the e-mail program and logged off the computer. "Now that we've finished all the chores, we can have some quiet time this afternoon. Or better yet, let's have some less quiet but peaceful moments while you play." For as long as Jane could remember, her sister had used music as a method for escaping stress as well as finding peace. Louise offered her playing as praise to God for the blessing of her talent.

Louise opened her mouth to decline, but Jane spoke first. "I miss the sounds of your music. The only notes I've heard coming from the parlor all morning have been scales. The notes were competent, I assure you, but they did little to appease my musical soul."

Louise pressed her lips together but still couldn't prevent a chuckle. It wasn't much of a secret in the Howard family that if Jane tried to carry a tune in a bucket, even the bucket would be offended. "The Erickson children were forced to play scales this morning so they wouldn't get rusty." She carefully avoided indicating who might have forced the repetitive drills.

"So much for the vacation." Jane shook her head sadly.

"I wouldn't even have minded hearing 'Chopsticks' if I thought they were having fun playing it." Louise's eyes took on a wistful look.

Clearly, Louise still wanted to help this troubled family. Her experience was the very thing that could make her most helpful. Still, until she found peace in her own troubled heart, she wouldn't be able to reach out to anyone else's.

"Well, are you ready for a recital?" Jane asked.

"I'll wait to play until later this afternoon. First, I have to do some shopping downtown. My Secret Santa recipient —I'm still not revealing any identities since you're being so secretive with yours—deserves to finally receive his or her first gift."

"You finish that, and then I'll run a few errands of my own. Later, you can relax and play while you're waiting. If I'm not back early enough, just go on with the recital without me." By tacit agreement, neither mentioned for whom Louise would be waiting.

Jane started toward the parlor to make sure all of the hospitality dishes were still filled with candy. Satisfied, she glanced over to where Louise stood in the doorway, staring transfixed at the seven-foot Douglas fir in the corner. Jane could understand what Louise found so mesmerizing. With daylight seeping into the room in thin streaks, the tree's handblown antique ornaments appeared translucent.

"It is beautiful," Jane said finally.

"Yes, but I still want to add more decorations. Perhaps you could bring out some of those other boxes while I'm shopping. Then while you're out, I could put a few of them up. Maybe I'll even ask the Ericksons if they would like to help me."

Jane could almost see the wheels in her sister's mind turning. "You keep thinking. You'll figure out an idea to help that family find their way. They're fortunate to have crossed paths with someone as caring as you are."

The high praise must have embarrassed Louise because at first she didn't answer. She turned away for a few seconds. "You never said which errands you still had to finish," she said when she finally turned back.

"I just have a few questions that I need answered."

"About the Quinlans?"

"It might be nothing. Maybe I just caught Meghan on a cleaning day at their house." Even spoken aloud, the excuse didn't ring true in her ears, but as she glanced down at the overalls and long-sleeve T-shirt she'd donned this morning for work, she had to acknowledge the possibility of it. The Howard sisters could certainly relate to wearing their oldest and most casual attire on workdays.

"Maybe."

Louise sounded no more convinced than Jane felt. Something about the whole situation involving the Quinlans just didn't sit right with her, but she would find some answers, today if she was particularly fortunate. If not today, she would keep asking questions until she did.

Chapter Nine

The pungent scent of newsprint and ink drifted into Jane's nostrils as she stood at a high counter and flipped through a bound stack of recent copies of the *Acorn Nutshell*. Her gaze drifted about the building that had housed the local weekly newspaper for more than ninety years. She paused to study the aging printing press and the Linotype machine collecting dust in the back. The equipment seemed out of step with the desktop computer on the L-shaped desk and with the printer, photo scanner and fax machine placed around the front part of the office. She turned the pages again, thumbing backward through the calendar, past feature photos of laughing children sledding after the first real snow, to Franklin High School football coverage, to the special pullout "Back to School" section. She had farther to go. If she remembered correctly, the headline came in the summertime, an article that she'd barely noticed, though it likely affected local families as well as those in Potterston and Riverton.

Editor Carlene Moss propped an elbow on the counter

and peered at the page Jane was studying. "You know, if you tell me what you're looking for, I can probably find it for you."

Jane smiled apologetically but shook her head. "That's all right. I'm almost there anyway."

Carlene tucked her coarse brown hair flecked with strands of gray behind her ears. "If you decide you need help, I *probably* know the reporter who wrote the article, the editor who penned the editorial, the ad salesperson, the photographer ... Well, you get the picture." When Carlene grinned over her joke, dimples dotted her heart-shaped face, making her appear more a teenager than a woman in her midfifties.

"And chances are, I'd be looking right at her?"

"Did I ever tell you what a smart woman you are, Jane Howard?" She was staring down at the page on which Jane's hands had come to rest.

"You're just dying to know, aren't you?"

"Guilty." Carlene blew out a sigh. "What can I say? I'm a born and bred newspaperwoman. I'm nosy to the core." When Carlene left to answer a ringing phone, Jane returned her attention to the pages. She scanned through June newspapers, back to May and then to April. Maybe she'd flipped too quickly and missed the article. She turned a few more pages, and there it was. Under the April 14 headline, "Warehouse layoffs cut workforce in half," was an article about twenty-seven employees from Potterston Feed and Grain who would receive only minimal severance packages.

As she read, she thought of twenty-seven families cut off from funds for food, clothing and shelter in a job market where help-wanted signs were few and far between. Were the Quinlans among those families?

Her gaze rose to the date at the top of the page again. April? Eight months had passed since the layoff. How many families had enough savings to withstand eight months without income? Not many she could name.

"Oh, you're interested in the warehouse layoffs?"

Jane was startled when she discovered Carlene looking over her shoulder. She didn't know when the editor had approached again, let alone begun reading right along with her.

"Well, why didn't you say so?" Carlene didn't wait for a response but moved to a row of metal cabinet drawers below the counter. About halfway down, she slid out a drawer, flipped back through files and pulled out a yellow envelope. "Here you go. They're all here."

"What?" Jane let the editor press the envelope into her hand. On a neatly typed label at the top, it said, "Potterston Feed and Grain."

Carlene bent her head to look at the newspaper clippings Jane was pulling from the envelope. "What specifically are you looking for? More details on the layoffs?"

Jane didn't want to embarrass Meghan's family by making public inquiries about their financial situation, so she chose her words carefully. "I didn't see any articles on it, but were the people affected by the layoffs recalled?"

"No, those were permanent layoffs."

"That must be so hard for the families. Do you know how many of them were from Acorn Hill? There weren't any statistics or lists of names or anything."

"That's not how it's done, Jane. Everything is always hush-hush. The companies announce no names, and employees keep quiet in case they might be called back. At least most employees do." She paused a few seconds and then studied Jane, understanding. "Are you asking about anyone in particular?"

Jane's mouth dried up. She couldn't tell Carlene, but she had to know too. "I just wondered how they're doing. Eight months is an awfully long time to be without a regular income."

"But it's not long enough for people to get over their pride. I'm having trouble finding enough people affected by the layoffs who would be willing to be interviewed for an article about it. How can I inform Acorn Hill what these people are going through if no one is willing to admit he's struggling?" Carlene stared off into space and continued as if talking to herself. "Just this morning I thought I had a great family willing to be interviewed, a young family that lives right outside of town. But then Logan Quinlan called me back and said there's no way he'll put his family through that humiliation."

Suddenly, Carlene looked at Jane. From the editor's shocked expression, it was clear she'd revealed information that she hadn't planned on sharing. "Oh my goodness. I'm letting this get to me."

Jane waved her hand as if to brush away the awkwardness of Carlene's blunder. "Don't worry about it." Somehow she managed to make her voice sound calm. "I'm sure someone will be willing to talk with you."

"I hope you're right." A melancholy smile settled on Carlene's lips. "It's a story that needs to be told."

"Thanks so much for your help—"

Carlene's laugh interrupted her. "I wasn't that much help. Hey, you never said why you were looking for information on the warehouse layoffs."

"I just learned something about the situation, and I was curious."

It wasn't the whole story, and the editor didn't appear convinced, but the part that Jane had said was true. "Anyway, thanks again. I have to get back to the inn. My niece is coming in from Boston tonight."

"Too bad the rest of your family won't be here to see her. Have you heard at all from Alice and Ethel about when they'll be home?"

"Not yet." She wasn't surprised the local newspaper editor already knew about her sister and aunt's adventure. Acorn Hill was a small town after all. "We hope they'll be home for Christmas."

Stepping outside the frosted glass door where black, gilt-edged letters spelled out the words *Acorn Nutshell*, Jane finally allowed herself to digest the information swirling in her mind. She couldn't decide whether to be happy or sad. Of course, she was sad. She hurt for Meghan and for her sisters and parents. The idea of them suffering and, worse yet, suffering in silence because of their pride, seemed intolerable to her.

Still, she couldn't help feeling comforted that she knew the truth about the Quinlans now. With the information she could at least try to help this family in crisis. She wasn't sure how she could help them and spare their feelings at the same time, but she was convinced that with God's help, she would find a way.

Melodious sounds filled the parlor late Tuesday afternoon as Louise let her fingers pass over the keys of her beloved piano. The music filled her ears and warmed her heart, bringing comfort the likes of which she hadn't experienced all day.

She began with "Silent Night" and "O Little Town of Bethlehem," then moved on to Bach's "Jesu, Joy of Man's Desiring" and selections from her favorite oratorio, Handel's Messiah.

Louise was still singing the "Hallelujah Chorus" when she opened the door to the parlor. "Hallelujah! For the Lord God omnipotent reigneth. Hallelujah!"

She felt wonderful. For a solid hour, she'd forgotten to feel sorry for herself or to worry about Cynthia. She missed having Jane as an appreciative audience, but her sister was right to recommend that she play, because while her fingers moved over the keys she felt closest to God and surest that He was in control. Loud sounds coming from the living room, on the other hand, seemed to be God's reminder that He had work for her to do.

"What now?" she whispered as she crossed the house to the living room.

"Would you stop pacing?" Paul Erickson was asking his wife in a louder than usual voice as she stood by the window. "Can't you just sit for five minutes?"

"I can if you can take your nose out of that technical manual long enough to do something with your children," Sandy said.

The two Erickson children sat on the burgundy sofa, staring into the fireplace and pretending to hear none of what their parents were saying. Louise hurried into the room before the accusations became more pointed.

"Oh, hi, everyone. Am I interrupting anything?" She stepped in front of the fireplace and warmed her hands.

"Nothing important," Paul murmured as he set his book aside.

Louise smiled the warmest smile she could manage. "Of course, relaxation is important. You must be feeling great after three whole days of it." That she could almost hear their internal groans expanded her smile. "We're awfully glad you chose Grace Chapel Inn as a place for you to find that inner peace that is so often missing in our busy lives." She paused for effect, waiting for all four of them to look at her. "That's why I'm so sorry to ask the four of you for a favor."

Claire's and Dylan's curly heads bobbed up. "Favor?" Dylan asked.

Louise took her time, planning as she went. She was playing this by ear. Playing piano by ear required one to really listen to the individual notes and the chords created when they blended. Similarly, this situation made it necessary for her to really listen to what the Ericksons had said as well as what important messages they needed to say but weren't. "It's just that Grace Chapel Inn was supposed to be closed over Christmas this year."

"I believe Alice mentioned that when we first called," Sandy said.

"Well, clearly it is not closed after all." She held her hands wide to signify that their presence made that so. "Your family is here, Kevin and Jill Ley will be in tomorrow, and as it turns out, even my daughter, who's coming tonight, is bringing a guest."

"No room at the inn, huh?" Paul laughed at his own joke, earning a frown from his wife.

"No *more* rooms anyway, and we don't even have a stable available for any overflow." Louise folded her hands to keep from fidgeting. "Not only that, but we're also going to be hosting the Secret Santa reveal party, again something we hadn't planned to do. With Alice unexpectedly out of town, it's even more difficult."

Sandy lifted an eyebrow. "What exactly are you asking, Louise? What do you need us to do?"

"Well, when we'd planned a simple Christmas, we decided to decorate simply. Now that things have changed, we'd like to put out the rest of the decorations, only—"

"Can we help, Mrs. Smith?" Claire called out.

"Yeah, can we help?" Dylan chimed. "We didn't get to do it at home."

Sandy frowned. "Children, you know better than to interrupt."

"Don't worry about that, Sandy." Louise didn't even care about the interruption if it meant the children were finally excited about something. "If you don't mind, though, I would really appreciate any help they could give me. You too, if you like."

Sandy smiled apologetically. "You see, there just wasn't

any time to put up a tree this year. Claire was in three performances of *The Nutcracker*, and Dylan had a hockey tournament just before school let out. With all of that plus our flying out right after school was dismissed, we just figured it wasn't worth it. You get the picture."

"Of course." Louise got it, all right, and it pierced her heart. The Ericksons had time for everything except each other, time spent just being a family. "I could use the help, and you've all missed out on the chance this year, so maybe it would be win-win." They were also helping by giving her a distraction until Cynthia arrived, but she kept that to herself. Little besides the music had kept thoughts of her daughter and her guest at bay today, but she was willing to give anything a try.

"Mom and Dad, can we?" Claire tilted her head in the cute way children do when they really want something.

"If it will help Mrs. Smith, then fine," Paul answered for them both. "It is Christmas, after all."

Indeed it was, and Louise hoped the experience would make it a happier one for the Ericksons.

The way the two children danced around the living room, one might have thought they'd just unwrapped the year's most coveted video game rather than been put to work.

"Where do we start?" Dylan asked. "This room already has a lot of stuff." He pointed to the oak mantel, where a trio of alabaster angels stood in chorus alongside creamy white candles in brass candlestick holders, their colors offset by evergreen boughs, holly and pine cones.

"You're right. Do you see those angels up there?" She pointed to them. "Those are very special. They belonged to my mother. She died when my sisters and I were little girls."

"That's so sad." Claire approached the mantel and looked up at the angels reverently. When she turned back to Louise, her eyes shone. "You won't have us put up anything that special, will you? I would be afraid of breaking it."

Louise was touched by the child's sensitivity. "Many of the things are special simply because they belonged to my family members, but most of them aren't fragile."

Dylan nodded eagerly. "We have stuff like that at our house. Mom even has an old bell ornament that belonged to our great-great-grandmother. It hangs on a piece of kite string, but it's still really cool."

Claire peeked again at the three angels before adding, "Usually we don't get it out because it doesn't go with the year's theme. Last year it was blue and gold. The bell's red, and it's kind of dented and stuff."

"Oh, that old thing," Sandy said with a toss of her head, "I've had it forever. My great-grandmother probably got it in a late 1800s version of a dime store."

Though she scoffed at their mention of the old ornament, Sandy's cheeks flushed. If only she could realize that little things often mattered more to children than grand gestures did. Time mattered more than a frenzy of activity. Still, Louise doubted that their mother's embarrassment would bring the family closer. She turned to Sandy. "A lot of people like to decorate with special themes. I know I do."

"I know," Dylan said. "I saw your tree in the piano room. It's pretty fancy."

"I guess it is." Louise was smart enough to realize that "pretty fancy" was not high praise coming from an eleven-year-old boy. To an adult, the seven-foot Douglas fir made an elegant statement with its white lights and handblown antique ornaments, but to a child, the decorations probably looked more like an accident waiting to happen. "Then I have a question for you. When you grow up, you'll get to choose how to decorate your own tree. What kind of theme would you use?"

Dylan didn't hesitate. "Race cars and hockey players."

Claire wrinkled her nose and shook her head. "No, silly. Not just those things. It should have all kinds of kid things. Funny cartoon ornaments, soft things that wouldn't break, stuff kids made at school, Dylan's race cars and hockey players and Great-great-grandma's bell."

Louise had to swallow her emotion. The little girl had said so much. She hadn't given her tree a theme, but Louise might have called it "Family and Tradition." She wondered if the child's parents heard the same plea in her words. "Why, those ideas are lovely," she said when she trusted herself to speak again.

Because the Ericksons seemed eager to start, Louise gathered the necessary items and helped them to get to work, wrapping additional fresh greenery along the staircase railing and draping more on the doorway between the living room and the dining room. Louise offered direction but made excuses to slip away once they seemed to be enjoying themselves.

Claire and her mother appeared to have fun carefully dressing some of the ladies in the antique porcelain-doll collection for the holidays. They gathered the dolls, showcased on a three-tier, nineteenth-century carved burl walnut table, around a miniature tree decorated just for them. Laughter filled the air as Dylan helped his father string more white lights outside.

Too soon the activity was over, and the family returned to their status as caged vacationers, but those brief signs of family connection assured Louise that there was hope for the Ericksons after all.

Chapter Ten

Alice stared out the sunroom window late Tuesday afternoon as rain pelted the glass and wind made the hibiscus shrubs shimmy and sway. The longer she scanned her surroundings, the more the images moved in and out of focus in the downpour. This was not at all the way she pictured sunny Florida during winters when she'd dreamed of some tropical escape from a northern freeze. How suddenly appealing her chilly home seemed now, with tiny snowflakes dancing to earth and icicles sparkling like diamonds on bare tree branches.

"Into each life some rain must fall." The quote from Longfellow fell easily from her lips, surprising her. She glanced at her aunt, who slept contentedly on the wicker sofa, a floral-print pillow stuffed beneath her head. To Alice's left, Darlene appeared far less comfortable, dozing in one of the side chairs, her chin pressed uncomfortably against her chest. Satisfied she hadn't awakened either of them, she thought again of the quote and smiled, knowing how proud Louise would be that she was quoting Longfellow. The poet must have understood a day like this, when hope wasn't brimming and rain fell in sheets. Still, she liked his upbeat line: "Behind the clouds is the sun still shining."

She chose to concentrate on that line as she sat in the sunroom feeling like a hostage to the storm. Inside the house, Ronald and Florence still sat or paced or occasionally yelled as they had most of the day while Alice, Ethel and Darlene waited apart, involved but regarding the situation as the outsiders they were. They'd brought the couple this far, by car and by persuasion, but the outcome of today's discussions was entirely up to the Simpsons.

They were still talking. Alice could be grateful for that at least. They hadn't even come out to the sunroom and asked their friends to intervene. They also hadn't come out to offer any food, and Alice's stomach rumbled with the lack of it. Before she'd settled in for a nap, Darlene told Alice and Aunt Ethel that because she couldn't get inside to prepare a meal, the five of them would go out to dinner together.

To keep her mind off her hunger, Alice flipped open Ronald's laptop, which she'd had the foresight to bring out with her earlier. At least she could feel close to her sisters by reading one of their e-mail messages. Excitement filled her as she downloaded messages, but the feeling was replaced by disappointment as soon as she read Jane's. It seemed so vague, so general. More than that, it felt as misleading as the notes she'd written since her departure. That had to end now. She needed to let them know what was really happening. Taking a deep breath, she began typing.

> Dear Jane and Louise,
>
> This trip has been much harder than I had expected. Please forgive my painting a happier picture in my earlier messages, but I hadn't wanted to upset you. I do still believe there is hope for our friends.
>
> "I wait for the Lord, my soul waits, and in his word I put my hope" (Psalm 130:5).
>
> As I write, Florence and Ronald are talking. I pray they keep talking.
>
> Yours,
> Alice

Alice had just sent the message when Florence and Ronald appeared in the doorway, standing close but careful not to touch. A sense of foreboding filling her, Alice straightened and closed the laptop.

"I hope everyone has had a lovely nap this afternoon," Florence said in a voice just loud enough to startle Ethel and Darlene awake. She smiled as the two women sat up in their seats. "Ronald and I have been talking for hours as you well know, and we have come to at least one conclusion. We're starving."

Because it was an obvious attempt at humor, the women did their best to laugh.

"Well, that's one thing we all can agree on," Ethel said as she patted her sleep-mussed hair back into place. "Darlene has offered to treat us all to dinner tonight at a local buffet restaurant."

Ronald folded his arms. "That isn't going to work for us."

Alice gripped the arms of her chair to steady herself. Would he insist on leaving right then?

His posture remained the same, but his expression softened. "The restaurant will be fine, but my wife and I insist on paying. It's the least we can do after . . . all this." He motioned with his hands vaguely.

Alice waited for him to say more. He'd said "my wife and I," but she didn't know whether it was out of habit or out of a conscious choice of words.

Ethel hauled herself off the couch and stood facing the Simpsons. "You two have been inside talking for"—she paused to glance at her watch—"more than five hours, and all you can agree on is that you're hungry? Well, I can tell you one thing—you'd better solve your problems quickly because no one else would ever put up with either of you." She lifted one hand to wave an index finger at them. "You two deserve each other."

Alice felt her lip twitch. *No, you cannot laugh*, she instructed herself. Perhaps she wouldn't have said it the same way, but she agreed with her aunt's comment, even the part about them deserving each other. Ethel didn't even look her way. She just continued staring down both of them and appearing more like a matronly gunslinger than a grandmother and upstanding member of the church board. Again, Alice's lip twitched, and this time a funny sound erupted from her throat. She cupped her hand over her mouth, but it wasn't enough to stop the sound from repeating itself, only louder.

Ethel turned on her niece. "So you think this is funny, do you? After driving two days and listening to hours of complaining, I bet you're thinking this is downright comical. Those are the two most ungrateful so-and-sos I've ever laid eyes on." She indicated with a tilt of her head the two individuals now standing behind her. "And you." She pointed at Alice again. "You're … I don't know what you are."

Alice heard something that sounded like a snicker to her left and glanced at Darlene. There were tears in the woman's eyes. Tears of … mirth. Darlene fought to contain a laugh but was no more successful at it than Alice had been.

Another snicker broke the silence, but it came from the other side of the room. All heads turned in time to see Ronald cover his mouth. That was too much for Alice. Another chuckle escaped before she could stop it. Like a dam weakened by floodwaters, everyone's control gave way, and laughter burst forth, filling the room. Darlene had twin paths of tears running down her cheeks.

"What?" Ethel held her hands wide. "What are you all laughing about?"

Alice opened her mouth to answer and then realized she didn't know what to say. How could she explain that they needed to laugh to find relief from the tension that had been crowding this house? They were reacting to the same stress that had caused Ethel's outburst, but she probably wouldn't see it that way.

Ronald rested a hand on Ethel's shoulder. "You're right."

She stiffened, causing his arm to fall away. "Right about what?"

"Florence and I do deserve each other."

The four women turned to face him, none more surprised than his wife.

"Excuse me, Ronald?" Florence's gaze narrowed as she looked at her husband.

Ronald's eyes sparkled. "I only mean that we deserve to be together, and our marriage deserves a fighting chance."

"Is that what you decided in there?" Alice pointed to the interior of the house. She needed to distract them from starting another argument. "I mean besides the fact that you were both starving?"

Florence shook her head and rolled her eyes. "That starving business was a joke. Don't any of you understand humor?"

Alice might have mentioned that the joke wasn't all that funny.

A few seconds ticked by as Florence studied them, appearing to consider. "I suppose it has been an awfully long day to spend on an enclosed porch. I probably wouldn't be in the best humor either."

"Thanks for understanding." Darlene's voice held a sardonic tone. "Now don't you think it's about time for you to tell us what's going on with the two of you?"

Ronald stepped forward and spoke for both of them. "We have decided to keep talking."

It wasn't everything that Alice had hoped for, but it was something. The Simpsons were at least willing to try. *In his word I put my hope.* The words from Psalm 130 made their way into her thoughts again. Their hope hadn't been in vain, and their prayers had been heard. Little by little, God was softening the hearts of two stubborn individuals, who, as Ethel said, truly deserved each other.

Alice knew her aunt preferred more, but Ethel kept that frustration carefully hidden as she slapped her hands together. "Now that we have that settled, did someone mention food? I have a particular fondness for free food, though at this point I wouldn't consider any cost too high."

"Did you hear that, ladies?" Ronald asked. "Ethel is buying dinner, and the sky's the limit. Is there anywhere nearby we can get surf and turf?"

"Wait, I didn't say—" Ethel stopped herself when she saw the mischievous grin on Ronald's face.

He pointed an index finger at her. "Gotcha. No, I said dinner is on us. The buffet sounds like a good idea too, because I really am starving, and a little of everything sounds wonderful right now."

Alice was pleased to learn that Ronald's appetite had returned. He'd barely eaten since leaving Acorn Hill. Maybe he too, was beginning to believe there was hope for his marriage.

As Florence turned to go through the doorway, Darlene rested a hand on her shoulder. "Before we go, I need to know something. What are you two planning for tomorrow?"

Florence hesitated, glancing briefly at Ronald before turning to face her aunt. "Talking," she answered finally. "We need to do a lot of that."

Instead of giving her niece a supportive hug, Darlene only smiled at her. "Well then, you'd better hope it doesn't rain tomorrow, because you two will be the ones stuck out on the porch."

When Jane returned home just after dark, she found Louise in the Sunset Room, checking on details one last time to make sure everything was perfect. "Why on earth are you fussing over this room when we already made sure it was spotless this morning? A little nervous, are we?"

"I'm not nervous," Louise claimed. Her denial didn't sound convincing. She took her time straightening pictures on the wall before she spoke again. "Is it that obvious?"

"Probably not to the strangers shopping alongside you downtown today and maybe not even our current guests, but it is to me." Jane took Louise's hands in hers. "Oh, your hands are so cold." She squeezed. "Don't worry. Everything's going to be fine if you can manage not to collapse in a heap the moment they come through the door."

"Thanks for the vote of confidence."

"I'm always here to help. Have you been like this the whole time since I left?" Jane took a final appraising look around the room and, deeming it perfect, ushered Louise out the door.

"You might be surprised to hear this, but no, I haven't. I played for a while, even Handel, and then I had the Ericksons help me with decorations. I barely thought about . . . tonight at all."

"I'm sorry that I missed your performance, but everything really looks great. Did all of the Ericksons help?"

Immediately, Louise's face appeared more animated. "You wouldn't have believed it. Claire and Sandy were smiling as they worked together on the doll display. Paul and Dylan didn't argue once while they unraveled the hopelessly tangled strings of lights."

"And you forgot your worries, if only for a little while. It sounds like a magical time for everyone. You see, Louise, you do have a good idea every once in a while."

"It's unfortunate that they're so rare." Louise pulled out

her master key and opened the Garden Room, which they had prepared for the Leys's arrival on Wednesday. Her gaze followed the floral border along the wainscoting and then flitted over the rosewood bedroom suite. "Did you see the Ericksons as you came in?"

"They were in the living room, doing their best to ignore each other."

Louise frowned before her expression became resigned. "I do have another idea for the Ericksons if you don't mind adding something a little more casual to our decorations this year."

Jane studied her sister. "Of course I don't mind, but you're sounding as cryptic as you did in your message to Alice. Speaking of Alice, did you hear from her again?"

"She sent another e-mail. Paul was kind enough to assist me with the computer. This time she didn't try to hide how difficult the situation in Florida has been. She also reported that talks between Ronald and Florence are making progress."

Jane couldn't help chuckling at that. "Sounds more like international peace talks. Poor Alice."

Louise moved past the Sunrise Room, flipped on the light to the shared bath at the end of the hall, and stepped inside. Seconds later, she popped her head back out again. "You never told me if you found out anything about the Quinlans."

"I thought you'd never ask." Jane's joy faded as she con-templated the seriousness of the situation for this young family. "Carlene helped more than she intended, but now I know for sure that Logan was one of those who lost his job in the layoffs. The rest I can only guess based on Meghan's appearance. According to Carlene, most of those who lost their jobs in April still have not found work."

Louise shut off the bathroom light and returned to face her. "Now that you know, what do you plan to do with the information?"

"I've been thinking a lot about this. Carlene said Logan and several others like him were too embarrassed to be interviewed for a newspaper article. I want to help the Quinlans, but I want to find a way to do it anonymously so it won't offend them."

"That sounds like a tall order," Louise said as they walked toward the stairway. "Maybe Rev. Thompson will be able to offer you some ideas."

"I have one of my own, combining a spirit of giving with the Secret Santa program that we already have in place." If only she could make the idea work, it might really make a difference for the Quinlans. Thoughts of Meghan's too-small coat and those gifts of underwear and socks made Jane even more determined.

Louise was studying her. "Does this mean you're not going to share your idea with me? Another secret?"

"I'll tell you when the plan is ready. I'll even let you help if you like."

"Good." Louise started down the stairs. "I'm probably going to need a lot of distractions over the next few days."

Jane followed her sister, her plan forming in her mind. It would work a little like the telephone game, except that it would be in written form so the message didn't become distorted. Excitement began to replace the worry that had filled her heart since discovering the truth at the *Nutshell* office. The people of Acorn Hill were kind and generous and always willing to help. She would have to count on that generosity as she started the ball rolling and hoped its momentum would build. The whole project would begin with a little note.

Chapter Eleven

I wonder if something happened to them, Louise thought as she sat on the edge of the living room sofa and waited. All day she'd puttered around the house making preparations, but now she realized she hadn't taken the time to watch the news to see if Cynthia would be driving through rough weather. Of course, she would have called if they had car trouble. A smart city woman, Cynthia was never without her cell phone.

Louise might have stayed trapped in her own counter-productive thoughts if young Claire hadn't put aside the *Little House in the Big Woods* she'd been reading in front of the fire to come and sit between her and Jane. "I had fun decorating, Mrs. Smith," she said shyly.

"I'm glad."

Dylan put aside the handheld video game he'd been playing. "Ms. Howard, did you see the lights that Dad and I put up outside?"

"I did see them, Dylan," Jane said. "They look great."

Louise exchanged a look with her sister over the top of Claire's head. Maybe her latest idea might work with the

Ericksons after all. She didn't know about Sandy, who was flipping through a magazine while sitting in the rocker in the corner, or Paul, who'd been in Father's study since returning downstairs, but at least the children would enjoy it. "I was thinking about adding more decorations over the next few days. Would you mind helping me again?"

"More?" Dylan asked.

"Can we, Mom?" Claire chimed.

"It's fine with me." Sandy lowered her magazine and turned to Louise. "Now that you'll have less work hanging over your head before Christmas, maybe you'll even find time to give a few piano lessons."

Out of her peripheral vision, Louise caught Paul stalking through the doorway. "Would you please, please stop bothering her about that ridiculous piano?" he said.

An awkward silence settled in the room. Louise sensed the children's gazes on her, as if they waited for her to acquiesce. Of course, she wouldn't do that, but she also didn't want to offend Sandy, no matter how tedious her requests were becoming.

"Well, I just thought..." Sandy let her words trail off as headlights flashed through the front window. "Someone's here," said Claire.

Louise would have prayed a prayer of thanksgiving for that narrow escape if she could have focused on anything but the front door and the guests about to come through it. "Maybe your daughter's here, Mrs. Smith." Claire ran to the window to get a closer look. The headlights darkened and a car door opened. "It's a man and a woman. He's hugging her. Ew!"

Dylan joined his sister by the window. "They're coming up to the porch now. They're carrying suitcases."

"All right, you two," Paul called out. "That's enough of the play-by-play." He turned back to Louise. "We'll just say hello and get out of your way."

"You don't have to leave," she began, but he shook his head to allay her polite reply.

"You need time to spend with your daughter." He waited for several seconds before adding, "And her friend."

Louise glanced quizzically at the young father, and he smiled. She nodded her gratitude and made her way with Jane to their front door. After they had stood quietly for a few moments, Jane asked, "Is someone going to let them in?"

Claire and Dylan, who had followed the sisters, didn't have to hear the question a second time, and they pulled the door open. Cynthia Smith stood on the porch alone, her hand poised to knock. A blue down parka and a stocking cap nearly swallowed her slim form and covered much of her dark hair. Louise, though, would have known those keen blue eyes anywhere.

Cynthia's face glowed. "Hey, Mom, we finally made it." She started to step forward and seemed startled by the two children in the way.

"Are you Mrs. Smith's daughter?" Claire asked as she looked up at her.

"Yes, I am. I'm Cynthia." She grinned down at her. "And who are you?"

"I'm Claire." She indicated her brother. "And he's Dylan."

The boy pointed out the door. "We put up those lights today," he said proudly.

Cynthia took her time scanning the front porch area. "You did a great job of it too."

"Come on, everybody," Jane said, taking a step back. "Let my niece come inside. She has to be freezing out there, and this old house is breezy enough without holding the front door open."

Cynthia hesitated a moment and then stepped aside instead of through the door. Standing at the bottom of the steps was a tall, pleasant-faced man, every bit as bundled as Louise's daughter. "I'd like you all to meet my friend, Greg Hollister."

"Hi, Greg," Dylan and Claire called out in unison before anyone else had the chance.

Louise was too busy replaying her daughter's words to catch her own cue. Cynthia had called him her *friend*, and she hadn't hesitated the way women do when they're deciding whether to refer to a fellow as a boyfriend or simply a friend.

Jane interrupted Louise's musing by stepping forward again. "It's nice to meet you, Greg. I'm Jane Howard, Cynthia's favorite aunt, except when my sister Alice is in town to argue otherwise."

"Where's Aunt Alice?" Cynthia looked back and forth between her mother and aunt. "I thought she was supposed to be here."

"It's a long story," Jane told her, "one best told after the two of you come in from the cold."

Greg's first response was a laugh—a good, hearty, baritone one. "Sounds like a great idea to me, Ms. Howard. Cynthia didn't tell me we'd be spending Christmas on the porch."

"Your friend here has a sense of humor. I like him already." She winked at her niece and then turned back to Greg. "And please call me Jane."

Cynthia stepped inside with Greg following behind her, carrying two suitcases. She didn't bother to slip out of her coat before rushing to her mother for a hug. "I have missed you so much," she said, giving Louise an extra squeeze. When she pulled away, Cynthia wrapped her arm around her mother's shoulders and turned to face the newcomer. "Greg, I would like you to meet my mother, Louise Smith."

He yanked off his stocking cap, sending dark blond hair flying with static. "It's great to finally meet you, Mrs. Smith." He removed his glove and gripped her hand in a firm handshake.

"It's nice to meet you too, Greg." Her voice sounded strained to her ears, but he didn't know her, so perhaps he wouldn't notice.

She probably should have offered him the courtesy of using her given name, as Jane had, but she preferred the formal distance until she knew a little more about this man.

"We're pleased you are able to spend the holidays with us." *Pleased* might have been a strong word, but she wasn't about to forsake her manners.

Greg chuckled, his posture still relaxed. "I wish my folks were as pleased by my being away from their home. Mom probably won't speak to me until Easter."

Cynthia turned to him as she pulled off her hat and patted her shoulder-length hair back into place. "You didn't tell me that. I didn't want you to make your mother mad by coming here with me."

"She's not mad," he said as he shrugged out of his coat and stepped over to hang it on the coatrack. "Just disappointed. She likes us all to be together at the holidays."

So Greg had a family that would miss him, and yet he was willing to disappoint his mother in order to make this trip to Acorn Hill. That at least suggested Cynthia was important to him. Louise tucked that information away to consider later. The man was handsome enough. She would give him that much. Taller than Eliot had been, Greg was trim but sturdy looking in jeans and a moss-colored sweater that brought out green specks in his hazel eyes. His hair, when it finally lost its static electricity, was trimmed in a neat, traditional cut. When he grinned, which was pretty much constantly, twin dimples popped out on his cheeks.

". . . you've met Aunt Jane, Dylan and Claire," Cynthia was saying when Louise tuned back in to the conversation in the entry. "I would introduce the others, but I'm afraid I'm at a disadvantage."

Again, Jane stepped in, introducing the rest of the Erickson family. Conversations continued around Louise— about weather, travel conditions, even the current temperature in San Diego—before the Ericksons made their excuses and went up to their rooms.

"Why don't the three of you take a seat in the living room? The fire will feel good after that trip." Jane stepped closer to the door and hoisted the two heavy-looking suitcases. "I'll get your things settled in your rooms."

Greg stepped forward. "Here, let me get those."

"Wait, I can—" Jane stopped after Greg deftly removed both bags from her hands.

"Just tell me where to go." He took a few steps up the stairs and paused as if waiting for direction.

Jane turned to her sister and niece as if looking for advice.

Cynthia waved a hand at her. "Oh, let him, Aunt Jane. He likes to play the gentleman. Besides, he's going to flip when he realizes he has to carry my bag all the way to Mom's room on the third floor."

Greg shrugged and continued up the stairs.

"When we're done, I'll make you some tea and a snack," Jane said as she followed him. "If you're anything like my niece, you're probably dying for something sweet."

Greg stopped to stare down at Cynthia. "And here she's been trying to convince me she's a healthy eater."

Cynthia grinned. "Every woman has her secrets."

Louise waited until Jane and Greg had climbed to the second-floor landing before she turned back to her daughter. "Indeed."

Cynthia drew her eyebrows together. "Excuse me?"

"Apparently, one woman around here has a lot of secrets."

Her daughter shook her head. "Greg's not a secret. We've been together for a while now. I was intending to tell you about him before . . ." Her hesitation seemed to change the meaning of all she'd said prior to that last word.

"Before what?"

Cynthia started toward the living room, rubbing her hands over her upper arms as if she was cold. Pausing, she turned her head and spoke over her shoulder. "Before I decided at the last minute to invite him to spend Christmas with us."

Louise waited, watching as her daughter moved close to the fire and started warming her hands. The scene reminded her of another long ago when she and Eliot had visited Acorn Hill with their preschooler. Cynthia was mesmerized by the fire, always wanting to get too close, so Louise tried to stay within arm's reach to protect her. Cynthia had long ago grown past a need for her mother's protection. When did a mother ever grow past wanting to provide it?

Louise took a few steps more so that the two women stood sharing heat and space next to the fire. "Why did you invite Greg?"

Cynthia turned toward her, wearing a mock-scolding expression. "Mother, since when is it not acceptable for the Howard family to welcome guests over Christmas?" She turned and walked toward the peppermint candle still burning on the windowsill, melted wax forming bumpy rivulets down its sides. "I thought that candle meant that you innkeepers would never turn anyone away over Christmas."

"I never said anything about turning anyone away. None of us would ever do that," Louise replied. "I only asked why you invited this particular guest."

"Why do you ask?" Cynthia continued staring into the candle.

Now she was being purposely vague, and it was beginning to annoy Louise. "Because he has a family of his own who would have preferred he spent time with them."

"True. He could have gone there." Cynthia turned to face her mother, straightening her shoulders. "But I thought this might be a good time for you and Greg to meet."

"Now and not *before*?" she asked, stressing that word her daughter still hadn't explained to her satisfaction.

"Look, Mom, I know you're mad at me for not telling you about Greg sooner." She reached out and took her mother's hands. "But please don't form a negative opinion of him because you're upset with me. He's a great guy. You'll find that out if you give him a chance."

Cynthia tilted her head in a pleading look that brought even more memories flooding back to her mother. Louise couldn't help smiling. "Is it really important to you what I think of him?"

"Of course it is. You know that."

Louise's heart fluttered. Cynthia was asking for her approval of this young man she obviously regarded as special. She had always imagined a young man taking Eliot aside and asking for their daughter's hand in marriage. That would never happen. He would never escort his daughter down the aisle. Yet, Louise could take some comfort in Cynthia's seeking out her opinion. For both of their sakes, Louise hoped that Greg turned out to be the kind of man Cynthia deserved. She hoped with all her heart she would be able to give them her blessing. If she couldn't, she might lose her daughter in the process.

"Fine. I promise to be on my very best behavior," Louise said with a playful salute.

Cynthia grabbed her in a strong hug. "Thanks, Mom. This is going to be a great Christmas. I promise."

"You should have seen your daughter on that photo scavenger hunt with the Christian teens group." Greg laughed so hard that it took several seconds to compose himself before he could continue the story. "There she was, still dressed in her suit from work and doing push-ups with a bunch of teenagers on the walk outside Wal-Mart. Cynthia should be grateful to me. If I hadn't donated twenty dollars to the group's mission-trip fund, the leader would still have Cynthia's picture posted on his bulletin board."

"I'm forever in your debt," she said, her voice laced with sarcasm.

"As long as you realize that." Sitting next to Cynthia, he reached over and patted her hand.

Over the last two hours, Louise noticed that Greg had touched Cynthia's arm or hand several times, not possessively but with affection. It was hard to dislike someone who treated her daughter with such tenderness and made her daughter laugh with such regularity. She was beginning to suspect that some of her preconceived notions about Greg were incorrect, but still she planned to reserve judgment until she knew more.

Her sister and even her father's cat Wendell had been far easier to impress, it appeared. Jane was chatting with Greg as though he were an old friend of the family, and Wendell, the disloyal feline, hadn't even bothered to play coy and observe their guest from his place by the fireplace.

He promptly settled himself in Greg's lap. The newcomer gave the gray tabby a nice long rub behind the ears, and they were best friends.

Cynthia gestured widely then, her hand accidentally brushing Wendell's ear and interrupting his nap on Greg's lap. "Hey, I wasn't the one who ended up with a footprint on his head when he tried to stuff ten people into a phone booth. I don't know how you even *found* an actual phone booth."

"We called a bunch of people on our cell phones until we found someone who knew where an old phone booth was located. You know, modern technology solving age-old location problems. I don't even know if the phone in the booth worked."

"Probably not after all of you squeezed into it."

"That's what phone booths and compact cars are made for, to squeeze in as many people as possible."

Jane, who had pulled the rocker from the corner to be closer to the young couple, appeared riveted by their stories. "Do you two ever run out of things to say?"

Cynthia smiled at her mother and her aunt. "Even if we're on our best behavior, somebody else in the group steps up to fill the void. We're an active bunch."

"You mean the Christian teens group? I thought that was just for high school students."

"They could probably call us honorary members, but I

think the correct term is *chaperones*," Greg said. "The group leader asks for volunteers from our singles group when he needs extra adults for activities."

"The day of the push-ups incident, Greg didn't warn me about the type of activity he'd volunteered us to help with." She nudged him. "Otherwise, I would have changed first."

"So the two of you met at church then?" Louise couldn't resist asking.

Cynthia, Greg and Jane appeared surprised. She hadn't asked a single question since they'd gathered together in the living room. But then a person could hardly get a word in edgewise with Greg and Cynthia telling funny story after story, and with Jane egging them on to tell more.

After two hours of listening, Louise knew several details about Greg. He couldn't make par on a miniature golf course to save his life, he made up for the deficit by soundly beating her daughter at bowling, and he was allergic to shellfish. As for the important things, Louise still didn't know if Greg was even gainfully employed or if he'd ever been married, let alone what his intentions were concerning her only daughter.

Cynthia smiled at Greg before turning back to her mother. "No, our meeting didn't happen that way. I'd like to say it was somewhere interesting like an encounter at the Museum of Fine Arts in Boston, but the fact is we met at work."

"I'm a literary attorney, and I had a lunch meeting with Cynthia and a few of her colleagues," he continued for her, as he often did.

"An attorney? That's a nice, responsible career," Jane commented, glancing sidelong at Louise.

Louise frowned in return.

Greg missed the exchange. "It pays the bills, anyway, and my student loans. It helps that I'm single and that I don't eat much."

Cynthia rolled her eyes at him and continued the story. "Since Greg was new in town, he asked about churches. I told him about mine and how it had an active singles group."

"And the rest is history," Jane said with a sweeping gesture of her arms.

Cynthia shook her head. "If you say so, Aunt Jane. You're so dramatic. We did find out something interesting that we had in common, though. We were both born in Philadelphia, just a day apart."

Greg squeezed Cynthia's hand again. "Fate. That's what it was. We were supposed to meet."

Again, a look passed between Louise and Jane, and Jane smiled knowingly. This was serious all right.

Louise had to admit that she'd been wrong on a few things. A literary attorney would not need an editor to support him, and Greg turned out to be a Christian after all. Guilt filled Louise as she remembered how little faith in her daughter she'd shown by worrying Cynthia would choose someone who didn't share her convictions. Louise should have known better and shouldn't have prejudged Greg.

Cynthia didn't appear to have caught the sisters' exchange. "So what's on the agenda for the rest of Christmas week? We could go caroling."

"Okay." Jane leaned forward and rested her hands on her knees. "I could sing lead but only if we want doors slammed in our faces." They all laughed, except for Greg who had to be let in on Jane's joke about her singing disability.

"Perhaps our energy would be best spent on other endeavors," Louise said, trying to keep a straight face. "We're having a community Secret Santa program this year, and we'll be hosting the reveal party before Christmas Eve services. We need to bake cookies for the party, and we would welcome your help with that."

"Oh, Secret Santas. That sounds like fun," Cynthia said. "Is the whole community brimming with secrets?"

"One particularly intriguing secret is the identity of my Secret Santa," Jane said. "I still haven't received a single gift from mine. No note. No card. Nada."

Louise shook her head. "That just doesn't make any sense. I wonder if your name really was left out of the hat. Even my Secret Santa recipient received a first gift today and will be surprised twice tomorrow." She turned to the others to explain. "I'm playing catch-up. I had a bit of a late start."

"I guess we'll find out all the answers at the reveal party," Jane said. "I sure hope Alice makes it back for that."

Cynthia turned to her mother. "Wait, we've been here for hours, and you still haven't told us the complete story of why Aunt Alice isn't here."

"When would we have had the chance, dear?"

"Is it a big secret? Did she elope with a handsome stranger or join the space program?"

Jane leaned forward in her rocker so it stopped its gentle movement. "Nothing that romantic, I'm afraid." She proceeded to fill them in about Florence and Ronald's marital crisis and Alice and Aunt Ethel's road trip south to help save their friends' marriage.

"Well, that also explains where Aunt Ethel is. That was going to be my next question." Again, Cynthia turned to her guest. "She's actually my grandaunt—my grandfather's younger sister." For a few seconds, Cynthia fell quiet, seeming deep in thought, and then she smiled. "I don't know about you, but I think their adventure seems pretty romantic too, going to extremes to help a friend save her marriage."

"I suppose it is," Louise agreed grudgingly, though she suspected that Alice's reality was far less romantic than the plan sounded.

Greg, though, nodded enthusiastically. "Yes, marriage is a sacred thing, and friends like that are a blessing." He closed his hand over Cynthia's, and he squeezed gently before letting go.

Louise studied the two of them for several seconds. Their fondness for each other was evident.

In addition, Greg was a kind man, a Christian man and one who could support her daughter if she chose to leave the workforce to raise a family. For how much more could a mother ask? Again, Louise wished Eliot were present to share this moment. He would have been so proud. This young man was so like him in his kindness and fun-loving spirit. Cynthia was a lucky young woman.

Louise smiled at the thought, guessing that her daughter might have had good reason for not telling her about Greg earlier. Maybe she worried that once Louise had met Greg, she would have pressured Cynthia into choosing him before she decided he was the right one for her.

Fortunately, Cynthia wouldn't have to worry about that now. Louise had been a patient mother and now she could be delighted in the blessing God had brought into her daughter's life. Cynthia said she thought this would be a great Christmas. Louise, it seemed, was beginning to agree.

She glanced again at the young couple, who for a moment seemed oblivious to the others in the room, sharing a private exchange. If Louise's suspicion was correct, Cynthia would be receiving an extraspecial gift this Christmas—something that came in a tiny gift box and glistened with the brilliance of newfound love.

Chapter Twelve

*J*ane got an early start Wednesday morning, slipping down to her computer before the rest of the house stirred and before the winter sky transformed from black to daytime gray. *He that riseth late, must trot all day, and shall scarce overtake his business at night*, she recited silently, smiling at one of the many tidbits of Benjamin Franklin wisdom she had committed to memory. The inn was quiet except for the rumble of Wendell's purring from her lap.

"I'm glad you found a nice place to rest," she murmured to the cat as she rubbed under his chin. He stretched his neck to give her better access and then yawned and curled back into his napping position when the attention stopped.

Jane stifled a yawn of her own. They'd stayed up unusually late the night before, sharing stories and laughter with Cynthia and Greg. She would have liked to believe thoughts of her own plans drove her from under the covers so early this morning, but memories of the evening before had unsettled her a bit as well.

Her sister had eventually warmed to the delightful Greg, but something about the young couple struck Jane as strange. Though they chatted at length about their escapades with other members of the group, they never mentioned anything about even having dinner together just the two of them. Also, though they exchanged a few friendly touches while they sat together, Jane wondered why they never held hands, as young couples in love were wont to do.

She pushed the niggling thought away as silly. Never one to approve of the public displays of affection that were all too common these days, she felt that she should commend rather than question a couple who preferred to keep tender moments private.

Besides, she couldn't think about her niece's romantic life now when she had a note to write and a few Secret Santa gifts to deliver before making breakfast for her guests. She couldn't resist checking e-mail before she began, but she was only disappointed not to find a note from Alice.

Of course, Jane lacked her aunt's optimism for this trip in the first place. Marriages were neither built nor destroyed in simple steps, so she of all people understood that it would take more than a simple remedy to repair Florence and Ronald's. She hoped her aunt and sister could deal with the disappointment if even their best efforts failed to mend what had long been broken.

Not wishing to further discourage Alice, Jane typed a message to her, updating her on Cynthia's young man and the family's plans to add more decorations to the inn. After weighing her decision for a few minutes, she described in brief detail her discovery about the Quinlans and her plans to find a way to help them. She closed with an assurance that prayers were indeed headed south to Alice.

At the creaking sound of movement on the second floor, Jane hurried to open the computer's word-processing software, and she began a different message. A simple note, she decided, just wouldn't do. So in clever Secret Santa fashion, she began a poem to encourage her neighbors to share the spirit of the season with those around them.

Dear member of the Acorn Hill community,

In this season of gift-giving and sharing,
Our game offers a chance for true caring.

I tell you now what none has known;
A need has arisen in one of our own.

To respond to this need is an act of
   compassion,
But it must be met in a stealthy fashion.

The true spirit of Christmas, we can deliver;
Joy can be shared by receiver and giver.

On Christmas Eve, please do what you can.
Deliver help and hope to the below-listed clan.

Your Secret Santa

Satisfied, Jane added the pertinent information at the bottom of the note—brief details on how the Quinlan family had fallen on hard times; names, ages and approximate sizes of the family members; and suggestions for gifts of food and supplies. She also suggested the Secret Santa benefactors forward copies of the note to their own recipients but otherwise remain quiet about any help they might provide until after their clandestine deliveries late Christmas Eve.

The first copies of her document were coming off the printer when a touch on Jane's shoulder caused her to jump.

Claire Erickson stood next to her, barefoot and wearing a long nightgown. She had morning eyes, and her curly hair was even messier than usual.

"Oh, Claire, you startled me," she whispered.

The little girl grinned. "Sorry." Claire spoke in a soft voice as well. "Why are you up so early?" Instead of waiting for Jane to answer, the child stepped to the printer and glanced at the note. "Is that a poem?"

"It's a part of a game really, but an important game that will help a family in need."

Claire read the whole note without realizing she hadn't been invited to share it. She looked up when she had finished. "I like your poem. Can I help?"

"You understand that it's a secret, right?"

"I can keep a secret."

"That's good. I'll have to talk to your parents first, but

if they say it's okay, then I'll let you help make a gift basket for the family."

Excitement glimmered in Claire's eyes. "We should always help people when we can. I learned that in Sunday school."

Jane digested that interesting bit of information. She and Louise wondered if the Ericksons attended church, and it appeared they did often enough for Claire to learn that valuable lesson about giving.

"We don't go to church anymore," Claire continued as if Jane had asked the question. "We have games on Sunday mornings."

She nodded. She didn't begrudge parents the difficult decisions they had to make these days when weekends were getting shorter and lists of activities were growing longer. Every choice came with repercussions.

"A lot of churches have services at different times, so people who work don't have to miss so often."

"Our church has that too, and Mom says we'll go when we find the time."

Famous last words, Jane thought, a twinge of sadness touching her heart. She understood the tragedy of not finding the time to do the important things in life. "I'm sure you'll find it." She hoped that Claire's parents would discover what was important before their children were grown and living on their own.

She whispered to Claire, "I have a few Secret Santa

deliveries to make before breakfast. Do you think you could sneak back into bed for a while longer until your parents are awake?"

"I'll think about ways to help."

"You do that, but remember, we have to keep this work quiet. After breakfast I'll talk to your parents about helping."

Jane could feel the child's gaze on her as she tucked three copies of the letter into gift bags for Nia Komonos, Zack Colwin and Rev. Thompson.

"Nobody should be sad at Christmas. Not when we celebrate Jesus' birthday," Claire said.

Jane reached down and ruffled the child's curls. Paul and Sandy were probably making some mistakes with their children, but they'd gotten at least one thing right if Claire understood the true meaning of Christmas. "You're right about that. Now off to bed with you. Quietly."

Claire tiptoed away, turning back once and pressing her index finger to her lips. Jane watched her climb the stairs and then collected her coat from the coatrack. One of her recipients, Rev. Thompson, would probably move the project along, but Jane was counting on the good hearts of all those in the Acorn Hill community to truly make a difference for the Quinlan family.

She drove through town as quickly as was safe, rushing to make her three stops before the sky brightened too much. Besides the actual assistance she and her sisters would provide, Jane had done all she could to help involve others. From this point on, she wouldn't know the degree or quality of help the Quinlans would receive or even if her message would reach its intended targets. She said a little prayer as she left the gift bags in a location where each of her recipients would find them. The project was truly out of her hands now . . . and in God's.

"'God bless us, every one!'" Jane lifted her coffee cup in a toast to everyone gathered at the table. Though Jane didn't often quote Charles Dickens, Louise appreciated her sister's selection at this special time. The spirit during that morning's breakfast did feel like the Christmas morning described in *A Christmas Carol.*

Even the gray skies promising yet another layer to the blanket of white covering Acorn Hill did nothing to cloud her sunny outlook. Jane laid out a lovely breakfast, and she and Louise joined the Ericksons, Cynthia and Greg at the table.

"Here's to Tiny Tim, our chef." Louise did her own toast with a forkful of the scrumptious concoction of eggs, smoked cheddar and Canadian bacon that Jane had named Better Morning Soufflé. "You really outdid yourself this morning." The soufflé was lightly browned, puffy and as light as her mood.

"Hear! Hear!" Paul Erickson responded as he lifted a

bite of his cinnamon-topped delight. "What did you say this masterpiece was?"

Jane grinned, flattered by the praise for her culinary talents. "Topsy-Turvy French Toast à l'Orange. It's delicious and low in calories."

"The delicious part is what's important to me. Do you think you can give Sandy the recipe for it?"

Next to him, Sandy elbowed him. "You mean so you can make it when we get home?"

"Of course, dear." A mischievous smile lit his lips.

"I just want more biscuits," Dylan said over a mouthful.

"Please don't talk with food in your mouth, Dylan," Sandy said with a frown. "Besides, those are scones." She lifted one off the china platter and bit into the flaky pastry.

"Scones?" Dylan took another big bite, but following his mother's demand, he chewed and swallowed with a gulp before speaking again. "They're good."

Enjoying the boy's enthusiasm if not his manners, Louise chuckled. "Scones are a special kind of biscuit. Jane's orange-raisin scones are my favorite."

She snuck another peek at the far end of the table where her daughter sat with her beau. Greg leaned over and whispered something into Cynthia's ear, and they both giggled. Louise couldn't help smiling with them, though they seemed oblivious to her sharing the moment. If her daughter chose to spend her life with this young man, Louise liked knowing they would probably have a lifetime filled with laughter. She only wished she could have had the chance last night to talk to Cynthia about her new love, but her daughter appeared so exhausted that Louise withheld her questions. Now she couldn't wait to get Cynthia alone so she could learn more.

Greg stood up from the table and performed an exaggerated bow. "If you did all of this for me, Jane, then I am duly impressed and awed by the gesture."

"As am I with yours." Jane blushed, her pleasure obvious, and she stood and executed a nearly perfect curtsy, her ponytail bobbing.

As Greg lowered into his chair, Cynthia poked him with her elbow. "You silly, they go to this trouble for all their guests. Not just you."

Greg put his hand to his chest in feigned shock before he started laughing.

Paul, who was in a particularly good mood this morning, chuckled with him. "Why, Greg, don't you think the rest of us rate scones and soufflé?" He held his chin between his index finger and thumb, appearing deep in thought.

"I stand—or it's sit, I guess—corrected," Greg responded with a smile.

Paul settled back into his chair. "Well, as long as we have that settled."

Louise pushed back from the table. "I just remembered that the Leys should be here sometime this afternoon.

Well, the more the merrier." She stood up and started stacking dirty plates and collecting silverware.

"Here, let me get some of that." Greg's arm brushed Louise's as he relieved her of part of her load.

"You don't have to do that. You're a guest." Still, she was impressed that he had. In addition to all of Greg's other attributes, he helped in the kitchen too. Even Eliot, with all his wonderful features, had considered the kitchen hostile territory. Cynthia was one lucky woman. "*I'm* not a paying guest." He paused and drew his eyebrows together. "Or am I?"

"Oops, forgot to mention that," Cynthia said, grinning. She collected several glasses and started toward the kitchen, pausing to turn back to him. "I hope you brought your gold card."

"Sorry. I guess I'll be washing a lot of dishes while we're here."

Jane came up behind them. "What wonderful timing you have. Did I mention our dishwasher is on the blink?" She laughed, and Cynthia and Greg joined her.

When the four of them returned to the dining room, the Ericksons had stacked all the remaining dishes and were wiping up a few crumbs off the damask seat cushions.

"We *are* paying guests," Paul was quick to point out.

Jane accepted a serving plate into her arms. "And particularly helpful ones at that."

Claire sidled up to Louise and tugged at the sleeve of

her light blue cardigan. "Mrs. Smith, do you need us to help decorate again today? We had fun yesterday."

"I was just thinking about that. What does your family have planned for today? More relaxation?"

"We sure are enjoying it," Sandy said, but even her enthusiastic voice sounded strained.

"More of it might kill us all," Paul murmured.

Louise swallowed a laugh before she risked a suggestion. "I had this wonderful idea for a Christmas activity with my family and thought your family might like to join us."

"Can we, Mom?" Claire tilted her head pleadingly. "Please."

"Yeah, can we?" Dylan chimed.

Louise held up her hands to slow them, already chuckling. "How do you two know I'm not planning a basement-cleaning day? Don't you want to wait until I've told you my idea?"

"Well, what is it?" Claire asked in an excited voice.

"Yeah, tell us." Belatedly, Dylan added, "Please." Louise couldn't have been more delighted. They were clearly up for any adventure this morning. She herself hadn't felt this excited by a Christmas surprise since Cynthia was in pre-school and she and Eliot played Santa Claus for her.

This outing might be just the thing to help the Ericksons reconnect as a family, and it was doubly good that it would give her a chance to become better acquainted with Greg.

"She's right, guys," Paul said. "Let's hear her idea and then decide."

Louise indicated that they should follow her into the living room and waited to explain until they were all seated. "I owe the idea to you two." She nodded at the two children sitting cross-legged on the floor. "When you were talking about the theme you would have for your own Christmas trees someday, you both said something to the effect that you would like a children's Christmas tree, with unbreakable things and things made by children." She held her hands wide. "I thought it would be fun to have a tree like that this year."

Seated on the couch opposite Louise's chair, Sandy tilted her head to the side. "You're not going to take down all those lovely handblown ornaments, are you? I think that tree in the parlor is beautiful."

"I agree. I don't want to change a thing about it, but that doesn't mean we can't have another tree in the living room." Louise caught Jane's gaze and watched a smile spread across her face. She didn't have to announce to her sister that this was the plan she'd been considering, because it was clear Jane understood.

"Will you get the tree at Wild Things? I think Craig still has a few." Jane turned to the others to explain. "Craig Tracy, the store owner, sets up a tent behind his store and sells Christmas trees every year."

"I have an even better idea," Louise said, her excitement growing. "I called the North Pole Christmas Tree Farm in

Merriville, and I found out they still let you cut your own tree there. They even supply saws and axes."

Greg took a mock swing with an imaginary ax, landing an imaginary injury on his foot. "Sounds like a dangerous proposition to me."

"I don't know," Jane said. "I think it sounds like fun." She and Louise exchanged smiles that reflected memories of family Christmas trees.

"Oh, can we, Mom and Dad?" Claire asked.

Dylan studied Greg's technique before taking an imaginary swing of his own. "Can I cut down the tree?"

The mother in Louise was shaking her head before she even conferred with the boy's parents. "That's probably not a good idea. We'll leave that hard job to the men this time. I think Greg and Paul can handle it."

Paul appeared intrigued with the idea. "Why not. Let's do it," he said to his children's cheers. "But are you sure you want to do all this, Louise? You're going to an awful lot of trouble for us."

"It's no trouble, and it isn't only for you anyway. I want the chance to share this experience with my daughter and her friend. With just the three of us sisters living here, we usually don't have anyone around who can, or perhaps *should*, wield an ax."

Sandy appeared far less enthusiastic than her children. She didn't seem to get the warm family-togetherness angle of the plan.

"Of course, getting the tree is just part of the activity," Louise continued, focusing on Sandy. "I thought we could decorate it with ornaments and garland we make ourselves, particularly with special pieces made by the children. We can celebrate the joy and delight children have at Christmas by having a tree themed just for them."

Her gaze connected with Cynthia's. "I have a few ornaments in the attic that Cynthia made when she was a girl. I even found a few pieces that my sisters and I made when we were children. I guess Father couldn't bear to throw any of them away."

Claire appeared perplexed. "What will we put on the tree? All of the pretty things we've made are at our house. In boxes." When she added the last, she glanced at her mother, likely as a reminder that they hadn't had the time to dress a tree this Christmas.

"Well, we won't be able to get your great-great-grandma's bell, of course, but you can still have things that are yours. We'll make them." Louise held her hands wide for emphasis. "Cinnamon ornaments. Clay ornaments." She gestured toward her sister. "Of course, Ms. Howard here will probably have to help with some of that. She is the most handy with crafts among the Howard sisters."

"I highly doubt that."

"Well, Jane, you are the artist among us after all, a very talented artist at that."

"Does anyone here think I'm being buttered up for something?" Jane asked with her eyebrow raised.

"Oh, I think so," Paul said.

"Yeah, me too," Greg agreed.

"Just what I thought. What do you really want, dear sister?"

"Well . . ." Louise paused to direct a guilty look at her sister. "Someone needs to stay at the inn to greet the Leys when they arrive."

Jane pouted. "And you think *I* should be that someone?"

"I was rather hoping."

"Hmm." Jane placed her hand below her chin and tapped her index finger on her lips. Finally, she turned back to Louise. "Well, I did have my heart set on tromping through the snow alongside Sandy and sharing the joy of frozen ears and numb toes, but I guess I can make this very big sacrifice for you." She made a long-suffering sigh. "I'm sure I'll find something to do here all alone . . . by myself . . . without anyone else."

By the second redundancy, all of the guests were beginning to chuckle, and Louise was happy to join them.

Sandy shook her head sadly at Jane. "I just can't bear the thought of you being so *alone* here. I would be more than happy to stay back with you and would even be willing to make the sacrifice of sitting with you by the fire if you need me to."

"Oh no," Louise said quickly. "I mean it won't be necessary for you to miss this great family experience, Sandy. Besides, how can Jane appear to be the magnanimous sister, giving all for family and guests, if she doesn't spend the afternoon alone?"

"You know, on rare occasions, my dear sister is right, and this might be one of those times."

Louise's smile returned. "Thanks, Jane, for your undying show of support. We'll honor your sacrifice by allowing you the privilege of setting the tree in the tree stand when we get home."

Rubbing her hands together in imitation of an excited child, Jane said. "Oh, would you? By the way, she's not sharing our family joke about how our father could never get a Christmas tree to go straight in the stand. I'm sure I'll do Father proud with my own skills in that area."

"That's right," Cynthia said. "In every Christmas picture I've seen of the three of you and Grandfather in front of the tree, all of you were leaning." The look in Cynthia's eyes suggested that she might be recalling other happy family Christmas memories as well.

"Don't worry, Jane," Greg told her. "We'll help you get that tree straight."

Jane waved a hand in his direction. "I knew I liked you. Okay, you guys go on."

Louise glanced at her watch. "Can you all be ready in about an hour? We'll have to take another car in addition to mine, I'm afraid."

"We can take my car," Greg offered.

"Thank you," Louise responded. "Before we leave, I have to run downtown." She turned to Jane and winked. "I have a very *secret* errand."

"You remembered to put the note in your package, right?"

"The note is in there." She smiled at Jane, feeling privileged that her sister had let her in on her plan and asked her to be a part of it by passing the poem along to her Secret Santa recipient. Perhaps later, when all of the secrets were revealed, she would ask Jane when she'd added writing poetry to her list of creative skills.

Louise started back toward the kitchen, but her daughter put a hand on her shoulder. "Why don't you get going on your errand? Then you'll be back sooner. Greg and I will help Aunt Jane finish up with the dishes."

Grateful for the offer, Louise slipped on her coat and collected the gift she had been keeping in Father's study. Once outside the inn, she couldn't resist smiling up into the sky, no matter how gray and dull it appeared. The snow capping nearby buildings appeared fresher and whiter somehow. Christmas decorations looked brighter than she remembered, even in the daylight.

She hummed the first few bars of "It's Beginning to Look a Lot Like Christmas." Before she started her car, she took a moment to offer a prayer of thanksgiving, both for God's gift of the special young man in Cynthia's life and for His inspiration in how to help the Ericksons reconnect. She had the excited, almost giddy feeling that today would be a day to remember.

Chapter Thirteen

*W*hy, Louise, I haven't seen you around here in days. I wondered what had become of you."

Louise flinched, feeling a bit like the proverbial child caught with her hand in the cookie jar, as she turned to face her friend Viola Reed. Because Viola was busy with a line of holiday customers when Louise made her stealthy entrance into Nine Lives Bookstore, she'd hoped to have plenty of time to hide Viola's Secret Santa gift before she was noticed.

She wanted to hide the package near a copy of *Jane Eyre* or *Wuthering Heights*, because Viola's love for the works of Charlotte and Emily Brontë was well-known, but Louise was forced to settle for a hiding place behind a face-out copy of an Eleanor Roosevelt biography.

Having missed Louise's guilty reaction, Viola's brown eyes brightened as they peered over the top of her bifocals. "Merry Christmas, dear one."

"Merry Christmas to you, Viola." Louise gave her friend a quick hug, breathing in her fresh lilac scent. Her cheek brushed a red silk scarf that was decorated with Santa heads, the accessory adding a festive touch to her friend's black velour tunic and matching slacks.

In fact, the whole store looked especially festive this year with its boughs of greenery and a tinsel-draped tree.

"I was just admiring your lovely window display," Louise said when the silence stretched longer than was usual between the two of them. "Who knew Kipling, Shakespeare and Twain wrote all those holiday books?" She added with mock seriousness.

Viola chuckled as she touched her short, steel gray hair. "You know as well as anyone in Acorn Hill, better than most, that great works of literary fiction are meant to be enjoyed year-round. They happen to make wonderful Christmas gifts as well."

Louise was relieved that the awkward moment had passed. "There are certainly a number of titles on my own Christmas wish list." As she scanned the portraits of some of Viola's favorite authors spaced along the wall, the face of Charles Dickens caught her attention, bringing pleasant memories of that morning's breakfast to mind. They were blessed, indeed.

"Have you been busy at the inn?"

"It's been a bit hectic this week." Louise purposely took a few steps away from the location of her hidden gift, and Viola moved with her.

"I sure can relate to that." Viola looked toward the cash

register to see if anyone needed service before she turned back. "This place has been so busy this last week that I've considered trading that front door for one of those revolving models they have in big department stores." She paused and bent down to collect her tiny black-and-white cat Kane.

"Not that I'm complaining about a good shopping season, and I'm not going to complain about making a living when some people in our area are still out of work." She looked up from her furry friend to meet Louise's gaze. "Carlene Moss told me the other day she's doing an article on people laid off in the spring from Potterston Feed and Grain. Many of them still haven't found decent work."

"I'd heard something like that," Louise said, trying to avoid giving details.

"Carlene didn't mention whether the layoff involved anyone we knew, and I didn't want to pry."

The bell atop the store's door jingled to announce the arrival of more customers. Viola glanced first at the door and then at her cash register, where one of her customers had just deposited a pile of books. "I better get back to work. Were you just browsing today, or is there something I can help you find?"

Until Viola asked the question, Louise hadn't really considered that she did have a little last-minute shopping to finish. She hadn't purchased a single gift for Greg. She couldn't let him be forgotten on Christmas morning.

"I'm shopping today, but go ahead and help the other customers first." She scanned the wooden shelves with signs that read TRAVEL, REFERENCE and BIOGRAPHY and wondered what types of books Greg might enjoy. Did he share a love of the classics with Viola and her, or did he prefer mysteries as Alice did? "This might take a while."

Viola stopped midstep and turned back to her. "Okay, Louise, you've been acting very strangely, and I insist that you tell me right now what is going on."

Louise couldn't help smiling. "I need to select a Christmas gift for my future son-in-law."

$\sim$

Alice brushed her fingers back through her bobbed hair, surprised to find it damp with perspiration.

Darlene looked over from where she was tucking stray strands from her loose ponytail behind her ears. "It gets hotter out here than you'd expect when you're walking, doesn't it? By noon, it should be seventy-three degrees, and that's normal for December."

Alice nodded, pulling at the collar of her floral top. During their long walk through the neighborhood, pinks, lavenders and reds spread before them, not to mention varying hues of green. She found the combination of scents amazing, so heady and sweet.

Glancing up, Alice enjoyed the warm sun on her face. "This day is just beautiful."

"I thought you'd never get back," Ethel called from the front porch where she sat on a wrought-iron bench, clad in a light pink exercise suit. "What took you two so long?" Aunt Ethel patted the bench as a signal that she'd been first to arrive back at the house.

Alice crossed her right arm to her left side in a long stretch. "We just decided to enjoy the journey instead of sprinting home."

"Can I help it if the two of you can't keep up?"

Shaking her head, Alice narrowed her eyes at her aunt. "Now you be careful, okay? I don't want you to hurt yourself while we're down here."

Ethel glanced up at her. "You just don't want to do any nursing on your vacation."

Darlene, who had clasped her hands and was stretching above her head, glanced at Alice. "I didn't know you were a nurse."

Thoughts of her job brought a smile to her face. "I just love caring for patients. I only work part-time now, but I wouldn't give it up for anything."

Darlene indicated that Alice should sit on the bench next to her aunt, and she took a lawn chair for herself. "How did you get out of work the week before Christmas?"

Alice opened her mouth, but Ethel answered for her. "She begged and borrowed from her coworkers and agreed to take a shift on New Year's Eve."

"I'm not much for funny hats, noisemakers and champagne anyway." Alice shrugged. "Even when I'm at home on the holiday, I'm usually dreaming happily by midnight. Our work day begins early at the inn."

Darlene stared at her wide-eyed. "You have two jobs?"

"My sisters and I own a bed-and-breakfast," Alice answered. It was odd that they still knew so little about each other though they'd spent so many hours together.

Darlene turned and glanced at the emerald green rental car. "When do you have to be back to work?"

"At the hospital, my first shift is Tuesday, the twenty-sixth. But I promised my sisters I would be back at the inn on Christmas Eve."

Darlene placed her finger alongside her nose and appeared deep in thought. "That means you'll need to get on the road by . . ."

"Saturday," Alice finished for her. "That's the latest. It would be even better if we could get on the road Friday, so we can help with the Christmas celebrations. All the guest rooms ended up being filled even though we'd planned on having a private celebration with just family."

Darlene's smile was a sympathetic one. After the invasion she'd withstood this week—first a very upset niece and then a whole contingent from Acorn Hill—she understood having to make a change in plans. "Both of my girls—my twins—are coming home on Christmas Eve with their families."

"Karen and Sharon," Alice said, remembering what Ronald had told her.

Both Darlene and Ethel looked at her in surprise. Ethel was especially surprised that her niece could name Darlene's children.

"Ronald mentioned them in the car. My other passenger was asleep at the time," Alice explained, casting a look of feigned exasperation toward her aunt.

Ethel responded with a wag of her finger toward her tormenting niece.

"So Saturday at the latest and Friday at best," Darlene said.

It took Alice a few seconds to realize Darlene had returned to the subject of travel schedules.

"That gives us only one free day then."

"Free day for what?"

Darlene held her hands wide. "To go to the parks, of course."

Certain she must have missed something in the conversation, Alice glanced over at Ethel, but her aunt looked equally confused.

"Whatever are you referring to, Darlene?" Ethel asked finally.

Darlene looked at the two of them as if they were speaking a different language. "Have either of you been to Walt

Disney World?" When they shook their heads, she continued, "Then we have to go before you drive back. It's only an hour's drive from here. The timing is even good, because one of the least crowded times is just before Christmas."

Alice tried to think of a polite way to decline. "I don't think—"

Gesturing with her hand to interrupt her, Darlene pressed on. "You'll love it. Really. The place is amazing. It's as big as a city itself, with four major theme parks, two water parks, plus a bunch of hotel resorts and shopping and conference facilities."

Alice was chuckling but shaking her head by the time Darlene finished. "You sound like a great tour guide, but I'm not really one for amusement parks. Never was," she added quickly, lest anyone assume she was slowing down in her early sixties. Darlene waited patiently through each of Alice's excuses before she answered. "Believe me, Disney World is nothing like any other amusement park you can imagine."

"As lovely as it all sounds, Darlene, perhaps it would be best if we just stayed around the house," Ethel said. "We will be awfully tired on the return trip, and besides that, we don't even know if Florence and Ronald would be willing to go with us."

"Well then, shouldn't someone ask us that?"

Alice turned toward the sound of Florence's voice. Inside the screen door, the Simpsons stood together, looking out at them.

Darlene waved them out. "Florence, Ronald, what do you think about the five of us spending a day at Disney World?"

Ronald opened the door for his wife, and they joined the women outside. Florence turned to him as she answered. "I think that sounds like a fine idea, don't you, Ronald?"

"Absolutely."

"Then it's settled," Darlene said. "You'll love the parks at this season. They're all decorated for the holidays."

Alice, though, wasn't ready to give in. She straightened in her seat. "Aren't you concerned that we'll all be exhausted for the return drive to Acorn Hill?" Even with a couple of days until they needed to leave, she already dreaded that drive. "Also, we have only one more day when we could fit an outing like that into the schedule." She glanced at Ethel, waiting for her to come to her aid, but her aunt remained quiet.

Florence pursed her lips as if thinking and then nodded. "I think you're right, Alice. That would be a bad idea for us to have an adventure like that before making the return drive."

Alice had barely released her sigh of relief when Florence spoke up again.

"You've given very valid reasons why we should fly."

"Fly?" Ethel spoke up this time, her eyebrows coming together. "Florence Simpson, if you think I'm going to waste my good money on paying for first-class airline tickets just so we can work around this strike and not have to drive home, then you don't know me very well."

A smile settled on Florence's lips. "Ethel, I know you perfectly well. I also know, as you would if you happened to watch the news, that the baggage handlers have a tentative contract."

"That still doesn't mean you could even get tickets this close to Christmas," Ethel insisted.

"Well, let's just see then." Florence shuffled past her husband and headed into the house.

They waited in silence, wondering what Florence might accomplish.

"Our Florence could never resist a challenge," Darlene finally said.

"Don't I know it," Ronald agreed.

"She did choose you, Ronald," Ethel said, her voice playful with sarcasm. "I'd say that's proof she loves a challenge."

Becoming quiet, he glanced at the door through which his wife had passed. "As long as she keeps loving challenges," he said in a soft voice. He turned to Ethel and Alice. "You know, flying really wouldn't be a bad idea. We could easily turn in the car at a rental center at the airport."

"If you can get the tickets," Ethel said, doubt evident in her voice.

"What do you mean *if*?" Florence pushed the door open again and stepped out onto the porch. When they all glanced over at her, she smiled. "Four e-tickets to Philadelphia, departing at noon on Sunday. Confirmation should be available on Ronald's laptop."

Ethel stared at her incredulously. "How in the world did you get tickets on Christmas Eve?"

"If cost isn't a consideration, you can have whatever you

need. Besides, first-class is the only way to fly, and since I know that the payment for the car rental was taken care of by Ethel, the plane tickets are a thank-you gift from Ronald and me." Florence brushed her hands together as if to say the discussion was finished. "Now. Disney World. We all need to get out of this house, so we'll go tomorrow. Then we'll have two full days to recover before flying home. Is everyone agreed?"

"Sounds like a fine idea to me." Ronald said.

"We'll have a nice time," Ethel said. "And thank you so much for getting the tickets."

Though Alice was quick to pipe in with, "Yes, thank you both," Florence pinned her with a stare.

"You didn't say whether you were up for a Disney adventure."

"I can't wait." Alice hoped her voice sounded sufficiently sincere. It was pointless to argue once Florence made up her mind anyway.

As much as she was relieved not to have to repeat the cramped car ride home, with Ethel, Ronald *and* Florence this time, she still wasn't enthusiastic about a day in an amusement park.

⌒

"Let me see . . . cinnamon, applesauce, a megacontainer of salt, cornstarch, cookie cutters, paint, ribbons, string, needles, popcorn, Styrofoam balls, sequins and a straw." Jane used her index finger to take inventory as she surveyed the kitchen table, now crowded with her supplies. "That looks like everything."

She didn't even bother whispering as she talked to herself. It wasn't as if anyone was around the inn to overhear her private conversation and question her sanity. As long as she didn't feel compelled to answer herself, Jane figured she was just fine.

The inn had been quiet all afternoon. She'd spent much of the morning and early afternoon waiting for Kevin and Jill Ley's arrival, only to have the couple head out the door just as soon as they'd settled their bags in the Garden Room. She couldn't blame the young blond and blue-eyed pair for their eagerness to get over to Pastor Henry and Patsy's. They'd kept Jill's pregnancy a secret for four months and couldn't wait to show off her slightly rounded tummy.

Louise would be pleased to know how impressed Jill was with the piano and that she carried a violin case of her own to their room. Jane guessed that the two might have a lot to talk about—that is, if this busy week ever slowed down long enough for them to meet.

Jane should have enjoyed the peace and quiet she and her sisters had hoped for but experienced so little of this holiday season. In truth, she was feeling a bit lonely. She missed spending time with both of her sisters, even if Louise had been acting downright giddy since Cynthia's arrival or, more specifically, Greg's arrival. She missed seeing Alice's sweet face and hearing her sister's always positive take on the world. Jane even missed hearing a shrill, "Yoo-hoo, is anyone home?" as Ethel came through the back door.

She couldn't wait until Christmas Eve, when they would all be back together again. At least she still hoped they'd be together. Ethel and Alice would probably blame themselves if the Simpsons' marriage failed now, and part of Jane would blame herself for letting them run off to Florida.

Jane tucked those thoughts away. She had too many things to finish before their guests started returning. She didn't care to waste her only time alone worrying about Alice and Aunt Ethel. The Leys had assured her they wouldn't be back until evening, so Jane didn't worry when she locked up the inn to run errands.

For the better part of three hours, she combed through the best of Acorn Hill's shops, searching holiday sale racks and clearance bins, stretching her shopping dollars as far as she could.

As confident as she was that her sisters would be more than happy to share some of the cost, she wasn't sure she should have taxed their generosity so far. She couldn't help herself, however, when she thought that Meghan Quinlan and her even littler sisters might have empty stockings at Christmas. Handled shopping bags lined the counter where she'd set them while putting aside the materials for ornament-making activities. She'd purchased so much that she had to make three trips to the car to carry it into the house.

Jane opened the bags so that she could admire some of her purchases. Each child had one new outfit, a pair of brand-new pajamas and plenty of socks and underwear. There was even a nice, warm coat for Meghan, a pretty lavender one that a young girl would love. Jane hadn't forgotten Logan and Jessica either, purchasing a jogging suit for each.

Another bag contained necessary items such as combs and shampoo as well as small luxuries such as cologne and hand lotion. The final bag was her favorite, containing two baby dolls for the younger girls and a fashion doll for Meghan. "Dr. Maggie, Pediatrician," she read aloud from the script on the fashion doll's box. The doll itself sported a physician's lab coat and held a tiny infant patient. *I bet Meghan's going to love you*, thought Jane.

As she repacked the bags and lugged the first load to her room on the third floor, she couldn't help feeling pleased by the amount of progress she'd made in preparing help for the Quinlan family. She hoped Louise was having similar success on her outing with Cynthia, Greg and the Ericksons. They would probably all come home with rosy cheeks and filled with Christmas spirit, which would only make their ornament-making activity more enjoyable.

Jane returned to the kitchen and hefted her second load, feeling suddenly more confident that her plan to help the Quinlans on a large scale just might work. If even only one or two of the Secret Santa recipients became involved, she might be amazed by all they could accomplish. Still, she had no way to monitor whether her message had even reached all of the individuals for whom it was intended. Of course, if she received the letter back in a surprise gift from her own Secret Santa, that would be a positive sign.

"Fat chance of that happening," she said with a dry chuckle as she climbed the stairs a second time. Besides, it was only a matter of hours since she'd put the letter into circulation, and she couldn't imagine the wheels of charity turning that quickly.

She couldn't worry about any of that now. Already she had plenty to do to prepare baskets from the gifts she'd purchased. She needed to decide what to buy for a food basket. She would focus on what she believed to be God's will and let Him handle the rest. How many times had she entrusted Him with the problems in her life and then tried to take them back? It was almost comical.

Just as she had to wait for Louise and her companions to return with the Christmas tree before they could begin decorating it, she would have to wait until Christmas Eve to see the results at the Quinlans' home. Waiting, for Jane, was one of the hardest things in the world.

Chapter Fourteen

*S*now sculpted the landscape in rolling drifts, and blue spruce and white pine dotted the hillside, some so thoroughly coated that they nearly disappeared into their white backdrop. Clean, cold air fluttered branches and teased lungs with its freshness. In the center of all that natural beauty stood what had to be one of the more discontented groups of individuals ever to cut their own Christmas tree.

Sandy balanced on one leg with a booted foot hidden beneath several inches of snow. The other leg she'd bent and lifted behind her. Every few minutes she would switch legs. When she wasn't focused on preventing frostbitten toes, she was rubbing her gloved hands together briskly enough to create a spark, Louise thought wryly. Paul looked no better, with his down jacket zipped up over his nose. Even Cynthia had started grumbling and was complaining that she'd forgotten a hat. *If only you'd listened to your mother*, Louise thought as she resisted the urge to address Cynthia out loud.

Shaking her head, Louise turned in the most recent direction the Erickson children had run.

"Mom, I like this one," Claire called out from behind a row of thin firs. "It's perfect."

"No, I don't like those skinny girl trees. We need one of these." Dylan pointed to a mammoth Scotch pine that was more appropriately sized to fit in the governor's mansion in Harrisburg rather than in the living room at Grace Chapel Inn.

"Just pick one, would you?" Sandy spoke through either gritted or chattering teeth. It wasn't clear which.

She did have a point. They'd already stomped past row after row of perfectly acceptable trees, but no one could seem to agree on just the right one. In fact, not a lot about this excursion had turned out the way Louise imagined, and Paul, designated as the group's lumberjack, had yet to swing an ax. Everyone seemed to be missing the spirit of the activity and also would be missing the joy that could be buried beneath one of these heaps of snow. Even the sky was darkening by the minute to the color of steel as a snowstorm approached.

Part of her was tempted to load everyone back into the two cars and ride away to Acorn Hill. Craig Tracy probably still had a tree or two they could choose from at Wild Things. No, that would be too easy, and Louise was never one to take the easy way out of difficult situations. She was, however, a reasonable woman, and she decided she had better accelerate this family-bonding experience before the ties that bind snapped.

"Well, which do you think, kids, the Scotch pine or the fir? This is supposed to be a children's tree after all."

"Yes, children." Cynthia agreed. Her teeth were clearly chattering. "Pick a pretty one and soon, before we all become icebergs."

Paul set the ax aside and rubbed his gloved hands together. "Pick whichever one has the thinnest trunk," he urged.

Greg approached him from behind and patted his heavily padded shoulder. "Only because that means it's a younger tree, and younger trees stay fresh longer, right?" Even in the frosty temperatures, when his toes must be as numb as everyone else's, Greg still was in a good mood, his trademark grin in place.

"Absolutely." Paul hefted the ax again. "Okay, kids, which tree do I use this monster on? I can make quick work of it and be home for hot chocolate within the hour."

"I'm going to hold you to that," Sandy told him.

Louise had no doubt she would, and that for weeks to come she'd hold her husband accountable for taking her out on what she would see as a miserable excursion. So much for Louise's plan to help the Ericksons reconnect during this adventure. She would be lucky if the four of them were even speaking to each other by the time they returned to the inn.

"Okay, kids, it's time." With effort, Louise managed to keep her teeth from chattering. "You have one minute to agree on a tree. Otherwise, the grownups are going to have to choose."

Faced with that unacceptable outcome, the two children, who'd agreed on little since arriving in Acorn Hill, managed to find a perfectly suitable seven-foot Scotch pine well before the deadline. It was a little crooked, and one side of it had a significant bare spot, but the two of them danced around the tree, appearing thrilled with their choice. The adults exchanged amused smiles, but no one mentioned the tree farm owners would probably be pleased to let go of that prize.

Paul didn't waste any time sinking his metal blade in the sticky pine bark. Louise made sure the children stayed out of range for the tree to fall. The last thing they needed was to make a detour to Potterston Hospital.

He'd only taken a few swings when Cynthia stepped forward. "Any way you could speed that up?"

Instead of swinging his ax again, Paul rested it on the ground and turned to Greg. "Your friend here wants to help me out. Should I indulge her?"

"Never let it be said that I held her back." Greg glanced at Cynthia and lifted his eyebrow in challenge.

Amid a chorus of chuckles, Cynthia stepped forward and gripped the ax. "Sorry, Mom, I couldn't resist."

Louise glanced at her daughter. Perhaps Cynthia wasn't exactly the genteel lady she once endeavored to raise, but she was a fine, strong woman, and Louise was so proud of her. With a grin Louise gestured for her to begin. "Better get on with it. If you turn out to be a female Paul Bunyan, then all the better."

"I wouldn't go that far." Cynthia took a few good swings, letting the ax bite into the trunk. "Hey, that wasn't so bad." She returned the ax to Paul.

After only a few more swings, Paul was yelling, "Timber!" and the tree was hitting the ground with a *swish*. Applause broke out on the hillside, with a whoop or two added to the mix. Glee filled Louise's heart as she glanced at each of the faces. The outing was a success after all. She was tempted to cheer like the others, but because she wasn't the hollering type, she clapped instead.

"Okay, who volunteers to drag this humongous tree down the hill?" Louise asked. She scanned the group, stopping on the Erickson children.

Dylan lunged forward. "Me."

"Me too," Claire chimed.

Paul pointed to the bottom of the tree. "You'll want to drag it by its trunk so you don't break off any branches."

The children ran to the trunk and started pulling, but the tree barely budged.

"Here, let us men help with that." Greg reached inside the branches and grabbed the tree about halfway up.

With Paul holding from the other side, the four of them carried the tree down the hill, though one of the men could easily have dragged it alone. It was better this way, the group of them working together, just as all of them would decorate it together once they took it back to the inn. They had only to load the tree onto the roof of Louise's old Cadillac and secure it with a bungee cord. At least one thing on this adventure turned out to be easy.

The grumbling was transformed to laughter by the time they piled back into the two cars and drove onto the road back to Acorn Hill. *All's well that ends well*, Louise thought with a sigh of relief. It wasn't over, though. Part Two of her plan would begin as soon as they reached the inn, if Jane had collected all of the craft supplies. Behind the wheel, Louise offered a prayer that the second half of the plan would go a little better than the first.

The little Florida home that had housed so many voices for three days was strangely quiet for the lack of them early Wednesday evening. Alice paced its short halls and wondered if the time was right. Ronald had volunteered to fix a faulty outlet in Darlene's living room, so he and Darlene were off at the hardware store picking up supplies. Ethel had turned in early, the morning's speed walking having taken a larger toll than she would ever admit.

Florence had moved to the sunroom with her Bible the moment that Darlene's car backed out of the garage. Alice couldn't blame her for wanting to spend some time alone. The last several days had been emotionally wrenching enough for the spectators, let alone the principal participants.

Alice was reluctant to interrupt Florence's time for reading and perhaps meditation. Yet she couldn't shake the sense that she should do just that. Bad timing or not, she had to do it now. She might not have another opportunity.

"Florence?" she called as she neared the door to the sunroom.

The other woman cleared her throat. "Yes."

"I wondered if we might talk for a few minutes."

Her answer was an audible sigh. "Can it wait?" Her voice sounded tired, without the spunk it held earlier while they planned their outing for the next day.

Alice nearly lost her courage, but she straightened and stepped through the doorway. "It's pretty important."

Again, Florence sighed, but she indicated with a gesture for Alice to take a seat in the chair across from the couch where she sat. "What is it?" She leaned her head against the back of the couch.

Alice took a deep breath and pressed forward. "Ronald told me about the twins."

Florence straightened and frowned. "You mean our nieces? What about them?"

"How much you adored them. How much you and Ronald dreamed of having children of your own." Alice waited.

For several seconds, Florence said nothing. She only stared out the window into the magenta streaks of the setting sun. Then she met Alice's gaze steadily. "It just didn't happen." She waved her hand as if to dismiss the fact's importance. "That feels like a lifetime ago." She smiled wistfully. "Probably because it was. God had different plans for us. His plans are always perfect."

Perfect? Alice studied her, surprised by her words. The way she spoke sounded much like the way Alice thought of her own life. She once assumed she would marry and have a family, but God seemed to have other plans for her.

"I didn't need to be a mother to contribute to my community or church," Florence continued without prodding. "I might not even have had time for important work like the church board if I had been busy with a family."

Alice cleared her throat. She could relate to those feelings and often wondered if she would have been able to contribute to the same degree if her situation had been different. "Ronald also said you considered adoption but couldn't agree on the timing."

Leaning forward and resting her elbows on her knees, Florence settled her chin between her hands. "That was just another part of God's plan." She lifted her head. "I wonder why Ronald brought it up. Really, it was so long ago."

Alice shrugged. "Sometimes things like that cause resentment in a marriage."

"You mean childlessness?" Florence paused, her eyes glazed with memories from several decades before. "I suppose it can. It did in our case. No matter what he says, I knew Ronald believed I failed him by not giving him a child."

Alice blinked. That wasn't the way Ronald had said it at all. Could it be possible that some small part of the resentments in the Simpsons' marriage—at least the first ones— were based on mistaken beliefs? Could those tiny seeds of resentment have festered over decades? "I think you're wrong."

Startled, Florence studied her. "I don't think that's something that someone outside a marriage can ever know." For Florence, it was a diplomatic statement, a gentle reminder for Alice to mind her own business.

Though Alice loved confrontation about as much as

Wendell loved a kitty bubble bath, she couldn't back away from telling the Simpsons what they'd never had the courage to tell each other. "That's just not what Ronald said."

Florence opened her mouth, ready with a retort, but then closed it. She stared out the window again, likely seeing far beyond the darkening horizon.

"Would you like me to tell you what he did say?"

For several seconds, Florence said nothing. Alice supposed it was possible that she might not want to know what her husband had said, but she refused to believe Florence didn't care.

"Please tell me," Florence said finally.

"He said you both accepted God's will . . . eventually."

Florence tilted her head back and forth as if considering, but she didn't concede. "Why do I get the feeling that's not all my husband said to you?"

"I've always known you're a smart woman." Alice smiled, then continued. "He said that in the end you wanted to adopt, but he had become settled in his life and didn't want to change it." Alice cleared her throat again, wondering if she should say more, but she'd come this far. She couldn't stop now. "He said it was the only time he put his foot down with you, and you never forgave him for it." Bracing herself, Alice waited for the outburst that was certain to come.

Florence, though, threw her head back and laughed so

hard she hit her head on the white wicker behind her. "Ouch," she said and rubbed her head. "My Ronald, he's always been so dramatic. I *was* angry at the time. Furious. After a time, though, I let it go." She paused, eyes suddenly wide. "Do you think it's possible he really did do the same?"

"More than possible."

An amazed expression settled over Florence's features. Of course, she'd never considered the possibility that she was wrong about her husband, and yet she'd never asked. Over the last few days, Florence and Ronald had talked about a lot of things, but it was clear that they had a lot more to discuss. She hoped they would keep talking and sharing, reconciling the past with the present for years to come.

"Look at this one, Mrs. Smith."

From across the table where she was rolling out dark brown dough, Louise examined the tiny angel Claire held in the palm of her hand. "It's lovely, dear. Did you show that one to your mother?"

"No, she just went into the living room to see if the tree's standing yet."

Louise pressed her lips together, trying not to smile as she thought about the tree. Greg, Jane, Cynthia and Paul had been trying to get their precious Scotch pine into the stand for the last forty-five minutes. Apparently the "lumberjacks" had cut the trunk too short, so they trimmed off several lower branches to make it work. Adding to the problem was the fact that there were too many supervisors and not enough workers to get the job done, but Louise kept that little observation to herself.

"Well, put it on the cookie sheet with the others, dear, and we'll show her as soon as she gets back," Louise said.

Dylan looked up from a brown star with one very damaged point. "I have a better idea. Why don't you just eat that one and tell Mom and Dad what it looked like later. You know you want to." He laughed as if he'd just told the funniest and most original joke ever to be heard at Grace Chapel Inn, but because he had already tried the same joke three times in the last hour, it had lost its impact.

Claire didn't answer but pretended to stick her finger down her throat and made feigned gagging noises.

"Now, Dylan," Louise began, as she did each time he started his stand-up routine, "I told you when we started this project that cinnamon ornaments aren't edible, before or after they're baked. Believe me, you don't want to eat one."

Dylan pointed at his sister. "She's the one who wants to eat it, Mrs. Smith. I'm just trying to protect her." He seemed to be trying not to smile, but he failed.

Louise, much more practiced at sardonic humor than the boy, kept a straight face. "Well, aren't you a wonderful big brother. Claire is so lucky to have you."

Claire made an unpleasant face. "Yeah, really lucky!"

Now Louise smiled. "Are we going to waste our time chatting, or are we going to finish cutting out these ornaments?"

Claire picked up a cookie cutter shaped like a stocking. "I want to make ornaments."

"Me too," Dylan said. Already he was busy making another star.

"Don't forget to use that straw to poke a hole in the top of the ornaments, so we can hang them after they're dry," Jane instructed as she entered.

The other adults returned to the kitchen then amid cheers and applause. Greg lifted his hand to reveal forearms spotted with a red rash from handling the tree. "I'd like to thank the Academy, Mom and Dad and, of course, Cynthia. If not for her—"

"The tree would still be lying on the living room floor?" Cynthia scoffed. She turned back to Louise. "Don't worry, Mom. The Howard tradition is still intact. That tree is about as crooked as it could be while still standing."

"Good then." Louise shaped the scraps of dough into a ball again and rolled it out on the table for the children, who were already selecting cookie cutters for their next ornaments. "Christmas traditions are important."

Jane stood at the end of the table and examined the collection of shapes on the cookie sheet. "I thought you'd be done with these by now. I wanted to get these in the oven, so we can mix up the salt clay for other ornaments."

Immediately, Louise stood and offered her younger sister her chair. "Now that the rest of the grownups are back, maybe we'll make better time getting the work finished." With a wave of her hand, she encouraged the other adults to gather around the table.

Sandy leaned in between her children and pushed a Santa-shaped cookie cutter through the dough. "This stuff sure smells like cinnamon."

"Just wait until we put them in the oven," Jane said as she rolled the dough again. "You bake them slowly, at a low temperature, and it makes the whole house smell great."

Sandy closed her eyes and inhaled. "That will be special."

Louise glanced about the room, noting that not all of the adults were occupied. "Does anyone know how to operate an air popcorn popper?"

"I know how," Cynthia called out.

"I do too," Paul said.

Greg raised a hand as well.

Glancing at the three of them, Louise handed the bag

of unpopped corn to Paul. "Why don't you and Claire get started popping all this? When you're done, we can all start stringing the kernels."

"Can we eat some?" Claire asked as she scrambled up from the table and joined her father.

"Of course," Louise said.

"Hey, that's not fair," Dylan said with a frown.

Claire glanced over and shrugged. "You could always eat some of the dough."

Since the others hadn't been around to hear the comedy routine earlier, they laughed, but Louise only shook her head and continued orchestrating the work in the kitchen. Soon all of the projects were going smoothly. Sandy and Dylan sat at the table, cutting the last of the cinnamon-dough shapes, a small bowl of popcorn appeasing the boy while he worked. Meanwhile, Louise and Jane worked together mixing the salt-clay dough, and Paul, Claire, Cynthia and Greg worked an assembly line through the center of the kitchen, making long strands of popcorn garland. That left only the Styrofoam balls to be decorated with ribbon, sequins and tiny beaded pins.

Louise excused herself to make a quick trip to the attic. In a box clearly marked "Smith Christmas," she found the items she sought, the crafts that brought back the holiday memories of a little girl. There was a crèche formed of

Popsicle sticks and peanut shells, and a glittery snowman sandwiched between pieces of contact paper. Her favorite piece of all was a tiny wreath-shaped picture frame made of green-painted puzzle pieces. Inside was a picture of the sweet little girl Louise still saw when she looked at her daughter.

She collected the ornaments and a few others that were appropriately juvenile and headed downstairs. The sound of voices and the smell of cinnamon greeted her before she reached the first floor. Jane started an off-key version of "We Wish You a Merry Christmas," and some others filled in with the real tune. *Bless them*, Louise thought.

She closed her eyes and absorbed all of it before reentering the kitchen. Though the oven was only heated to a low setting, Louise felt warmer than she had in a long time. As she glanced around the kitchen, she sensed that the others felt the same.

Even the Ericksons appeared to have found a way to spend more than a few minutes in the same room without climbing the walls. They were enjoying the day as much as Cynthia and Greg were, and those two seemed to be having the time of their lives.

At the appropriate moment, Louise gave instructions, and they reconvened in the living room, where their special tree stood, its bare spot turned to face the wall. They wrapped lights and the popcorn strands around the tree and added Styrofoam ornaments as well as many of the pieces Louise had found in the attic. Jane, who'd done her own rummaging, contributed ornaments she and her sisters had made in school. They would have to wait on the ornaments in the kitchen until the cinnamon ones had baked for a few hours, and until the salt-clay pieces were dry enough to be painted. Already, though, the tree looked great—a child's tree with the love of Christmas draped over it like tinsel.

"Okay, Dylan, you do the honors," Louise said.

With a grin, the boy plugged in the extension cord, bringing colorful lights to life to a chorus of *oohs* and *aahs*.

"Oh, it's beautiful," Claire exclaimed. "Mom and Dad, we got to decorate our tree." There was no blame in her voice now, just joy.

"It's wonderful, kids," Sandy said with a truly contented smile.

This was the way Christmas was supposed to be, with families sharing time and building memories together. Part of Louise hoped the night would hurry forward so she could be alone with Cynthia, but another part wanted to savor each moment of the evening's gathering.

Chapter Fifteen

*L*ouise sat up in her bed with two lacy pillows propped behind her head, her Bible lying open in her lap. Under light from the pair of lamps on twin bedside tables, she tried to focus on the pages, but the passage in 1 Kings 10 that retold the Queen of Sheba's visit with King Solomon couldn't hold her attention. Instead, another story kept invading her thoughts.

Her gaze followed the room's floral wallpaper over to the door. Soon Cynthia would enter through that doorway, and the two of them would have the private mother-daughter time she'd been eager for all day.

So many questions filled her mind that she wasn't sure which to ask first. *When is the wedding?* That this particular question had worked its way to the head of the line made her smile.

Perhaps she shouldn't ask that one first, but there were several things she would ask once they were settled in for the night. She would ask about her daughter's feelings for Greg Hollister and about any thoughts Cynthia might have regarding her future with him.

Whether it was too soon to offer her blessing on their union, Louise wasn't sure. That would come later. She and her only child had more immediate things to talk about now.

The sound of her doorknob turning slowly pulled Louise back from her thoughts. Cynthia stood in the doorway, tightening the belt of her peach robe. With her face freshly scrubbed and her hair brushed until it shone, she still looked like a girl. As much as Louise missed that child, she loved the woman Cynthia had become, and she was proud of the choices she'd made.

"I wasn't sure if you'd be sleeping," Cynthia said as she closed the door behind her.

Louise gestured toward her Bible. "I thought I might do some reading." She had good intentions, anyway, even if she had read no more than half a dozen verses and absorbed even fewer.

"You're not tired?" Cynthia cocked her head and studied her mother. "It's been a busy day." Crossing to the bed, she slipped off her robe and slippers and climbed under the covers.

Louise half expected her daughter to turn away and settle in for sleep, ending her hopes for a conversation, but Cynthia propped up her pillow and leaned against it.

"Are you tired?" Louise couldn't help asking. "Because if you are, we can always talk—" When her daughter shook her head, Louise stopped herself.

"Really, Mom. I've been looking forward to spending some time with you—just us girls."

Louise swallowed, trying to ignore the emotion welling in her throat. "I have as well." Automatically, she brushed her fingers over her daughter's shoulder.

Cynthia reached up and closed her fingers over her mother's hand and then released it. "We don't see each other often enough."

The truth in that comment made Louise smile. If they spent more time together, they wouldn't be sitting here with so many unanswered questions between them.

"Greg seems like a nice fellow," Louise said to move the conversation forward. She hoped her daughter would pick up from there and save her from having to ask so many questions.

Cynthia nodded but said nothing.

Louise sensed that her daughter was about ready to open up, just as she'd intuited similar moments during Cynthia's teen years. She settled against the pillows, folded her hands in her lap and waited.

"Was it love at first sight when you met Dad?"

Louise blinked. She expected a discussion of relationships, but she hadn't prepared herself for it to be hers. She shook her head. "I don't really believe in such a thing. That's just infatuation. Besides, you know how your father and I met."

"I know, but I like hearing it."

Louise reached over and patted her daughter's hand. "Eliot was my professor of music theory at the conservatory. Yes, I noticed him when I first saw him, but I paid attention to all my professors."

"A little more to him though, right?"

"Not until after I was no longer his student." Louise frowned, doing her best to appear offended. "I did have my standards after all."

Her daughter grinned at her, and Louise couldn't resist smiling back. How fortunate she had been to know love and commitment such as she and Eliot had shared. She could wish no less for her daughter and was so pleased that she appeared to have found it.

"Have you developed your own theories on that at-first-sight nonsense?" Aware she was entering new territory with her daughter, she planned her next words more carefully. "Greg said you met at work, didn't he?"

"I haven't decided what I believe about that," Cynthia said in answer to the first question before addressing the second one. "We were friends first."

It was far from a full revelation of her relationship with Greg or their future plans, but it was a start. Louise squeezed her arms around herself in a hug, feeling content.

The two sat in companionable silence for a few minutes, but when Louise glanced at her daughter, Cynthia was watching her. Louise adjusted a pillow behind her head.

"I always loved watching you and Dad together. It was amazing how you both appeared to sense each other's needs. Just as you were getting up to pour a glass of lemonade, Dad would be carrying one out to you. He would be searching for his reading glasses, and you would lower them into his hands." She paused and studied her mother. "You really loved each other."

"Oh yes, we definitely had a bond. It helped us through the rough times."

"I can't picture the two of you even having rough times. Your marriage always seemed so perfect to me."

"No marriage is perfect. They all hit rough spots."

"You mean like Aunt Ethel's friends, Ronald and Florence?"

"I doubt any of our rough spots were as difficult as the one the Simpsons are facing now, but this is one thing you can know for sure: No marriage is exempt from them."

Again they both became quiet. Introspective. Louise almost regretted making the point about marital difficulties. Just as she didn't want Cynthia to see her and Eliot's marriage as perfect and unattainable, Louise hated having her dwell on the hopelessness that the Simpsons may have felt. It seemed premature to put that kind of pressure on Cynthia when her marriage to Greg was still only a possibility. She was about to apologize when Cynthia leaned over and placed a kiss on her temple.

"Thanks, Mom," Cynthia said, and then she stifled a yawn. Perhaps she'd talked enough for one night. "We probably should go to sleep. I know you have to be up early tomorrow." With that she flipped out the lamp on her side of the bed and snuggled under the covers.

Louise, though, didn't want to end their conversation on such a sad note. Her daughter deserved the chance to look at a future filled with hope. Louise wanted that for her, especially given that she suspected Greg's Christmas present for her daughter might well be a ring. "Don't let the fact that marriage is hard work dissuade you. It's also a wonderful blessing."

At first, Cynthia didn't answer, leading her mother to wonder if she was already asleep.

"I know," she said finally. "All my life I had two of the best examples a person could have."

She could almost hear her daughter's smile in her voice. Louise allowed herself to drift off to sleep wearing a smile of her own.

Jane set steaming bowls of nutmeg-scented oatmeal in front of Kevin and Jill Ley and tried not to be offended when the young woman winced and looked green. "If the cereal's going to give you trouble, I can make you something else."

Kevin rubbed his hand over his wife's back. "Unless you can bake saltine crackers, you might as well give up. She's been like this for days. The doctor said the morning sickness should end soon. We sure hope so."

"For now, how about I *bring* you some saltines? I made up a bunch of them earlier and stuck them in the box." With a wink over her joke, Jane started toward the kitchen.

"Sounds heavenly," Jill said with a sigh.

Jane hurried through the swinging door to collect the crackers and a pitcher of juice and glasses. She could have used a few extra hands in the kitchen this morning, but Louise and Cynthia hadn't come downstairs yet. They'd probably stayed up too late sharing mother-daughter talk and needed a little extra sleep.

Behind her, the kitchen door swung open, and Greg popped his head inside. "Is there anything I can help you with?"

Jane glanced at the strong, capable man in the doorway and then at the tray in her hands. She lowered the tray into his hands. "Thanks."

"No problem." Greg smiled at her. "Cynthia must have kept Louise up late talking."

"That's what I think too."

"A mother and daughter probably have a lot to talk about at times like these."

Jane glanced back to him from where she was preparing a grapefruit half for Paul Erickson. "What times are you talking about?"

He shrugged, but a secretive light danced in his eyes. "Oh, you know. Special holidays with family."

No, she didn't know, and she had the distinct impression that special holidays weren't what Greg really meant. Louise was right after all. Her niece and the young man were quite serious, and a proposal might be in his plans for Christmas.

Following Greg through the door, Jane carried a plate of saltines for Jill.

"Someone said you're expecting?" Sandy Erickson was saying when they reached the dining room table. "Congratulations. Is this your first?"

Kevin and Jill nodded, pride shining on their faces. Jane set the plate of saltines in front of Jill.

"Oh, bless you." Jill lifted a cracker and slipped a corner into her mouth so she could taste the salt. She sighed audibly.

"Greg, who knew it was so easy to impress our guests?"

Sandy used a knife to spread cream cheese on her bagel. "Children are amazing. They'll keep you busy, though, as you coordinate all their activities."

Jill looked surprised. "Activities? I've heard they sleep a lot at first."

Sandy chuckled. "Well, they do at first, but then there are so many fun things they can do—mom-and-tot tumbling and music programs, baby swim. You'll love all of it."

From the perplexed expression on the mom-to-be's

face, Jane doubted Jill would enjoy those things much at all, but then Jane had strong opinions about learning by nature and play.

Paul sipped a mug of coffee. "Don't let my wife scare you, Jill. Babies love being tickled on the floor and dancing in the kitchen just as much as those other things."

Claire and Dylan stiffened in their chairs, their spoons full of oatmeal stopping midway to their mouths. Jane couldn't help straightening as well. Instead of initiating an argument, though, Sandy took her last bite of food. Because they needed to pick up some things in Potterston, she hurried her family on their way.

Jane busied herself by clearing away breakfast dishes, glad the conversation had ended without fireworks. Louise would be disappointed when she learned about it, but Jane would try to provide her with some perspective on the matter. Change, if it ever came in people's lives, required tiny steps forward and a lot of time to go the distance.

Louise would point out that the Ericksons had made great progress toward reconnecting as a family during the activities the night before, and she would be right. Still, the underlying theory that had caused their distance in the first place—that only maximum activity and packed schedules would lead to happiness—probably needed to be revised as well. Jane wondered if Louise would be willing to initiate such a discussion with the Ericksons.

"Sorry to eat and run," Kevin began as he stood up from the table and helped his wife to her feet. "But Patsy and Henry have scheduled another day jam-packed with family-togetherness activities."

Jane glanced quickly toward the living room. "I'm surprised Louise hasn't made it down yet. I know she looks forward to meeting you, Jill. I told her you are a fellow musician."

"I'm sure our paths will cross soon enough," Jill said. She looked better after the crackers.

"Well, in case they don't right away, you wouldn't happen to be interested in doing a little playing on Christmas Eve, would you? I know Louise was going to ask when she met you. Louise will be playing here at a reveal party for the community members involved in the Secret Santa program, and you and Kevin are invited as well. Then we'll all head over to church for the Christmas Eve service."

At first Jill started to shake her head. Who could blame her? Besides being newly pregnant and probably exhausted, she was on vacation. She deserved a break. Then, Jill tilted her head and reconsidered. "Will Henry and Patsy be at that reveal party?"

"They'll be there."

"Then count me in. We were already supposed to be at the Christmas Eve service too, so why not?"

"Great," Jane said. "Louise will be pleased to have someone to share the occasion. She'll be even more excited to meet you."

Jill returned her smile. "I'm sure we'll meet either tonight or tomorrow morning." She waved good-bye, then joined her husband in the front hallway to collect their coats.

At the same time, Cynthia came out of the kitchen, having taken the back stairs.

"Well, look who's up," Greg said. "Did you get enough beauty sleep?"

She raised an eyebrow in an expression that resembled her mother's. "Why, don't I look like it? What gave me away, the dark circles?"

He shook his head. "I see no such thing. You look great to me."

For a few seconds, she appeared suspicious, but then she nodded. "Good answer."

"Nice job, Mr. Hollister." Jane winked at him before turning to her niece. "Any idea when I might see my eldest sister?"

"She'll be right down. Sorry. We were up a bit late last night." She stacked several dishes Jane hadn't cleared away yet. "Let's get these put away, and then we can check your e-mail to see if there's a message from Aunt Alice. I hope everything is going better for her and Aunt Ethel."

As Jane stepped up to the table, Greg lifted both hands to stop her. "Here, let me get these. You two go on, and I'll finish cleaning up and loading the dishwasher." When Jane hesitated, he continued. "Come on, Jane. Let me at least do this for you."

"You're sure?"

"He's sure, Aunt Jane. Let's go before he changes his mind," Cynthia said, tucking her hand under her aunt's elbow and hurrying her from the room. Over her shoulder, she spoke to the man who was already carrying a precariously stacked tower of dishes. "Thanks, Greg."

"Anytime," he said automatically. Then he paused as if to rethink his comment. "Well…sometimes anyway."

Once they were out of Greg's hearing, Jane stopped and faced her niece. "You picked well, sweetie."

Cynthia looked confused. "Picked what?" She paused as if she finally understood what her aunt had meant. "Oh." She sent an embarrassed glance toward the dining room. "I guess I did."

Funny, she didn't sound convinced. Jane might have lingered on the thought more if Cynthia hadn't started glancing around uneasily as soon as they neared the front hall. "You wouldn't happen to know where the old photo albums are, would you?" Her words were just above a whisper.

"How old? Are you looking for pictures of yourself as a child or of your mother and two favorite aunts before we realized what nonsense girdles and beehive hairdos were?"

"I'm looking for wedding pictures. It's been such a long time since I've seen them."

After her father's death, Jane could remember flipping through her parents' wedding album, trying to reestablish that link that felt broken between them and her, even if she found comfort in the assurance that her mother and father were together in heaven. Because Cynthia's loss of her father wasn't recent, Jane sensed that the curiosity might be something more. A woman who was looking forward to her own wedding might be looking for a way to share her parents' memories of theirs. "I'm pretty sure I saw that album in the library. It's white with gold trim, isn't it? It's on the lowest shelf directly behind Father's desk."

Again Cynthia glanced around her nervously. Jane sensed that her niece didn't want Louise to know she was looking for old photos. She'd stayed in her mother's room all night. If she had wanted her to know, she easily could have asked Louise where the family albums were. Questions filled her mind, but she tamped the need to ask them. Jane, of all people, understood the need for privacy.

"Why don't you head into the library and see if you can find the album? I'll check my e-mail, and if there's anything from Alice, I'll save it for you to read."

Uneasiness accompanied her as she logged on to her computer and signed on to her e-mail account. Now that Alice had come clean with them about the Florida trip, she almost dreaded an update. It was so hard to read that her sister and all of those around her were feeling pain when they were so far away. She wanted to help but felt her hands were tied. She found an e-mail from Alice sent the day before.

Dear Jane and Louise,

Happy to hear Cynthia has met a nice young man.

Look forward to an introduction on Christmas Eve.

Yes, you read correctly. The four of us—yes four —will fly Sunday. We'll arrive in time for the Secret Santa party. As for the Simpsons' crisis, I must say God is good. They have talked and agreed to keep talking. Tomorrow, we're planning an adventure at Disney World.

Spinning already,

Alice

Jane was laughing by the time Cynthia arrived, carrying a white album under her arm.

"What's so funny?"

She noticed that her niece set the photo album out of sight. "Here, read this." She moved the computer monitor slightly so Cynthia could get a better look. She'd read only a few seconds before she shifted. Without looking, Jane knew Cynthia would be blushing over the mention of the *nice young man*.

"I still don't see what's so funny," Cynthia said as she finished the note.

"Has Alice ever mentioned that she suffers from motion sickness on occasion?"

Cynthia shook her head.

"Well, she hates revolving doors, let alone spinning carnival rides."

"I get your point." Cynthia smiled but then added, "Poor Aunt Alice."

Jane hit *reply* to answer Alice's message.

"Here, let me." Cynthia tapped Jane's shoulder to indicate that she should let her take her chair. As soon as she sat, she started typing.

Dear Aunt Alice,

   Hope you love Disney World as much as Mom, Dad and I did. When you get home you'll be able to tell Aunt Jane how wrong she was to worry about you on the rides.

Love,

Cynthia

Rather than send the message, Cynthia typed a row of hyphens across the page to create a divider, then stood to let her aunt add to the note.

Jane read over her niece's message, trying to hold back a smile. Just when had Cynthia become an equal who could with dry humor put her aunt soundly in her place? "Wrong to worry?" Jane couldn't help asking.

"I wanted to give you the benefit of the doubt." Cynthia grinned. "I figure Aunt Alice wouldn't like knowing her little sister was laughing at her expense."

"She'll know."

"Of course she will."

"What will everyone know?" Louise asked, having come up behind them both without anyone's noticing.

"Our Florida foursome is going to Disney World today," Jane answered.

"You mean you *know* that Alice is going to love it?" Louise lifted her glasses into place and read Alice's message over Jane's shoulder. "She'll love all of it. I know Cynthia and I did. The shops, the shows, even the rides. Most of the rides are really shows that you go through in little cars."

Louise glanced at Alice's e-mail message again. "That's wonderful about Florence and Ronald. You don't think Alice is exaggerating, do you?"

Jane tilted her head, considering her question. "You know, I really don't."

"Then we're thinking alike," Louise said.

"Now I bet that's a rare feat." Cynthia joined her.

Louise was distracted a moment when she noticed the white album with golden trim. "Isn't that my wedding album?"

"Of course it is, Mom. Aunt Jane told me where to find it." Cynthia appeared neither upset nor surprised that her mother had noticed the album and now would probably want to look through the pictures with her. Running her hand lovingly over the slightly yellowed cover, she smiled at her mother. "I haven't seen these pictures in years and wanted to look through them while I'm here."

"Are you looking for some ideas?" Instead of waiting for an answer, Louise laid the book open on the desk and looked at the first picture of the smiling bride and groom. "Were we ever that young?"

"You were beautiful, Mom. Still are." For a few seconds, Cynthia stared down at the picture. "Sometimes I don't see Dad's face clearly in my memories. It's soft-focused, even a little blurry." She looked at the picture again. "I don't ever want to forget."

"You won't," Louise assured her.

Cynthia cleared her throat, but her eyes were shiny. She closed the album. "I'm going to take this upstairs. I'd like to look over the pictures before we go to bed tonight."

"That sounds like a great idea," Louise said. "I can't wait."

Jane watched as her sister and niece exchanged a warm glance. Her first impression had been incorrect, Jane realized. Cynthia was not trying to hide her looking through the wedding pictures from Louise, even if she probably would have to endure more of those comments about using the information to plan her own wedding.

Cynthia was acting secretive, though. Jane had no doubt about that. For whatever reason, the person she didn't want to know about the album seemed to be Greg.

Chapter Sixteen

A charming turn-of-the-century America, an escape to the rustic frontier, exciting outer-space missions and fantasy adventures inspired by one very special mouse, Walt Disney World's Magic Kingdom welcomed its visitors like the world of imagination opening its borders in all directions. With its soaring spires, Cinderella's Castle stood majestically in the center of it all, inviting guests—junior and senior alike—to enter the fantasy.

Transformed for the Christmas holiday with wreaths, bells, twinkling lights and boughs of green, the kingdom went a step further by becoming its own version of a winter wonderland. Flocked Christmas trees stood alongside palm trees, tall shrubs with gorgeous red and orange blossoms, and carefully shaped bright green hedges. Carolers performing on Main Street, USA, might have been bundled in long coats and mufflers, but the crowd they serenaded appeared far more comfortable wearing Bermuda shorts and sunglasses.

Disney magic even produced dancing snow flurries over the crowd during the afternoon parade, but they evaporated almost instantly on this day, when the mercury topped seventy-four degrees.

Of all the things Alice had come to love about the unique theme park, those contradictions impressed her most of all. She wasn't even disappointed that Florence had insisted they visit Disney's original theme park instead of Epcot, Animal Kingdom or Disney-MGM Studios, though all of them had attractions she might have enjoyed. "If you want to experience Disney World, you have to go to the original," Florence had said in a voice that didn't leave room for arguments.

Alice wasn't sorry to have spent much of the day enjoying the fantasy. She felt as if the five of them had stepped inside a storybook, and she still didn't have any inclination to close the book yet.

By afternoon, they'd sung along with banjo-playing bears in the Country Bear Jamboree and taken a relaxing cruise aboard the *Liberty Belle* riverboat.

Aunt Ethel posed with Ariel, star of *The Little Mermaid*, the two redheads smiling serenely for the camera, and they all lunched with Winnie the Pooh, Tigger, Eeyore and Piglet. Alice wasn't careless in her adventures, though. She took

Darlene's advice and avoided the spinning Mad Tea Party, and no one in the world could have convinced her to enter the line for Space Mountain, the roller coaster that raced through the darkness of a virtual outer space. The day passed with smiles and laughter, and Ronald and Florence spent a whole afternoon without having any major arguments.

Now, as they headed away from the Hall of Presidents, an amazing town meeting featuring lifelike figures of every US president from George Washington to George W. Bush, she ranked her favorite Disney attractions. It's a Small World won hands down.

"That was amazing," Ethel said as they followed the walkway leading toward the Haunted Mansion. "Could you believe how lifelike they all seemed?"

Alice glanced back at her. "I thought it was interesting how the presidents fidgeted and even whispered while Abraham Lincoln spoke. And the detail in their period costuming was great. Did you see the braces on Franklin Roosevelt's legs?"

"I don't know about you, but I'm glad that so many presidents couldn't really be in the same place at the same time," Florence said. "Could you imagine the shouting matches that would fill the room?"

No one mentioned that they'd experienced more than their share of shouting in Darlene's little home this week.

Alice didn't even want to imagine a situation where the first forty-three US presidents had a free-for-all. "How about going to an attraction where everyone gets along?"

Ethel cocked her head to the side. "You want to go to It's a Small World again?"

Alice put an arm around Ethel's shoulders. "Just one more time and I won't ask again. I promise."

"You said that last time," Ethel reminded her.

"Well, I mean it this time."

Ronald shook his head, an amused expression on his face. "I'm pretty sure you meant it last time too."

"I probably did," Alice said with a shrug. She glanced at the antique horse-driven hearse that was parked at the entrance to the Haunted Mansion. She looked up at the structure built to look like an eighteenth-century manor and winced. "My idea isn't as scary as this one."

"Don't worry," Ronald said. "It's more spooky than scary, and a lot of it's funny."

Darlene turned to the rest of her Pennsylvania guests. "Do you think that after we visit this one we should humor her and go to her favorite attraction one last time? You know how much she begged all of us to come so she could get her fill of thrill rides."

They all laughed at that. "I think we could do that," Ronald said finally, and the others agreed.

"We should have known she'd become addicted." Florence shook her head, then gave Alice a friendly swat on the wrist.

As they neared the entrance, Alice found the first hint that Ronald might be right. A small overgrown cemetery stood next to the walk, with comical but macabre inscriptions on the gravestones. From that point, she didn't mind being in the shrinking room, meeting her "Ghost Host" and taking a journey in a Doom Buggy through the rooms filled with ghosts dancing and having a jolly time.

Afterward, they took the short walk from Liberty Square to Fantasyland and moved back into line for Alice's favorite attraction. Happy musical strains greeted them as they boarded the wide, flat boat that would convey them through the exhibit.

"I'm going to be singing this song for the next week," Ethel grumbled.

"Me too," Ronald said as their boat floated slowly through the entrance.

Soon they were surrounded by moving dolls of every color and nationality, costumed in traditional garb from around the world, dancing and riding a Ferris wheel.

Wearing the same smile she'd sported each of the other two times they floated through, Alice glanced at Darlene and Ethel sitting next to her. They were smiling too.

Hoping they had that same contagious happiness, Alice turned to peek at the couple sitting in the row of seats behind them. Instead of glancing out at the huge collection of mechanical dolls, though, Ronald and Florence were smiling at each other. And they were holding hands.

"Hello?" Louise looked back and forth along the inn's front porch Friday afternoon and even down the steps to the walk. No one was there. *How strange*, she thought. She was sure that she had heard the doorbell, but then she'd been upstairs cleaning the guest bathrooms, so maybe it was just her imagination.

Again she glanced around the porch. She thought Dylan and Claire might have been playing a trick on her, but then she realized that Cynthia and Greg invited them to go sledding right after breakfast, and she hadn't seen signs of any of them since.

In fact, all of their guests had made themselves scarce throughout the day—the Leys, whom she still had not met, got up and out of the house before breakfast, and with the children gone for the day, Paul and Sandy took the opportunity to go into town by themselves. Even Jane was out purchasing food for their holiday meals as well as for the Quinlans' gift basket, but Louise expected her sister home soon.

As she started to close the door, Louise noticed a green-and-red gift bag with red tissue paper popping out the top. "Secret Santa strikes again." She retrieved the bag. "At least I haven't started hearing things." Though the bag looked similar to the ones she'd received on a regular basis since the Secret Santa matches were made, she hoped this gift was for Jane. Her sister's Secret Santa benefactor was running out of time to make a big gesture or even a small one.

Even Ethel and Alice continued to receive gifts despite their absence, but Jane was neglected. Again, the card on the package bore Louise's name. Closing the door, she carried the bag into the living room and peeked inside. For a few seconds, she considered pulling off the card and leaving her gift for Jane.

The idea, though, seemed dishonest. Instead, she decided to share whatever gift she received with her sister without the subterfuge. The giver was generous and appeared to know her well, filling the bag with a basil-musk candle, a lovely lace doily, a tiny box of raspberry truffles and a paperback copy of Dickens's *Nicholas Nickleby*.

She was trying to decide which of the items to keep and which to share with her sister when she noticed that the bag wasn't empty. Pulling out a brightly colored piece of paper, she discovered a present that her sister would love. She returned all the items to the bag, thrilled at the prospect of telling Jane the news.

A click of the kitchen door signaled a new arrival. "Jane, is that you?"

Her sister emerged with two brown grocery bags to ask, "Who were you expecting, Mrs. Claus?" Then she retraced her steps.

"No, but wouldn't a visit from that jolly woman be delightful?" She followed her sister into the kitchen, carrying the bag.

Standing at the counter where she had placed several additional grocery bags, Jane spoke over her shoulder. "I don't suppose that's a gift from my elusive Secret Santa." The humor in her voice suggested she was beginning to find the oversight amusing.

"No, it's yet another gift for your popular oldest sister, but I am willing to share, and there's something in here I think you'll like better than a modest gift."

Intrigued, Jane turned back to her and waited.

Louise pulled a folded letter from inside the bag.

"What is—" Jane began, but then she stopped as if the answer had suddenly dawned on her.

Louise unfolded the letter. The paper was different, bright red and heavy—impossible to miss. The message itself, though, was Jane's.

"It made it back." Jane's eyes shone.

"Yes, it did. We don't know if the letter made it to all of the Secret Santa participants because we don't know who has my name." She didn't want to suggest that the giver of the Dickens novel could be Viola, which would mean that she gave the letter to her friend only to have Viola return it. "But we at least know that someone saw the letter and thought it looked best printed on red paper. That's a start."

Jane nodded and pointed to the gift bag. "You said you'd share. Well, what did we get?"

One by one, Louise started removing items from the bag and setting them on the counter.

"Someone sure likes you—I mean *us*."

Louise lifted her head and stuck out her chin. "I'll share everything else, but the doily's mine."

For several seconds, Jane seemed to consider, but then she finally shrugged. "You drive a hard bargain, sister, but I can be bribed with truffles." She turned back to her grocery sacks and started putting away the food. She hoisted the turkey and rearranged items to find a place for it in the refrigerator. "I have a carton of nonperishable items in the car," she said as Louise helped her finish the job.

"I'll help you carry it in when we're done. You have finished shopping for the Quinlans now, haven't you?"

"I've done what I can. I mean, *we've* done what *we* can."

"I already told you I'm willing to share the costs with you, and you know Alice will want to help."

Jane took a long glance out the window. "I wonder if it really will help."

Louise stopped stacking soup cans in the pantry to study her sister. "Of course it will help. You've done a good thing to reach out to the Quinlans."

Jane shook her head, clearly not convinced. "But was it the right thing to send out that note? To go public with their private struggles? Carlene said Logan wouldn't even agree to be interviewed, he's so proud."

"You've done your best to help them. You became involved when a lot of people would have sat around just wringing their hands at the injustice of layoffs."

Jane rubbed her forearms anxiously. "What if I went too far?"

Louise glanced at her sister's tight posture. "Have you prayed about all this?"

Jane stared at the floor a long time before meeting her gaze again. "I've prayed," she said finally.

"Then relax and let God take care of it."

Louise's thoughts were still on Jane and the Quinlans later that afternoon when she started through the house toward her desk. With any luck she could finish some accounting work before the rest of the guests returned. Cynthia, Greg and the Erickson children were back from sledding with high spirits and rosy cheeks. They'd all scattered to their rooms to change into dry clothes, so Louise was surprised when she passed the parlor and found the door closed.

As soon as she opened the door, music drifted from the room. At first, she heard only musical scales, but then the notes transformed into song, much as a butterfly emerges from its cocoon. Louise slipped quietly into the room until she could see the person whose hands passed over the keys.

Young Claire sat playing an imperfect version of "Joy to the World" and wearing an expression Louise never expected to see when the Erickson children played the piano—happiness. After missing a few notes, Claire started over again, but it was clear she was having fun. The child's excitement drew Louise farther into the room.

Suddenly, Claire started as she caught sight of Louise, and her fingers faltered on the keys. "Uh, sorry."

Louise came closer then and rested her hand on the girl's shoulder. "Why are you sorry? I told you it was fine to play in here."

"I was supposed to be practicing, not goofing off playing other stuff by ear."

She started playing again, a perfectly acceptable tune that Louise might have assigned a student. Though Claire played the notes competently, her heart wasn't in the music. Eventually, Claire stopped playing and looked at Louise again.

"Do you like to play the piano, Claire?"

"Sometimes." Claire paused, as if considering her words, and then added, "Dylan really hates it."

Louise tried not to smile over the child's frankness, which she found refreshing. Children generally didn't self-edit the way adults did. "But you like it sometimes and dislike it other times." She had an inkling over which times those were, but she wouldn't criticize the child's mother aloud. "Do you like to practice?"

Claire looked embarrassed as she shook her head.

Louise rested her elbow on the top of the piano and regarded her. "That's why I play for fun too. Why learn to play the piano if you can't sometimes play music you like?"

Claire's eyes widened, and Louise felt her heart constrict. The child knew all about discipline and performance in music, but it was clear she never realized she might find joy in it. No wonder the Erickson children hated to play. This was work for them. She wondered how many of the other activities in which the "well-rounded" children were involved were about work rather than fun. Louise reached down and brushed her fingers lovingly over the keys, producing a fluttering melody. "I sometimes spend hours in here, just playing the songs I love. I never feel so calm, happy or close to God as when I'm playing."

"You mean it's okay to play just to play, even when you're a piano teacher?" Claire asked, the concept obviously foreign to her.

"Of course it is. Just like you enjoy kicking a soccer ball around only because it's fun." She paused as the girl seemed to digest what she was saying. "When you love something, it doesn't seem like work to do it, even when you invest a lot of time in it."

"It's like that when I juggle. I do it for hours."

It was Louise's turn to be incredulous. "You juggle too?"

Claire bit her lip, trying and failing to hold back a chuckle. "I don't juggle like a clown in the circus. Juggling is a soccer skill where you try to keep volleying the ball in the air, with kicks and bounces off your head, feet and knees. I could show you if Mom and Dad had let me bring a ball."

Louise started shaking her head, smiling. "A demonstration won't be necessary. I get it now. Sorry, I don't know the lingo for any sport, and you shouldn't quiz me on that."

"I won't, Mrs. Smith."

The girl appeared so serious that a chuckle started building inside Louise's chest. Finally, she gave in and let it out. At Claire's perplexed look, she explained. "I can't help it. I was picturing you as a seal with a ball on the end of your nose."

Claire giggled a bubbling waterfall of laughter, as only preadolescent girls can, and she sounded so much as Cynthia once had that Louise was moved. She glanced at Claire again, an idea forming in her mind. "So I don't make that kind of soccer mistake again, do you think you could teach me a few of those terms? I would consider it a real favor."

"Okay."

"Could you do me one more favor? Could you let me show you why I love playing music as much as you love"— she paused to search for the word—"juggling?"

At Claire's nod, Louise gestured for her to stand, so she could open the tapestry-covered piano bench. She withdrew several pieces of music that were quite a bit different from the Handel and Bach she played the other day. When she closed the lid, she motioned for Claire to join her on the bench. "Do you think you can turn pages for me?"

The first piece she played was a jazzy little original piece she'd once composed. She gave Claire a sidelong glance. "You see. It can be fun." She continued playing and blending seasonal music with different genres, including blues, rock and roll and contemporary Christian. Claire loved every selection, and she seemed to take pride in the special responsibility of turning the pages.

Soon they switched to carols exclusively, and the girl sang along with Louise in a sweet-toned soprano voice. They were halfway through the first verse of "Hark, the Herald Angels Sing," when the parlor door opened, and Jane, Greg,

Cynthia and Dylan joined them. They all wanted in on the fun, with Cynthia adding her rich alto voice to the mix and Greg offering an impressive baritone. Though less naturally gifted, Jane and Dylan joined in singing.

They were concentrating so hard on their separate parts in a version of "Silent Night" performed as a round that they didn't notice their circle had expanded until after the song ended and applause filled the room.

Paul and Sandy stood behind them, clapping loudly.

"Bravo!" Sandy called out, and Paul offered a two-finger whistle.

The couple looked happy, their outing appearing to have lifted their spirits. Louise couldn't help being pleased with herself. She shouldn't have questioned her ability to help a family in need of a reconnecting experience. She knew what she was doing after all.

Sandy caught her eye as she moved around the gathering and approached the piano nearest the side where Louise sat. "Thank you for all this," she said with a gracious smile. "You don't know how much our family has needed it."

"The pleasure is all mine," Louise said warmly. She truly enjoyed sharing her time and her love of music.

Sandy nodded her approval. "Now the children won't have to miss this week's piano lessons after all."

Chapter Seventeen

*Y*ou're hiding in the kitchen again, Louise admonished herself as she sat at the table where she'd retreated after the scene in the parlor. She hadn't exactly sprinted, but she came close to it, excusing herself to her chores. That she now avoided the family she sought to help frustrated her, but at the time she couldn't think of any appropriate way to respond to Sandy's remark. Or any nice way.

She still didn't want to face the situation. Why couldn't Sandy just join the rest of them in singing rather than insist on more? Was it for the same reason that she kept her children so busy and the family lived as strangers?

Louise was convinced that Sandy loved her children and that her intentions were good. Louise pushed aside uncharitable thoughts. Sandy probably didn't realize that her aggressiveness was hurting the people she loved.

Someone needed to help her to see this, if only for the children's sakes. As reluctant as Louise was to overstep her boundaries, she sensed she was the person God intended for the job.

"Lord, give me courage to do Your will," she whispered. "Please give me the words that You would have me say. Amen."

Finally ready to talk to Sandy, Louise rose from her chair and followed the sound of voices to the entrance of the dining room. Just when she was about to push the swinging door, it swung toward her. Sandy stepped inside, her lips pressed into a firm line. Louise swallowed hard, understanding that God had sent a challenge.

Sandy spoke before Louise had the chance. "I wanted to apologize for the misunderstanding earlier. Of course you weren't giving lessons. I should have realized that." Her expression suddenly brightened. "But Claire did tell me you were demonstrating for her what great skills she can have if she only practices."

Louise raised an eyebrow. "Indeed? Is that really what she said?"

"Well, not exactly."

"I only showed her that I love playing music as much as she loves to play soccer." Louise smiled when the other woman looked at her with confusion. She invited Sandy to the kitchen table, and they took seats across from one another.

Louise leaned forward and folded her hands together. "Why is it so important to you that I give lessons to the children while they're here?" She watched as their mother shook her head to disagree, but Louise pressed forward. "First the architecture, then the music."

Sandy pulled back as if the words had slapped her. "I only saw opportunities for my children to learn, to grow."

"Those are good goals, but so is taking the opportunity to slow down and spend time with your family. You said that was what you wanted to do when you arrived."

Fidgeting, Sandy didn't meet her gaze. "Perhaps slowing down is harder than I expected."

"Do you *want* to relax the pace of your lives, even for a few days?" Louise paused, studying Sandy. "You've said yourself that you wanted to escape the hockey, soccer, piano, voice and all the other activities; but then you keep trying to fill the space with more activity."

Sandy stiffened, pushing her chair back slightly from the table. "I'm not sure I appreciate your comments. You don't even know our family, so how can you make judgments about us?"

She was right, Louise decided. What right did she have to say these things? Still, the faces of Sandy's children appeared in her thoughts, encouraging her to continue. "I know your children have scheduled activities nearly every day, some they don't even enjoy. The four of you seem lost without your busy schedules and your frenzied pace." She watched Sandy's jaw flex in anger, but she'd started this, and she needed to finish it for the family's sake. "I think you'd like to slow down, but you don't know how."

Staring down, Sandy gripped the edge of the table. "Well, how fortunate for you that you have all the answers on parenting. If you think our family is such a horrible mess, then why have you made such an effort to involve us in your holiday activities, which look like pictures by Currier and Ives?" Then she looked up at Louise sharply. "Oh, I get it. You're trying to fix us, to help the poor Ericksons find their way."

"It's not like that," Louise said, shaking her head, but she couldn't help wondering how close Sandy was to the truth. This wasn't going at all the way she had planned. In over her head, she tried to explain anyway. "I wanted only to help the four of you to find your way back to each other —to reconnect. You seem to have made such progress."

Sandy pressed her hands on the edge of the table and stood. "I've always heard that bed-and-breakfasts are full-service inns, but you've outdone yourself, Louise. Maybe we should leave early. It will cost us a little more, but it might be worth it for us to get home immediately."

Louise's heart sank. Was she mistaken to think God was leading her to help the Ericksons? Or had she let her silly pride and her belief that she held some expertise in parenting cloud her wisdom? "Please don't go, Sandy. The children will be so disappointed if they don't get to have Christmas here. I'll stay out of your way. It wasn't my place, but please know I was only trying to help."

Sandy walked to the door that led from the kitchen to the hall. She left with one parting comment. "You can't meddle in people's lives unless you're prepared to deal with the consequences."

A sweet floral scent delighted Alice's senses as she sat on Darlene's front porch Saturday afternoon. She inhaled to preserve the last memories of her Florida trip. The day was nearly perfect with warm sunshine on her face, a nice cup of tea on the table at her elbow and a good mystery in her hands. The only thing that could have made it better was her sisters sitting in chairs on either side of her.

She returned to the pages of her story, an enthralling tale full of secrets, deception and an emerald ring that connected them all; but even great fiction couldn't hold her attention today, when less than twenty-four hours and a plane ride separated her from her sisters. Though she'd had a memorable trip, she longed for a tiny Pennsylvania town, snow-covered rooftops and the wonderful three-story house where the people most important to her were waiting for her return.

She would have to say the trip was successful. After their decision to reconcile, Ronald and Florence had spent every available minute in deep discussions and occasionally were caught exchanging secret glances. Maybe they were beginning to remember what they'd loved about each other in the first place. Their future wasn't etched in stone, but no marriage, or any life, offered guarantees.

Though all stayed close to the house since their return from Disney World, Alice was glad she'd declined Darlene's offer of a trip to the mall. It was better that Florence had the opportunity for an outing flanked only by her favorite aunt and her good friend Ethel.

Ronald remained with Alice at the house, and he busied himself with handyman jobs inside, so Alice felt as if she were alone. She took that opportunity to continue her ongoing discussion with God. "Thank You, Lord," she whispered. "Thanks for courage to do the right thing, for patience when Your way isn't ours, and for the hope and peace You always give."

Just as she whispered, "Amen," she heard the screen door open and close. She turned to see Ronald drying his hands on several paper towels. His eyes still bore the dark circles of exhaustion. Though her stress hadn't been half as extensive as his, she could relate to his fatigue. It had been a long week for everyone, and she was so ready to sleep in her own bed and take comfort in her own surroundings.

"Did you finish all the chores on the list?" she asked when he didn't speak.

"Afraid not. Darlene's honey-do list is awfully long. Now that Boyd is gone, she's had to learn to do a lot of repairs on her own."

Alice gestured for him to sit next to her on the bench and then waited for him to do it before responding. "My sisters and I have learned to do many simple repairs. It saves us a lot of money. Most aren't even that hard if we just follow directions."

"I don't like the idea of my wife fixing leaky faucets and climbing on ladders to clear gutters after I'm gone."

The image of Florence doing either of those things threatened to make Alice laugh, so she pushed the picture from her mind. "She doesn't have to do those things. You're financially set. She could hire a handyman."

Alice didn't mention that Florence confessed they hired out all but the easiest repairs these days anyway. Ronald was talking about more than mundane home repairs. He wanted to be there for his wife, and that desire showed just how much they'd accomplished in the last week.

"I bet you'll be thrilled to get home tomorrow," he said.

"It will be nice to be home again, especially on Christmas Eve," she said.

"I don't know whether Florence has mentioned it to you or not, but we're both grateful to you, Ethel and Darlene for forcing us to think before we threw away all we've built together. Thank you for that."

A smile settled on her lips. "Remember, I was just the chauffeur, and we discovered later that you could easily have flown."

"I was so furious at Ethel for that."

"I wasn't too pleased with her myself."

"Your aunt is a pretty determined woman, so like Florence. It's easy to see why they're friends."

Alice also found it easy to see why their friendship was stormy as well. It took a special woman to get that close to Florence. Alice had taken a few steps closer herself these past days, but it was her aunt who rose to the occasion so impressively.

"I don't doubt that this trip was Ethel's idea, but she wouldn't have been able to pull it off without you."

"Or you," she interjected before he could go on. She hadn't done all that much, and she didn't even want to confess that she'd tried to talk Ethel out of making the trip. If not for her aunt's insistence, they certainly would have failed to do God's work.

Ronald chuckled as he leaned back in the seat, spreading his elbows and linking his fingers behind his head. "You're right about that. I don't even know now why I was willing to give up so easily."

"Sometimes the challenge before us appears insurmountable, but with God's help, anything is possible." The words flowed from Alice's lips before she consciously planned them. She glanced at Ronald to gauge his reaction, and he was smiling.

"You sound so much like Pastor Daniel when you talk like that. He was a fine minister and an even better man. He raised three daughters to be impressive people too." He paused for a few seconds before continuing. "His little sister, Ethel, isn't so bad herself, even if she did nearly kidnap me to get me here."

Alice grinned at that. "Can she help it if you're such a stubborn fellow?"

"I suppose not." He leaned forward and rested his hands on his knees. "I know you told my wife about what I said in the car."

She blushed and sat forward on the bench. It had seemed like the right thing to do at the time, but now she was apprehensive. "I knew that you wouldn't. At least you didn't when you had years to tell her."

"I'm not upset. I just wanted you to know that I know you did it." He patted her shoulder. "I also wanted to thank you." He waved his hand to stop her before she could interrupt again and avoid his compliment. "You had to be uncomfortable bringing the whole thing up to my wife, and yet you did it anyway because you felt it was right."

Her cheeks felt hot, but Alice forced herself to respond. "I thought she needed to know," she said.

"She did. We both did. I wouldn't call it the key to all our problems, but it is a factor. Instead of talking to each other, we've often let small things fester until they become big things."

"I'm no relationship expert, but I would guess that a lot of people do that. Some just don't figure it out before it's too late. You two figured it out."

"In the nick of time."

"I know it's been a long week for the two of you—for all of us. Have you and Florence come up with any conclusions you will take home with you?"

"You mean other than that we're not willing to give up without a fight?"

"That's good enough." Alice didn't expect him to tell her more. He and Florence had already shared more than most couples would feel comfortable telling about their marriages, and she certainly didn't want to pry for more. She hoped that their commitment would remain strong when they returned home, where it would be easy to fall into old habits.

"Not quite good enough," Ronald insisted. "We have also decided to seek counseling with Rev. Thompson when we return home. Not just Florence this time, but both of us."

"That's wonderful, Ronald." Alice smiled, pleased by this level of commitment. "When we left Acorn Hill, you weren't certain your marriage was worth saving. What made you change your mind?"

"The stories did that. My wife and I have history—real history—the kind that young couples today can't even imagine. Florence and I have spent most of our lives together, building a lifetime of memories. I just realized there was no one else with whom I would rather share my golden years, no one who mattered to me the way she matters."

"That's wonderful." She turned and studied his profile. "Did Florence come to a similar conclusion?"

"She decided to forgive me for the scene that made her run in the first place," he said with a smile. "I sure didn't believe she would ever forgive me for that, so at least it's a start."

"A great start," she agreed, "and an even better Christmas present."

～

"Mom, are you still awake?" Cynthia asked late Saturday night as she crawled into bed beside her mother.

Louise made an affirmative sound but didn't lift her head. The bed bounced slightly with the shift in weight and then went still again. Funny, Louise had looked forward to sharing these special private moments with her daughter, and yet now all she wanted to do was to close her eyes and let sleep assuage some of her guilt.

The Ericksons had decided not to leave until at least the day following Christmas after all, but they had made themselves scarce all afternoon and evening. Jane assured her sister that she'd seen the family, and they even did a little shopping downtown for the gift baskets they would be taking to the Quinlans' home, but it was clear the Ericksons made a point to avoid the oldest Howard sister all day.

Cynthia switched off the lamp, and for several seconds, the two of them lay side by side, the darkness enfolding them. "Mom, are you all right?"

"I'm fine. Just a little tired."

Her daughter jostled the bed as she sat up and tucked

her pillow behind her back. "Do the Ericksons have anything to do with your being *a little tired?*"

Louise didn't answer but wondered how she'd happened
to raise such an intuitive daughter. If there was ever a time
she would have appreciated less intuition, it would be now.

"Should I take that silence as a yes?"

"If you feel so inclined."

She could sense her daughter smiling into the night,
and it rankled her nerves instead of calming them. Still, she
knew how determined Cynthia was. She would keep asking
until she had her answers, so Louise sat up and prepared to
give them to her. "I should never have gotten involved."

Cynthia remained quiet, likely turning the comment
over in her thoughts. "That doesn't sound anything like
what you and Dad taught me. We're supposed to get
involved. Wasn't that the focus of Grandfather's ministry?"

Louise shook her head in the darkness. *This is different.
My efforts were rooted in arrogance instead of God's will.* At least she
was beginning to believe that was the case. "This is different," she repeated, this time aloud.

"How is it different? Hasn't Grace Chapel Inn been a
ministry of sorts for you and Aunt Jane and Aunt Alice?
You even have that plaque on the front door." She paused.
"Now what does it say?"

Louise smiled in spite of herself. Cynthia knew very well what that sign said, but she humored her daughter anyway. "A place where one can be refreshed and encouraged; a place of hope and healing; a place where God is at home." For a few seconds, Louise pondered those words that inspired her so often. "It doesn't say, 'Come, stay here, and we'll tell you how to live your lives and raise your children.'"

Cynthia's laughter that always reminded Louise of tinkling ice cubes in a tall glass of iced tea filled their small room. "No, I'm sure it doesn't say that."

"Yet it's exactly what I did."

"With the best of intentions."

"That's no excuse. I hoped to help Paul and Sandy and the children rediscover each other and see for themselves the relationships they were missing out on."

"You were right. The choices ultimately are up to them, anyway. Right or wrong, we all have to live with the consequences of our decisions."

Louise glanced at her daughter's dark profile, sensing she might be speaking of more than Louise's unfortunate conflict with Sandy, but she shook the thought away. Sandy's words rang in her thoughts. Louise hadn't been prepared for her message to offend, and the consequence would be an uncomfortable Christmas celebration at the inn.

"Why did I think I was such a parenting expert that I

could push my views on a family raising children more than thirty years after I became a mother?"

"I happen to think you have valuable expertise to share. You and Dad were wonderful parents. You were involved in my life but not so involved that I turned in parent-made school projects or didn't make friends. You didn't push religion on me but simply lived your faith and nurtured mine. Though you loved your music, and Dad his academics, you were both so supportive when I chose my own path as an adult." Only their quiet breathing could be heard when Cynthia paused. When she spoke again, her voice sounded different. "I don't think I could have asked for better parents."

Though Louise didn't feel that she deserved any endorsement today, her daughter's testimonial was a wonderful gift. She reached across the bed until she found her daughter's hand and closed her fingers over it. "No, your father and I were the lucky ones. The greatest blessing God ever gave us was you."

"Do you miss him terribly, Mom?"

Louise was surprised by the turn in the conversation. "Not every minute of every day as I did the first few years after he passed. Sometimes a few hours go by and, occasionally, a whole morning or afternoon when I don't think of Eliot at all. Does it make you sad to know that?"

"Of course not, Mom." She squeezed Louise's hand. "I don't want you to spend all of your time missing him. That would make me sad. Dad too, if he knew you spent all of your days mourning him instead of finding joy in life."

Louise smiled into the darkness, Eliot's kind face appearing in her thoughts. He had to be so proud of their daughter as he looked down on her from heaven.

"When I think of Dad," Cynthia said, "it's always with happy memories of family activities, of him helping me with homework and insisting that I not give up too easily, even of outings with just Dad and me. Especially those."

She shifted and turned toward her mother. "It was different for you, though. You called Dad the love of your life. Can you think of him without missing him so badly you ache inside?"

Again, Louise smiled. Love was new for her daughter. She probably wondered what it was like to know that kind of commitment for a lifetime. "I will miss your father every day until I see him again in Paradise."

"That has to be so hard."

"It was at first. Still, thinking of Eliot now doesn't make me sad. Most of the time I don't see him as he was at the end, when the cancer had weakened him. I have so many more memories than those. They feel like nice visits with the past now rather than painful glimpses."

"Nice visits. I like that."

Louise patted her daughter's hand once more and released it. She resituated her pillow to settle in for sleep. "We'd better get some sleep now. Tomorrow's going to be a long day."

"I bet you can't wait to see Aunt Alice and Aunt Ethel again."

Louise smiled, her eyes already closed. "I didn't realize how much I would miss them. We haven't been apart for long since we decided to open the inn together."

"So the three musketeers will be back together tomorrow?" Cynthia said, repeating the moniker the Howard sisters gave themselves when they'd decided to go into the bed-and-breakfast business.

"Yes. 'All for one and one for all.'" Louise repeated the musketeers' slogan dreamily. Back together. It sounded nice. Unfortunately, with the tension that was filling the inn, it would probably not be the kind of homecoming she would have planned for her sister and aunt. If only there was something she could do to soothe the hurt feelings, but a sinking feeling inside her suggested that she had meddled enough.

"Don't worry, Mom," Cynthia said as if following her mother's dark thoughts. "Everything will be fine tomorrow. Maybe the Ericksons will be more forgiving than they usually would be. Tomorrow is Christmas Eve after all."

Chapter Eighteen

*E*arly on Sunday morning, Jane glanced out the living room window at a gray sky filled with heavy clouds of an even more ominous gray. A few flurries were already dancing past the window, some forgetting the journey downward and instead pressing their unique shapes against the glass. She loved having a white Christmas and wouldn't mind it if they received all eight of the inches forecast by tomorrow, if only Alice's plane landed before it started snowing in earnest. At least they were flying this time, she thought gratefully.

Taking a sip of her coffee, Jane sat at her computer and flipped it on. She had at least another hour before most of their guests arose, but there was no way she could have slept. In fact, she'd barely closed her eyes all night. Not that this was so unusual for Jane. She'd always had a childlike excitement when it came to Christmas celebrations.

As a small child, she awakened before sunrise every Christmas morning and sneaked downstairs to see what surprises Santa had left while the rest of the house slept.

She kept that enthusiasm as an adult, planning elegant holiday meals and elaborate table settings, attempting each year to top the last.

She should have been thrilled this morning. Alice and Ethel would be home by afternoon. They would all be together for Christmas. She had more than enough work preparing cookies for the Secret Santa reveal party to keep her busy until their arrival. The feeling she had inside this morning, however, was less like giddy excitement and more like doom. This wouldn't be the warm Christmas they'd hoped for when the Howard sisters started planning for it just after the fall foliage season. Tension would rule their gathering rather than joy. Everyone would be polite—she didn't doubt that—but the true spirit of Jesus' birth might be absent from this celebration.

If only there was something she could do. She'd watched Louise and the Ericksons the day before, separately, of course, and wished she could appease Sandy's anger and relieve Louise's guilt.

Now it was Christmas Eve, the day to carry out her plan for helping the Quinlan family, and she was suddenly worried that her sending out the letter had been a big mistake. What if Logan Quinlan didn't appreciate the do-gooders who reached out to help his family when he'd never asked for help? Too late now. She couldn't take back what she'd started.

Frustrated, Jane opened her e-mail program and checked for any messages. She guessed that Alice probably hadn't written more, as close as she was to coming home. Jane was surprised when a message from her sister appeared in her inbox.

Dear Jane, Louise and Cynthia,

Counting the hours to our return. What a wonderful Christmas celebration we'll have. Ronald and Florence have agreed to go into counseling with Rev. Thompson when we return. Ronald tells me they're willing to fight for their marriage. At first I worried about becoming involved, but God uses us all to His will, and we shouldn't question.

Missing you,

Alice

P.S. Has anyone been snooping for gifts in my closet?

Jane read the note a second time. It read more like a missive from God than one from her older sister. Alice was right. God did use them, even when they made mistakes while trying to do His will. Who was she to question, even if this promised to be the most uncomfortable Christmas in recent history? She would just go forward with plans for deliveries to the Quinlans and let God handle the rest.

For now, she needed to start preparing breakfast lest their guests arrive in the dining room to find a table barren of food. The minute she got up, Jane realized she was already too late. The whole Erickson family stood in front of her—clean, combed and in their Sunday best, though, according to Claire, they didn't attend church anymore.

"Good morning, Ms. Howard," Dylan whispered with a sly grin on his face.

"Happy Christmas Eve," she said, still studying him. Eventually, she turned her gaze on the other three members of the family. They too, were smiling, and they wore the same look—like the cat that had devoured the canary for his breakfast. "I'm sorry, but breakfast isn't ready yet. Even the Leys haven't come down."

"Don't worry about us," Paul said. "We have other plans this morning."

Jane felt disappointed. "Other plans? If you tell me what you'd like, maybe I can still fix a good meal for you."

"That won't be necessary," Sandy said in an odd-sounding voice that closely mimicked laughter.

"Then I don't understand."

Claire held out her hands to explain, as if she were the adult and Jane were the child. "We're here to help with breakfast."

"We're making Mrs. Smith breakfast in bed," Dylan added.

Now Jane really didn't understand. Had she missed something critical last night? Or had she watched too many episodes of *The Twilight Zone* as a youngster, and the program had addled her mind? She glanced at Paul and Sandy for an explanation.

Paul took Sandy's hand and answered for the two of them. "We want to find a way to say a really big thanks to Louise."

Louise hurried around her room getting ready to go downstairs. There certainly was a lot to get done before Alice and Ethel arrived, and with regular Sunday services this morning, they would have less time to complete each task. Standing in front of her full-length mirror, she smoothed her beige turtleneck tunic over her black wool skirt and added a rhinestone Christmas tree pin just above her heart. She brushed her silver hair into place, applied lipstick and a bit of blush, and, deeming herself ready, turned toward the door.

A loud clanging sound came from below, like pans being dropped. She pressed her lips together, slightly annoyed. Jane was usually quieter than that in the mornings in case their guests were light sleepers. Considering how much commotion she'd already heard, she guessed that the whole house was already awake. Even Cynthia, who enjoyed sleeping late when she was on vacation, was already getting ready. The Leys had probably left for the morning.

The spicy scent of sausage gravy wafted up the stairwell as she reached the second-floor landing. When she came to the main floor, Louise was surprised to find the dining room empty. Everyone was in the kitchen, not squeezed around the tiny table but fluttering about the room making breakfast.

Claire turned around first and smiled widely. "Hi, Mrs. Smith."

At her words, Jane and the other three members of the Erickson family turned to face her, guilty expressions appearing on all of their faces. Louise felt embarrassed. She was the one who should feel guilty for not being down earlier to help Jane prepare breakfast for their guests.

She hated to imagine the comments they might find regarding Grace Chapel Inn on the bed-and-breakfast Web site after the Ericksons' visit. *"Not only did the inn owners invade their guests' privacy, but they also forced them to make their own breakfast."* With an endorsement like that, they might be hanging a vacancy sign a lot in the coming months.

"Did I miss something?" Louise asked when none of the people facing her piped up with an explanation.

Jane lifted a platter of sausage patties. "I thought you'd be down a little later."

"From the way it looks in here, maybe I should have come a lot earlier. Our guests haven't been waiting long for breakfast, have they?"

The sides of Jane's mouth lifted. "This isn't how it looks."

Louise lifted a brow. "I surely hope not, because if it is what it looks like, it would mean we are using our guests to help us make breakfast."

Handing off the platter to Dylan, Jane instructed the boy to carry it into the dining room. Dylan used his back to open the dining room door, moved behind it and let it close behind him.

Jane turned back to her sister. "Well, that part would be right."

Louise folded her arms over her chest and directed her best look of disappointment at her younger sister. "Jane, what were you thinking?"

"I'd say I was following the adage that the customer is always right, and these customers begged me to let them help make breakfast."

Now that didn't make a bit of sense. The family was on vacation. "Why ever would they want to do that?"

"I believe the original plan was to surprise you." Jane explained. "Breakfast in bed was mentioned but ruled out when we all remembered you're sharing a room with Cynthia. Anyway, the surprise element went right out the window the minute you showed up in the kitchen at least twenty minutes before we thought you would."

Louise stared at Jane for several seconds, hoping that if she looked long enough her sister's comments would begin to make sense, but soon she realized it wasn't going to work. "Could someone else please translate for Jane?"

Her sister turned back to the stove where she was stirring the gravy.

Paul stepped forward then. "What Ms. Howard is trying to say is we convinced her to let us help make breakfast for you this morning."

"For me? Why me?" She had to be the last person for whom the Erickson family would want to do something nice.

Sandy spoke up next. "We wanted to thank the woman who helped us rediscover our family this week."

"I don't think I understand." Louise looked back and forth between Paul and Sandy for an explanation.

Sandy covered her eyes with her hand and shook her head before she pulled her hand away again. "First, I want to say I'm sorry. I was wrong to react the way I did when you reached out to me in concern. I shouldn't have pushed you to give the children lessons. I was wrong about that and a lot of other things."

"No, I was wrong," Louise said. "I shouldn't have forced my views about parenting on you."

Paul blew out a breath and then smiled. "If you hadn't said something to us, do you think anyone else would have? I don't think so. We probably would have wasted another seven years until Dylan went off to college and then wondered what happened to our family."

Louise couldn't help glancing back at Sandy. What had changed in little more than a day? She just had to know. "I don't understand. When we had our talk—"

"I was embarrassed and angry," Sandy finished for her. "I couldn't believe that someone would actually think I wasn't doing the best for my children when that's all I've ever wanted to do."

Louise started to interrupt her, to tell her there was good too, in all the activities Sandy planned, but Sandy was eager to explain herself.

"I needed to step back, to think and to evaluate whether any of the things you said had merit. Then yesterday while we were out shopping for some gifts for that young local family that is struggling, I asked Paul and the kids what they thought about our visit here." She ruffled Dylan's hair when he came close enough to touch. "I sure got an earful then.

"They told me they'd had more fun since we've been together in Acorn Hill than they could remember. They asked if we could string popcorn when we get home and if they could make cinnamon ornaments for Easter."

Paul approached his wife and put an arm around her shoulder. "Dylan begged to quit taking piano and voice lessons as well as art classes. Claire wanted to quit dance and voice. I even suggested that Sandy and I quit those tennis lessons we've been taking for two years." He shrugged. "I've always hated tennis."

Sandy sighed. "All this time I thought Dylan and Claire were doing all these things because they loved them, and they were really doing them because they loved *me*." At the last word, her voice sounded strained.

For the first time since the conversation began, Louise noticed that Sandy's eyes were red and puffy, the way eyes look the morning after someone has had a good cry.

"My children wanted me to be proud of them for all their accomplishments, when I was already proud of them for being who they are. I just neglected to tell them so." A tear escaped, and Sandy let it trail down her cheek without trying to wipe it.

Louise pulled out the lace handkerchief she'd tucked up under her sleeve and handed it to her. Louise patted her shoulder while Sandy used it to dab at her eyes. "Does this mean the children will be giving up all their activities?" She hoped not. That would only send the family to another extreme that probably wouldn't make them happy.

"Dylan still wants hockey, and Claire doesn't want to give up soccer or piano."

The last had Louise shooting a quizzical look at the youngest Erickson. Claire looked bashful.

Paul answered for his daughter. "She said she wants to practice so she can play well enough to love it the way Mrs. Smith does."

Glancing at Claire again, Louise winked. Then she looked again at Sandy.

"We have decided to add one activity as a family, now that we'll have all this free time available."

At Sandy's strange announcement, Louise tried to keep her expression calm, but she wasn't sure if she could manage it. She could just imagine what the family would take up now—mountain climbing, archeological digs, perhaps performances like the von Trapp family in *The Sound of Music*. She hesitated before asking, "What will your new activity be?"

"We've decided we need to get back to church," Sandy said. "We let church take second place to all the other activities that filled our schedules, and we don't want to do that anymore."

Paul lifted a basket filled with fresh biscuits from the

counter and started toward the dining room. He turned and spoke over his shoulder. "Since we're planning on starting back to church this morning after we serve breakfast, I would suggest we pick up the pace here."

They all chuckled at that and followed him out of the kitchen. Greg and Cynthia were waiting in the dining room, looking happy about the conversation they overheard. Once they'd all taken their seats and Paul said grace for them, they started into the Erickson-prepared breakfast of biscuits and gravy along with scrambled eggs and country sausage.

After everyone had taken a few bites, Paul turned back to Louise. "I noticed you seemed nervous when you heard we'd be taking up a new activity. What did you think we would say, that we'd chosen family bungee jumping?"

"Of course not," she said, but her warm cheeks gave her away. "Well, something like that." She became serious then, glancing first at Paul and then at Sandy. "I do think your decision to go back to church is a good one for your family. You won't regret it."

"I certainly don't regret the mix-up that led us to Grace Chapel Inn."

When Sandy smiled, Louise returned it. She had no regrets, either. She was now convinced all of it had been a part of God's plan. She was even glad she'd taken the risk to try to help the family find their way. Sandy had told her she needed to be prepared for the consequences when she became involved like that. As she glanced around the table at these people she'd come to care about, she saw the consequences of her meddling clearly. She'd made some lifelong friends.

"Good-bye, dear one," Darlene said while she hugged Florence just outside the security checkpoint at Orlando International Airport. Around them, a flurry of activity filled the echoing halls as other Christmas Eve travelers hurried to their gates, but Florence and her aunt clung to each other.

Ronald, Ethel and Alice stood to the side and waited for the two women to share their moment. Briefly, Alice felt like an outsider peering into the window of a private family occasion, but then she relaxed. She'd been a part of the situation all along, and she was pleased to have shared in it.

When Darlene finally pulled away, there were tears in her eyes. Florence's eyes shone just as brightly. "We'll never be able to thank you enough for opening your home to us, listening to us battle and helping us to find our way back to each other."

Darlene smiled through her tears. "Just keep loving each other, okay? That's thanks enough."

Ronald stepped forward and, wrapping her in his arms, spoke against her shoulder. "Now *that* we can do." He pulled back but still held her forearms. "You'll be all right, won't you?"

"I'm fine," she assured him as they stepped away from each other. "The twins and their families visit as often as they can. I would, however, love to have company more frequently." She looked first at Florence and her husband and then at Ethel and Alice. "Family and friends."

"Don't worry," Ronald told her. "You won't be able to keep us away."

Alice stepped forward then. "Thank you so much for your wonderful hospitality. We'll accept your invitation, but with one condition—if you're ever near Acorn Hill, you come stay with us at Grace Chapel Inn."

"Then it's a deal." Darlene gathered Alice into her arms.

Ronald glanced down at his watch. "We have to get going; we need to get to the gate."

"Not before I get to say good-bye to my new friend," Ethel said as she pressed forward.

She gripped Darlene in a firm hug. The lookalikes, who were so different and yet so similar, had grown very close. "Yes, please come. It would be wonderful to have you."

Soon they moved into the line for security checks, and Darlene stood waiting for them to go through screening. As she prepared to pass through, Alice glanced back at Darlene and waved. The trip that seemed like such a mistake initially had produced such happy results. Not only had they helped the Simpsons restore their relationship, Alice and Ethel also made a wonderful friend in Darlene.

Alice stared out the small, oval-shaped window just past noon while the aircraft waited its turn on the tarmac. As eager as she was to be home with her family for Christmas, she was nervous about the idea of cruising there at thirty-six thousand feet.

She never could understand people who loved to fly, who were exhilarated rather than uneasy when an airliner propelled itself into the skies, its flight crew and passengers praying for the best. Alice could, however, understand the appeal of a flight lasting a mere two hours and eighteen minutes, compared with a drive of nearly seventeen hours plus stops. In less than one-sixth of the time, they would land in Philadelphia, meet up with the driver Florence had hired and be on their way back to Acorn Hill—that is, if the jet got off the ground.

Squirming in her wide first-class seat, Alice glanced at Ethel next to her, who had already settled in with a pillow behind her head and a blue airline blanket tucked over her knees. She had her nose in a new romance by her favorite author and appeared not to have a care in the world.

Just as Alice was about to look away, her aunt glanced up. "Would you stop wiggling and read a magazine or something? How am I supposed to get into the story and picture Amanda welcoming Claude back after the Battle of Gettysburg when you can't sit still?"

Alice grinned. "Sorry about that."

Ethel frowned at her niece and returned to her book.

Alice glanced across the aisle to where Florence and Ronald were having a conversation. From their mild expressions and soft voices, she surmised that they were enjoying their chat. *So far, so good*, she thought.

She covered a yawn with her hand. She couldn't be tired already. They still had a whole day ahead of them. They'd had an early start, though, attending the first service at the huge modern church where Darlene was a member. Alice enjoyed the guitar music and especially the choruses projected on a huge screen, but she looked forward to the simplicity of tonight's service at Grace Chapel.

As the airplane rolled a little farther forward and the engines roared with the sound of increased throttle, Alice stiffened. *Lord, please lay Your hand on this flight*—She stopped herself. Wouldn't God's hand be on flights that crashed just as surely as they were on those that landed safely? *Dear Lord,* she began again, *please bless those on this flight and give them safe arrivals at their destinations. Amen.* She felt the sudden urge to chuckle at the irony there. A safe arrival at her *final* destination could just as easily involve a plane crash.

Pushing such thoughts aside, she focused on her more immediate destination of Acorn Hill and all the wonderful events scheduled there tonight—the reveal party, the Christmas Eve service, even the secretive gift-giving trip that her sisters had described. She wanted to be a part of all those things, but she couldn't get there until the pilot got this plane in the air. Taking a deep breath, she braced her hands on the arms of her seat and closed her eyes. She was ready to go.

Chapter Nineteen

"Are they here yet?" Claire asked as she scrambled into the living room, having worn a path in the carpet from the kitchen, through the dining room and to the front of the house for the last hour.

"No, they're not here yet." Annoyance filled Dylan's voice as he answered the same question once again, but he hadn't abandoned his post by the front window, either. When the car did arrive from the airport, they would be right there to give the announcement.

Paul glanced at his children curiously and turned back to Jane. "If I didn't know them better, I would guess that they were waiting for their own sister to come home instead of yours."

Jane held open the kitchen door, a platter of decorated sugar cookies and gingerbread cutout cookies in her arms. She could understand their excitement. She was feeling downright filled to bursting with Christmas spirit herself. "At least we have a pair of good lookouts. Not everybody has good lookouts on their payroll."

"Payroll?" Dylan turned his head away from the window to look at her. "Are we getting paid for this?"

"Absolutely." She paused and waited as a glance passed between Dylan and his sister. "In cookies, of course."

Claire looked back at Jane. "But we helped make those."

"And you both did a great job of it, especially the part about making sure the beaters and the mixing bowls were extra clean when we finished." She rested the tray on the dining room table that was decorated with a long lace tablecloth accented with a narrow red runner and a huge poinsettia centerpiece. Glancing into the living room, she surveyed the other preparations for the party. Folding chairs borrowed from the church basement had been hauled over and arranged along all the living room walls.

Claire approached the table and watched as Jane arranged her tray with butter cookies, tiny tarts and fudge brownies, and placed it alongside several others. "Doesn't everyone at the party get the cookies anyway?" she asked.

Jane tapped her forefinger on her lips and tried to appear in deep thought before glancing down at the child again. "You know, you're right. Well then, I guess watching for the car from the airport will just have to be your Christmas gift to me."

Claire shrugged. "Okay."

Dylan answered with a shrug as well and turned back to the window.

Sandy pushed through the door, carrying a pitcher of punch to the drink service on the buffet table against the dining room wall. "Shouldn't they be here already?"

"Should be." Louise said as she passed through the dining room. "First, the flight was delayed in Orlando because of technical problems with the luggage-compartment door. Then their landing was delayed because of the snowstorm, and they had to circle for a half hour. Finally, there was some mix-up with the luggage."

"At least Alice called to let us know she would be delayed," Jane said. "She probably didn't think of it as an emergency, but I guess she decided she'd cause some emergencies—her two sisters' heart attacks—if she didn't let us know everything was all right."

"Now if only their driver can manage to avoid ice and snow drifts long enough to get everyone home . . ." Louise let her words trail off, worry in her eyes.

Cynthia crossed to Louise and squeezed her arm. "They'll be just fine, Mom. Can you imagine Aunt Ethel letting something as insignificant as a snowstorm make her miss a party? I know I can't."

"She's right about that," Jane answered with a chuckle.

"But she is going to be late to this party. We already know that."

"A car's here," Dylan said, causing everyone to start and Claire to run back to the window and squeeze in beside him. He watched for several seconds. "Wait, here's another one." Then he turned away from the window, a frown on his face. "I thought you said they were coming in a limo. Those are just regular cars."

Jane stowed her apron in the kitchen and smoothed her hands over her red cotton blouse as she approached from behind Dylan and glanced out the window. "Those are the guests for the Secret Santa party. See that couple coming out of the first car?" She indicated with a nod toward a round woman with a tall, thin man walking next to her. "They're Fred and Vera Humbert. Mrs. Humbert is in charge of the whole Secret Santa program. She'll announce who was Secret Santa to whom for the last several weeks. It will be fun."

"I wish we had Secret Santas too," Claire said as she watched. "It would have been cool to sneak fun gifts to someone."

Jane patted her shoulder. "I know, but this game was really for grownups. Sometimes we forget how much fun Christmas can be, so we have to be reminded."

Claire cocked her head to the side. "Is that why you wrote the secret, special letter?"

"What letter?" Jane stared at her with wide-eyed innocence. "I don't remember any letter."

The little girl moved in closer and spoke to her conspiratorially. "I don't remember shopping for any secret gifts for tonight, either," she whispered.

They turned as the front door opened. Vera and Fred entered the house, Vera cradling a treasure chest-shaped box. She greeted Louise with a hug. "Thank you again for agreeing to host the party." She glanced around the room. "As usual, you've outdone yourselves."

Louise smiled as she stepped back from the woman who wore a red Santa hat on her head and a flashing Rudolph pin on her colorful holiday sweater. "Is your box filled with secrets, Vera?"

She grinned and patted the box. "A lot of surprises in here."

"But all will be revealed this evening," Jane said in a deep, ominous voice.

Vera glanced around the room. "Have Alice, Ethel and the Simpsons made it back yet? I hate to make the announcements before they return."

Soon introductions were made, and the front hall filled with guests, chatting and wishing each other season's greetings. Since the coatrack couldn't contain all the heavy outerwear, Louise carried several coats into the library and rested them on their father's office chair.

With so much laughter and happy voices filling the room, Jane was pleased they had agreed to host the reveal party. She was also happy that Vera had suggested the Secret Santa program in the first place. It brought together so many members of the community. Some of these faces she would see again at the church service later, but this way she had the chance to see Acorn Hill community members who attended different churches as well as those who didn't attend at all.

If only Alice, Ethel, Florence and Ronald would arrive soon, the party would be perfect. It didn't seem right to enjoy herself while they were still making their way along the treacherous roads from Philadelphia.

In the living room, Rev. Thompson stood chatting with his landlords, Rachel and Joseph Holzmann. Though the minister appeared comfortable in one of his trademark pullover sweaters, he no doubt would change into one of his well-tailored suits before the evening service. Rachel looked especially lovely tonight in a red cashmere sweater and black crepe slacks, her mane of heavy dark hair arranged high on her head with Victorian hatpins.

Rev. Thompson caught Jane watching them and made his way over. "Hello, Jane," he said. "Lovely party, as usual. I love all your beautiful decorations, but I must admit I especially like this Christmas tree." He indicated the children's tree. "It looks like a lot of work and love went into this one."

She glanced over at the tree and smiled. It was special in its awkward homemade way. "You'll have to give Louise credit for that one. Also, make sure to compliment our young guests, Claire and Dylan, on their work for that project."

"I will." The minister studied her in that intense way he had of spotting trouble in his congregants' souls. "Have you heard anything from Alice and Ethel yet?"

"We're expecting them at any time." Jane poured decaf for him and handed him the cup and saucer.

He thanked her and watched her again. "You're worried, right?"

She glanced out the window at the snow that was continuing to fall. "Wouldn't you be?"

He patted her arm. "Have a little faith, Jane. They'll be here soon."

"I'll try." She would also try to remain a sane hostess while she waited, which was just as hard to accomplish.

In the span of that short conversation, the living room had filled with most of Acorn Hill's familiar faces. Near the Christmas tree, Viola Reed was showing off her holiday scarf, covered with a dozen kitties in Santa hats, to a laughing Nancy Colwin. Craig Tracy was crouched at the base of the tree, checking the stand, likely to make sure the plant was getting enough water. Others were chatting, joking and, in general, having a wonderful time.

Jane crossed to the front door just in time to see Pastor Henry and Patsy Ley enter with several relatives in tow. "Stop. Hold it right there." Several members of the Ley clan seemed taken aback. She addressed Kevin and Jill, who'd come through the door last and were still wearing their coats. "Wait right here. There's someone I'd like you to meet."

She wound her way through the crowd and returned a few moments later, pulling along Louise, who wore an expression of combined surprise and mild irritation. "Louise, I would like to present our guests, Kevin and Jill Ley."

Louise smiled and extended her hand. "So you're the elusive Ley family. It's so nice to finally meet you. I was certain you were a figment of my sister's imagination."

Jill shook her hand. "And I was beginning to believe that Jane had invented a sister whom she described as an extremely talented musician."

"That part she might have invented," Louise said with a laugh. "She does have a sister though. Two in fact."

"D-d-d-don't let her k-kid you, Jill," Pastor Henry said, his stutter more evident in the crowd than it usually would have been when he was visiting with just the Howard sisters.

"Oh, I won't let her, Henry." She turned back to Louise. "I'm looking forward to accompanying you." Jill reached down and patted her violin case.

"I'm counting on it," Louise said.

"Excuse me. May I have some quiet now, please?" A voice could barely be heard over the din of conversation, and its efforts to rise above the noise met with little success.

Jane returned with Louise to the living room, where Vera stood, trying to gain everyone's attention. Having entrusted her precious treasure box to Fred, Vera clapped her hands together in a way that was probably effective in her fifth-grade classroom at Acorn Hill Elementary School. The adults in the room, however, took a little longer to quiet.

"Thank you," Vera said when she could finally be heard. "I know all of you have had a wonderful time this holiday season with the first-ever Acorn Hill Secret Santa program. Who thinks it would be worth repeating in the future?"

The quiet was replaced by cheers and applause, but the crowd was easier to settle a second time. Vera glanced at Louise and pointed to her watch. They'd all hoped Alice and the others would be back in time for the reveals, but it was getting late, and guests would have to leave soon to get ready for the Christmas Eve service. With a glance out the window, Louise nodded for her to go ahead.

"Now who's ready to find out who their Secret Santas are?" Vera asked.

Again, a chorus of cheers broke out, but it died away quickly as guests moved to the places where they'd deposited thank-you gifts for their sponsors. Jane collected hers as well, though she wasn't sure why she'd even purchased one. Not having received a single gift, she knew her Secret Santa didn't exist. Still, she just couldn't ignore the directive to bring along a gift to the party. She could always add it to the gifts for the Quinlans later, she supposed.

Vera opened the box. "This is how it will work. I will draw a name out of the treasure box. On one side is the printed name of the recipient. On the other side in small script is the name of that person's Secret Santa. When I call your name, get ready to go thank your Santa."

The room became quiet as she dug in the open chest and pulled out the first card. "Hope Collins," Vera called.

"Woo-woo!" Hope hollered as she bopped to the middle of the room, a reindeer-decorated gift bag in her hand.

"Go thank your Secret Santa, Dr. Hart Bentley."

Hope rushed over to the beloved town doctor and threw her arms around him. "I loved the candy, Doc." She handed him her bag. "I hope you like cucumber lotion."

He grinned and adjusted his spectacles. "It's my favorite."

They made it through a few others on the list without anyone in the Florida contingent being called. Sylvia Songer, the owner of Sylvia's Buttons, had played Secret Santa for Pastor Henry; and Craig Tracy, owner of Wild Things, had only to cross Hill Street to leave secret gifts for Clarissa Cottrell, owner of Good Apple Bakery.

"Zack Colwin," Vera called out and then scanned the room after peeking on the back of the card. Disappointment lined her features, but she continued anyway. "Your Secret Santa was—"

"Me!" A voice from the doorway interrupted the announcement. Alice stood just inside the door, still in her coat. "Alice Howard," she clarified for anyone who might not know.

Alice braced herself as several in the crowd came out of their seats and hurried her way. Though Jane had twice the distance to cover as Louise, they both reached their sister at about the same time. In seconds, Alice, coat and all, found herself in the center of a suffocating hug.

"You made it," Louise said before she squeezed her again.

"You didn't think I would?" There had been plenty of times when Alice herself hadn't believed she'd make it home to spend Christmas with her sisters, but she chose not to bring that up now. She was just glad to be back in Acorn Hill, home where she belonged. From the moment they'd driven into the town limits, she was barely able to stay in her seat, and when the driver pulled into the lot and parked, she rushed into the house without collecting her bags.

"Oh, uncertainties crossed my mind a time or two. I'm glad one of us is always so sure," Louise said.

Alice turned to Jane for a second hug. "Did you miss me at all?"

Jane glowed as she answered, "No, not too much. Except perhaps when I was folding linens and there was no one to hold the other end."

"Wow, you did miss me."

Cynthia made her way through the crowd then. "I came all the way to Pennsylvania, and I haven't seen you at all. Do you have any hugs left for me?"

Alice didn't waste any time showing her that she did. Then she pulled away from her niece and studied her. "I hear there's a young man I should be meeting."

Greg came in closer and offered his hand. "Hi, I'm Greg. I've heard so much about you these last few days. I'm glad to finally meet you."

Alice grinned at him. "I haven't heard enough about you, but we'll remedy that soon enough."

"I've been looking forward to introducing you and Aunt Ethel," Cynthia began. "Wait, where is she?"

"Over here." Ethel stood just inside the door with

Ronald and Florence coming through it behind her. "*Someone* had to wait outside until we gathered the luggage."

Alice's cheeks warmed. "Sorry."

"Well, I should hope so," Ethel said before her stern expression softened.

The whole welcoming scene was repeated with Ethel, Florence and Ronald before clapping in the living room interrupted their warm homecoming.

"Excuse me," Vera said pleasantly when she had everyone's attention. "We're delighted that all have made it home safely, but could we please finish the Secret Santa reveals so we'll have plenty of time to eat before Rev. Thompson's Christmas Eve service?"

The announcements went smoothly after that. Jane received extra applause for having filled in for Alice and Ethel, stealthily providing gifts for three recipients. Wilhelm Wood, owner of Time for Tea, turned out to be Alice's Secret Santa, and Rev. Thompson was Santa to Ethel.

Surprise lit Louise's eyes when Vera announced that Carlene Moss was her Secret Santa. She'd been convinced it was her friend Viola Reed or, if not Viola, librarian Nia Komonos.

"Don't be shocked, Louise," Carlene said with a smile. "All good newspaper women do their research, so I knew exactly what books you read."

Alice glanced around. Almost all already knew the names of their benefactors, and many were discussing their best, sneaky gift-giving techniques, but Vera cleared her throat again. "Ladies and gentlemen, we're not quite finished. I have one last name in my box, Jane Howard."

Jane moved to the center of the room, appearing nonplussed.

"Your Secret Santa is—"

"Oh my goodness!" From near the door where she'd stood since they'd arrived, Florence Simpson stood with her hands covering her face.

Vera cleared her throat and began again. "Uh, Florence Simpson."

For a second, Jane stood there, surprise evident in her eyes, but then she turned and strode over to the couple standing next to the door.

Florence was shaking her head before Jane reached her and handed her the thank-you gift. "Oh, Jane, I am so sorry. With everything else going on, it completely escaped my mind. I don't—"

Jane raised a hand to stop her fussing. "Florence, please, don't worry about it. I certainly understand."

"Really, I'm sorry. I even purchased a few items, but I never got around to delivering them. I still plan to give them to you."

Jane shook her head. "It's not necessary. I'm fine. It wasn't a problem at all." She looked around nervously, her cheeks and neck taking on a girlish pink color. "Please accept my gift."

"Thank you, but I also want to give you some of the cuttings from my prize hostas when I divide them in the spring."

Again Jane shook her head, appearing desperate. "Really, you don't have to do that."

But Florence wasn't listening, Alice noted. Apparently some things never changed.

"The Blizzard Hosta is streaked and beautiful," Florence began. "Or maybe you'd want some of the Princess Anastasia with its gold center and blue green margins. If you like more wild varieties, you'll love Wild Bill with its large leaves and streaky colors."

"Florence, please," Jane said with strain in her voice. "This isn't necessary."

Ronald cleared his throat then. "Uh, Jane." He waited for her to look up before he continued. "You might want to go ahead and say yes because my dear wife isn't going to give in until you do."

Florence glanced back at her husband, but no rebuke followed, as might have been expected. She simply watched Jane and waited.

Vera stepped forward then. "What do you say, Jane?"

"Yeah, what do you say?" several crowd members repeated.

Jane shook her head. "Florence, I would love some of your hosta cuttings."

With that, the Secret Santa reveals ended, accompanied by enthusiastic applause.

Chapter Twenty

The party at the inn continued with conversations and refreshments in the living room, and music and praise in the parlor. Florence, Alice observed, didn't appear to be taking part. Instead, she moved about the rooms, seeming to search for someone. When her gaze stopped on two women in the front hall and the women turned to face her, Alice found herself holding her breath.

Florence had never pulled any punches before, so Alice didn't expect her to start now, especially with Hope Collins and Nancy Colwin, two women she probably despised.

Theirs was the conversation she overheard when Ronald had failed to come to her defense in a timely fashion. Theirs were the words that set off a chain reaction of events, sending a couple with a rocky marriage to the edge and requiring friends of that couple to intervene.

Florence approached them more slowly than Alice thought she would, and she wrung her hands instead of planting them on her hips. Alice stayed close by in case she was needed.

"Could I talk to you two for a moment?" Florence asked.

"Um, well . . ." Hope began.

"Well, I . . ." Nancy started.

Florence lifted a hand to stop them. "Please, let me," she said.

Both of the other women closed their lips.

"I overheard the two of you talking about me last week."

"I know you did, and I'm so sorry about that," Nancy said, her expression serious. "I should never have—"

Florence tilted her head to the side and studied her. "Which are you sorry about, having said these things or my overhearing them?"

"Well, both," Hope answered for the two of them. "We were wrong to say those hurtful things."

Again, Florence appeared to be studying the other two women. "Even though everything you said was true?"

Both women gaped at her.

Finally, Hope recovered enough to speak. "Well, I suppose they were true, but that doesn't mean we were right to criticize you by repeating them. I'm sorry—I really am— and I know that Nancy is too."

Instead of adding more, Nancy nodded her agreement.

"Not any more than I am about my part," Florence said.

Nancy lifted an eyebrow. "Excuse me?"

"I'm sorry for saying *a lot* of unkind things over the years. What good did any of them do anyone?"

Hope shrugged. "They offered information?"

"Well, that's nicer than the truth anyway." Florence smiled.

Nancy's face, though, became serious. "I don't want you to think that Ronald didn't come to your defense that day, though. He did."

"I know."

"He was right too," Hope continued for her. "You do contribute so much to Acorn Hill through the church board and your support of other agencies. We appreciate what you do. We're only sorry we made it appear as if we didn't."

"That's very kind of you to say," Florence said politely. It was clear from her expression that she was touched by the words.

After a pleasant parting, Florence returned to her husband, who was waiting in the living room with Ethel. Perhaps Ronald had purposely stayed out of the conversation because he believed she needed to heal those relationships herself. As far as Alice was concerned, she was doing a pretty good job.

Strains of "Away in a Manger" filled Grace Chapel later that night, with soft yellow lights and burning candles providing the only illumination as Joseph and Mary made their difficult journey to Bethlehem. The choir sounded beautiful as Louise played the soulful tune on the organ with Jill Ley's mellow accompaniment on the violin.

Without the overhead lights, all the church-decorating committee's lovely work—the red velvet bows with sprays of baby's breath that adorned the window sills and ends of pews, and the multicolored poinsettias flanking the altar— was hidden in shadow. Even the spotlight that usually focused on the lifelike crèche that was Florence's gift to the church had been shut off, directing everyone's focus to the center aisle and the coming of the Lord. Jane closed her eyes and let the peace of the moment wash over her.

High school senior Ingrid Nilsen and youth group member Bobby Dawson, this year's Mary and Joseph, walked barefoot along the rich red runner that led to the manger at the base of the altar. In Ingrid's arms was a newborn named Michael, who slept away his first volunteer effort for Grace Chapel.

Jane's heart warmed as she thought of another baby, a gift from heaven and a promise of redemption once cradled in His mother's arms.

Rev. Thompson read from Matthew 1:23. "The virgin will be with child and will give birth to a son and they will call him Immanuel—which means, 'God with us.'"

Alice leaned close and touched her arm. "It's beautiful, isn't it?"

Jane nodded and smiled at her sister.

"We come tonight to give thanks for God's greatest gift to a dark world," Rev. Thompson continued in a soft voice that sounded different from the one he usually used to bring the message of God to his congregation. "In John 1:14, we read, 'The Word became flesh and made his dwelling among us. We have seen his glory . . .'

"We give thanks tonight for so many things but that gift most of all—God's only Son. We are humbled by God's sacrifice that, begun in a lowly manger, would lead to a cross and would purchase the price of salvation for us all. Can we not as God's children seek out ways to give of ourselves during this blessed time of year?"

Jane couldn't be certain what else Rev. Thompson said in his sermon, but the part about giving thanks spoke to her heart. She and her sisters had much to be grateful for tonight—a family back together where they belonged, good health and more than life's basic needs, even the opportunity to help others.

That last reason for gratitude stayed with her well after the benediction, when church members were dismissed with words of new beginnings and restored hope. She and her sisters would help to bring that hope to another family tonight. She couldn't wait to get started.

"Wasn't Rev. Thompson's sermon wonderful?" Louise said thoughtfully as she and Cynthia changed in her room prior to their late-night outing to the Quinlans' rural home. "New beginnings. I like to think there are a lot of new beginnings for all of us at the inn this Christmas season."

The truth was, she could barely contain her excitement. When would Greg propose? Would he ask Louise first for her daughter's hand? She pulled a dark sweater over her head and tried to imagine how she would answer him if he did ask.

"Mom, did you hear me?" Cynthia asked to regain her attention. "I said Greg and I won't be getting married."

"Of course not, sweetheart," Louise responded before she even realized what her daughter was saying. "Wait. What do you mean?" The realization was staggering. "I expected him to propose to you before the weekend was out."

"He did propose, but tonight I told him I couldn't marry him."

Louise shook her head and sat on the edge of the bed. "I don't understand what you're saying. You brought Greg here because you wanted me to meet him, didn't you?" Louise didn't wait for her daughter's answer, because she already knew it. "Greg has all the things you've ever said you wanted in a husband. He's a good Christian man, a good person. He's a man with qualities like your father's, someone Eliot would have been pleased to know you've chosen."

With a sigh, Cynthia sat next to her mother. "He's a wonderful man. I know it. You're the one who convinced me I couldn't marry him."

Louise raised an eyebrow. "Would you mind explaining?"

Her daughter's smile was a sad one. "Greg proposed a few days before I planned to come to Acorn Hill, and I had every intention of accepting his proposal while we were here. He's my best friend, and I do love him in that way. We didn't really ever date, you see. We were always together as friends."

"A lot of loving marriages develop from friendships," Louise said.

"I know you're right about that. Greg's such a good, Christian man, someone I truly respect. Could I ask for more, especially when I'm not getting any younger? But then I listened to the way you talked about Dad, heard the way you loved him in your stories, and I realized there was something missing. I want that. I want the kind of love you and Dad had, even the kind of love that Florence and Ronald are beginning to find again."

Louise glanced at Cynthia, suddenly worried that the stories had led her daughter to expect too much from relationships. No, she couldn't believe that. She had to believe that God had someone else in store for her daughter. "Have you told all of this to Greg?"

"We talked before the reveal party."

Louise shook her head, understanding even less than

before. "He's been in such good spirits all night. How could he have recovered so well after such devastating news?"

A chuckle rose in her daughter's throat. "You know, I think he was relieved. He admitted he'd wondered too, if he was settling for a convenient marriage with a friend just because of our shared faith and marriageable age, when God might have other plans for the two of us. We decided we were willing to wait for the partners God has planned for us. We didn't even have to lose each other as friends in the process."

Louise reached out and touched her daughter's cheek, incredulous to think she once worried that Cynthia would settle because of a ticking biological clock. Her daughter wouldn't settle for any reason until she found the husband God chose for her. If He determined she was to remain single, she would gladly accept His will in that situation as well. Louise didn't think she'd ever been more proud of her daughter.

"Now keep it down, everyone," Jane admonished as she climbed out of the car a few hundred feet from the Quinlan's home. It was bad enough that two cars were needed to cart all of their gift baskets plus the four other adults who insisted on helping Jane to deliver them—Louise, Alice, Greg and Cynthia. They certainly didn't need to awaken the Quinlans before Christmas morning.

At least Ethel had finally admitted to exhaustion. She decided to rest before they gathered again at the inn to share their Christmas Eve tradition of reading the account of Jesus' birth from the Book of Luke. Paul and Sandy had sent their children off for baths with promises of staying up late for the event, so the four Ericksons remained at the inn as well.

"We'll just deliver the baskets as quickly and quietly as possible and then hightail it out of here, right?" she whispered. As she glanced around at her fellow Secret Santas, she had to force herself not to laugh. They looked more like a group of has-been cat burglars than a group delivering Christmas spirit.

Louise hefted a sizeable basket from the trunk of her car. "At least they left the Christmas lights on. It's so dark out here that we wouldn't be able to find the porch."

Jane glanced over at the house with lights blinking along the railing of its long, sheltered front porch. Now if they could only get from here to there and back without crashing and spoiling the surprise, they would really have accomplished something. "Do you think we can get it all in one trip?"

"Barely," Greg said. He hoisted the heaviest basket, the one filled with canned goods and other nonperishable items. "If we just stand around here, we're definitely going to get caught."

Jane let Greg lead, and she took her place at the back of the line. As stealthily as possible, they sneaked in single file along the bushes near the fence. At what appeared to be the least visible spot, Greg turned toward the house, approaching from the rear. Jane glanced down for no more than a second and was surprised when she came into contact with something solid—Alice.

"Ouch," Alice whispered.

"Sorry. Well, are you going to get moving?"

"I can't. They've stopped in front of me."

Forgetting their plan to remain inconspicuous, Jane stepped out of the line and moved to where Greg and Cynthia were standing and just staring. When she followed their gazes to the porch, a brief gasp escaped Jane's throat. She'd hoped her message reached the others, but she never imagined this. Obviously she'd underestimated the caring hearts of the people of Acorn Hill. Boxes and baskets of all shapes and sizes lined the porch, some filled with clothing, others with food and even toys. Each one had a card attached that read, "From your Secret Santa."

Before long, they were back at Grace Chapel Inn, warming themselves by the fire. Claire and Dylan had on pajamas and had wet hair, but, true to their word, their parents allowed them to stay up for the evening's special event.

Aunt Ethel was back as well, looking refreshed and comfortable in her pink jogging suit.

"You wouldn't have believed it," Jane was telling Sandy when Alice returned downstairs. "There were baskets everywhere. It was just amazing to see how much the people around here care for others."

"Yes, we've been pretty amazed by that ourselves," Sandy said.

Alice could see why Sandy might have been surprised by a small town's generosity, but she wondered why Jane appeared so shocked that God had answered her prayers in such a remarkable way. Still, complete trust had always come hard for Jane, and Alice could only hope that the sister she adored could someday place her confidence in God without reservation.

They had petitioned God for so many needs this week—the renewal of the Simpsons' marriage, peace in the Erickson family, help for the Quinlans, guidance for Cynthia and Greg, and even that the Howard sisters would be together again for Christmas Eve. God had answered each prayer in His own way, in His own time.

"Are we going to get started?" Alice asked. "Who would like to read tonight?" She collected the Howard family Bible from the mantel where she'd set it earlier.

Paul raised his hand. "Would you mind if I did? It's been too long since my children have heard me reading aloud from God's Word, but they're going to hear it more often now."

She handed him the Bible, with Luke 2:6 already marked. He began reading about Joseph and Mary's arrival in Bethlehem. "'While they were there, the time came for the baby to be born, and she gave birth to her firstborn, a son. She wrapped him in cloths and placed him in a manger, because there was no room for them in the inn.'"

Jane cocked her head to the side when he paused. "You never told us you were an actor," she said.

Alice noticed it too. When Paul read, the story seemed to come alive, though they'd seen and heard the verses so many times before.

"You never asked." When they continued to watch him, Paul added, "Just some small community-theater work."

He continued through the angels' message to the shepherds and concluded with baby Jesus' presentation in the temple. Finally, he closed the Bible.

"It's late, and we have another big day tomorrow," he said.

Funny, but after the evening's celebration, Alice couldn't imagine that there was more to come. They had already celebrated the "reason for the season" in a real and powerful way. The reality was far different from the celebration she'd told Rev. Thompson that she and her sisters were looking forward to, but she wouldn't change any of it.

Grace Chapel was filled with exuberance and many worshippers Christmas morning, the latter at least partially owing to Rev. Thompson's wisdom in scheduling the service closer to lunch than breakfast. At Grace Chapel Inn, they'd already had a wonderful morning, with a delightful breakfast and plenty of time to exchange gifts before preparing for the service. Now, even with Louise off playing the pipe organ at the rear of the chapel, there were still too many owners and guests representing the inn to be seated in one row.

Jane sat sandwiched between Alice and Ethel and wished Louise didn't have to play so that she could be with them as well. Next to them, Cynthia sat with Greg, the two appearing comfortable in their newly defined roles as friends. Jane didn't tell Louise she'd been concerned about the relationship when her sister informed her that the two had decided not to marry. Sometimes people see what they want to see, and at the time Louise had wanted to see her daughter with her son-in-law. Greg would be a wonderful son-in-law to someone someday, just as another family would one day be privileged to include Cynthia—in God's time, though.

Jill and Kevin were on the opposite end of the pew, behind a full row of Pastor Henry and Patsy Ley's relatives. Jill rested her hand on her tummy. By this time next year, the two of them would be old pros at balancing the diaper bag and car seat and would be celebrating their first Christmas as parents.

Over her shoulder, Jane smiled at the Ericksons, who were all sitting together. Somehow Paul and Sandy had managed to convince Claire and Dylan to leave their brand-new, MP3 players at the inn until after church. Those were the children's main gifts under the Christmas tree, but one slender package for both of them featured a picture of the trampoline they would find when they returned to California.

Turning her attention back to the altar as Louise began playing the prelude, Jane caught sight of the Simpsons. She wasn't sure, but they seemed to be sitting closer than they usually did, and if she wasn't mistaken, that was a smile on Florence's lips. Jane glanced around once more, wishing she could see the Quinlan family in the congregation. Of course, they didn't attend church as far as she knew. Still, she was happy for the amazing gift the family would have found on their porch this morning, and she hoped they received it with the same spirit of joy in which it was given.

The opening hymn, "Joy to the World," reflected the feelings in her heart. She had a feeling some people never experience in a lifetime—she was content.

Rev. Thompson stepped to the front to begin speaking. "Merry Christmas!"

"Merry Christmas, Pastor!" the crowd called out.

"An angel had a message to the shepherds in the field recorded in Luke 2:10-11." The minister glanced down at his Bible and started reading. "'Do not be afraid. I bring you good news of great joy that will be for all people. Today in the town of David a Savior had been born to you; he is Christ the Lord.'"

Instead of reading further or asking them to turn to another carol in their hymnals, Rev. Thompson motioned with his hand for them to be seated. "When I arrived at church this morning, I found this note tucked inside the door. Mayor Tynan said he also received a copy to go out to the downtown business district, and Rev. Rogers at the Methodist church informed me that his church and the Presbyterian church have received copies as well. I wanted to share it with you. 'To all Secret Santas who delivered God's love on Christmas Eve,'" he began. "'On behalf of myself, my wife and our three daughters, I wish to thank the people of Acorn Hill for reaching out to our family during this holiday season. I am a proud man, which is my failing, so I had a hard time asking for help, even when our family fell on hard times after my job loss.

"'I deeply appreciate everyone's kindness in meeting our family's basic needs and so much more. When we saw our daughters' smiling faces this morning, we thanked God for you.'" Rev. Thompson paused to take a steadying breath before finishing. "'God bless you all, Logan Quinlan.' In a postscript, he thanks individuals who offered him contacts to help secure employment."

Jane brushed tears from her cheeks, wishing she were in the habit, like Louise, of carrying a handkerchief. The Quinlans weren't ashamed of the outpouring after all. They were pleased and grateful. She glanced up as Rev. Thompson refolded the letter. Of all the lovely presents she'd received that day—the books, the picture frame from Cynthia, two new beaded necklaces—this letter was by far the best.

Louise was relieved when they returned to the inn following the church service. She almost wished they could cancel Christmas dinner and simply share some quiet time reading by the fire and drinking tea. How so much activity and so many emotions could be packed into one week, she wasn't sure.

When their group reached the front door, a small wrapped gift was waiting propped against it. Louise picked it up and studied it. "Jane, it's for you. It's probably that gift Florence said she bought for you before she went to Florida."

Jane frowned. "Oh, I wished she hadn't gone to the trouble. I have to remember to tell her I won't hold her to her offer to share her hostas when she divides them."

"Are you joking, Jane?" Ethel asked from behind them. "Take my advice and accept the plants gratefully. They're absolutely beautiful."

Jane blew out an exasperated sigh as she stepped inside and stomped the snow off her boots. The delicious smell of turkey wafted through the house, promising a wonderful Christmas dinner for all, including the Ericksons, who had received a special invitation. But Jane didn't seem to notice. "Okay. Okay. I'll take them. I'll be on my best behavior."

The others followed her inside and started removing their coats. Claire came to stand next to her after she'd hung her coat. "Ms. Howard, aren't you going to open your present?"

Smiling down at the child, Jane picked up the package that she'd set aside and pulled open the loosely taped paper. "It's a tin of some kind." She lifted off the lid to find chocolate-chip cookies.

Claire was down on the floor, examining the wrapping paper. "Wait, you forgot the card." She handed it to Jane.

Drawing her eyebrows together, Jane pulled open the envelope and opened the card. Whatever she read must have touched her, because her hand flew to her mouth and tears immediately welled in her eyes.

"What is it?" Louise reached for the card, and her youngest sister lowered it into her hand. In a child's scrawl, the message inside said, "Secret Santas never tell."

"What does it mean, Jane?" Alice asked, pressing a hand to her shoulder.

Tears skimmed down Jane's face. Louise suspected the note had to do with little Meghan Quinlan and the conversation that inspired Jane to action, but they would have to wait for her to explain it later, when her emotions weren't so close to the surface.

Moving in close to her sister, Louise placed her arm around her shoulders and squeezed. "You finally got a Secret Santa gift after all." At least that got a chuckle out of her.

Louise directed their guests to relax while the three Howard sisters escaped to the kitchen together to put Christmas dinner on the table.

This year's celebration was nothing like what the three of them had planned, but Louise wouldn't have traded any of these moments—of families becoming reacquainted, of reconciliations and of sharing their bounty with others who were struggling. She glanced at Jane, who was chopping the celery, and Alice, who was wiping the china, guessing both of them would agree. They had truly experienced the spirit of the season.

About the Author

ana Corbit is the author of eleven inspirational novels and the winner of the 2007 HOLT Medallion award. A wife and the mother of three daughters, she lives in southeast Michigan.

Tales from Grace Chapel Inn

Back Home Again
by Melody Carlson

Recipes & Wooden Spoons
by Judy Baer

Hidden History
by Melody Carlson

Ready to Wed
by Melody Carlson

The Price of Fame
by Carolyne Aarsen

We Have This Moment
by Diann Hunt

The Way We Were
by Judy Baer

Once you visit the charming village of Acorn Hill, you'll never want to leave. Here, the three Howard sisters reunite after their father's death and turn the family home into a bed-and-breakfast. They rekindle old memories, rediscover the bonds of sisterhood, revel in the blessings of friendship and meet many fascinating guests along the way.

A Note from the Editors

Guideposts, a nonprofit organization, touches millions of lives every day through products and services that inspire, encourage and uplift. Our magazines, books, prayer network and outreach programs help people connect their faith-filled values to their daily lives. To learn more, visit www.guideposts.com or www.guidepostsfoundation.org.